D0393757

The Maverick's Bride

**Center Point
Large Print**

Also by Catherine Palmer
and available from Center Point Large Print:

Love's Haven
Leaves of Hope
The Heart's Treasure
The Briton

The Haven Series
Thread of Deceit
Stranger in the Night

**This Large Print Book carries the
Seal of Approval of N.A.V.H.**

The
Maverick's Bride

CATHERINE PALMER

CENTER POINT PUBLISHING
THORNDIKE, MAINE

ISBN: 978-1-60285-647-9

Library of Congress Cataloging-in-Publication Data

Palmer, Catherine, 1956-
  The maverick's bride / Catherine Palmer.
    p. cm.
  ISBN 978-1-60285-647-9 (library binding : alk. paper)
  1. Large type books. I. Title.
  PS3566.A495M38 2010
  813'.54--dc22
2009033103

Delight thyself also in the Lord;
and he shall give the desires of thine heart.
—*Psalms* 37:4

For Tim
With all my love
Always . . .

Chapter One

———

1898, British Protectorate of East Africa

"Oh, Emma, what shall I do?" Priscilla Pickering lifted her tear-rimmed blue eyes. Sniffling, she raised her white lace handkerchief and dabbed at her cheek.

Emma sighed inwardly as she looked at her sister. "You will do as you've always done, Cissy. You will put on your brightest smile and bid him farewell as if he didn't mean a thing in the world to you." Stepping back from the open trunk, Emma tossed a pink ostrich-plumed hat onto the bed. "This will have to do, Cissy. We haven't time to look for the white one. Father is already waiting on deck."

"But, Emma, you don't understand. Dirk is different. I do love him—truly."

Emma buckled the trunk and picked up her own lavender hat. How many times had she helped her sister recover from a broken heart? She pursed her lips for a moment. "I know you love him. But, Cissy, honestly—you've loved them all. You insisted you loved that awful what's-his-name who tried to take you off to Sussex. And you loved that banker chap who was going to carry you to France if Father hadn't ordered him away and locked you in your room."

"Emma, Dirk isn't like those other men." Cissy sniffled again and ran her delicate fingers through the ostrich plumes. "Dirk is good and kind. He loves me, Emma. We want to be married."

Stifling another sigh, Emma crossed the floor of the steamship cabin and knelt before her sister. "Cissy, dear, you must try to accept the truth. Dirk Bauer is a soldier. He has no money at all. He's leaving the ship in less than an hour for his post along the border. And Cissy—he's not even English."

At this Cissy burst into renewed sobbing. "Oh, Emma, I know it's hopeless! We'll leave this ship so Father can survey his silly railway—and I'll never see Dirk again."

Emma took her sister into her arms. "There, there. It's not so bad."

She reflected for a moment upon that morning—was it only three weeks ago?—when she and Cissy had been promenading on the deck. They had rounded a corner and come upon a cluster of young German soldiers. She smiled, remembering the awkward introductions, the men gazing in awe of Cissy, as men always did, and Cissy's hat blowing, as if on cue, into the arms of the handsomest of them all.

Emma had gone off on her own then—preferring the ocean breeze and the rolling waves to flirtatious chatter. She recalled climbing to the top deck and standing alone beneath a brilliant azure sky. She had stared out across the endless ocean as if she might catch a glimpse of her future.

Subsequent meetings between Dirk and Cissy had been a great secret, although of course Emma had known. It was her responsibility to keep Cissy in hand. As the practical sister, Emma had attempted to dissuade her sibling from the fruitless course. But perhaps it had been the sea air, or the glorious sunshine. At any rate, Emma filled most of her hours with contemplation and study of the land to which God had led her.

The British Protectorate of East Africa.

Books, geographical society pamphlets, maps— as she devoured them, Emma shivered at the wonders in store. But the land held more than beauty. It was a place of hidden promises. God had laid out His plan for Emma's life nearly two years before. While making her debut into society at St. James's Court, she had heard someone coughing as she stepped down from the carriage. Wearing nothing but rags, a little girl huddled alone against the cold iron fence that surrounded the palace.

Despite longing to help the child, Emma had heeded her father's command to *stop dawdling*. When she emerged several hours later, she saw two men lifting the girl's lifeless body into a cart. That moment had propelled Emma on a journey that led her to Africa and the hope of finding a hospital where she could practice her hard-won skill as a nurse.

"It's lovely for you, Emma!" Cissy pouted, breaking into her sister's thoughts. "This is just your sort of thing—savages and wild animals. But where does it leave me? You'll never get married—and Father won't let me marry until you do."

Emma wished for the thousandth time that her sister would follow the example she set and take hold of her emotions. At age twenty, Cissy should not be weeping and flailing about all the time. Common sense kept trouble at bay. Emma had learned that lesson the hard way.

"Cissy, you know Father dotes on you," she said. "He'll let you marry soon enough, I'm sure he will."

"But I won't have Dirk!"

"But you will have *someone*. Someone who will take care of you. You'll have children and a happy home and everything you've dreamed of."

"I want to marry Dirk." Cissy wadded her handkerchief into a ball and set her jaw.

It was a look Emma knew well enough. With a grin, she gave her sister a hug and set the pink hat on Cissy's head. "There now. Dry your eyes and put on your smile. We must leave the cabin soon. Father will be growing impatient."

Rising, Emma shook out the folds of her lavender silk skirt and stepped to the mirror on the bulkhead beside the door. Cissy joined her, and together they adjusted and pinned their hats to the rolls of hair coiled on their heads. Emma watched Cissy dab at her soft blue eyes—twin sapphires set in the palest porcelain—and pinch her cheeks to bring out the roses. It was easy to see why men went mad for Cissy, Emma thought. Her sister's hair shone like the sun and she had curves in all the right places.

Cissy smiled at her reflection, a flash of pearl-white teeth between pink lips. "When I have my inheritance," she declared, "I shall hire servants to tend me wherever I go. Then I shall never be without the proper hat for each dress."

Emma watched her sister fussing with the plumes. Did Dirk know Cissy would inherit half of their father's money? She would have half, too—if she married a man of her father's choosing. The very thought threw cold water on the embers of hope burning in her heart.

For a moment Emma gazed frankly at her own reflection, then she turned from the mirror to pull on her gloves. Her olive-green eyes were an advantage, but her hair waved so wildly and it was that awful wheat color. Her legs were simply too long, her neck too thin and her back too straight for popular fashion.

But what did she care for hats and gowns? Emma would much prefer diving into a pond, perching atop a hay cart or riding a horse, given a choice. But then, she never had been given a choice.

Picking up a lavender parasol from beside the trunk, Emma wandered from the mirror toward the other side of the cabin to wait for Cissy to finish her primping. From the porthole above her bed she had gazed out at the turquoise Indian Ocean, longing for a sight of the protectorate.

Finally, just that morning, they had made port. This raw, untamed territory on the east coast of Africa held her destiny on its burning plains. And she was determined to answer the call of God that flamed in her heart.

"Emma, do you think this pink gown is suitable today?" Cissy asked. "Perhaps Dirk will think it too bright. Perhaps he won't believe how sad I am to lose him."

"You look lovely," Emma said absently as she lifted her skirts and placed one knee across her bed to move closer to the porthole. Pushing back the curtain with one hand, she leaned up to the round window.

Through the film of salt on the glass, she gazed at the busy harbor of Mombasa. An array of small wooden craft bustling with Arab traders surrounded the steamship. From one of its upper decks, a long gangway stretched to the pier. Down it, crewmen carried bale after bale, crate after crate of goods brought up from the hold of the ship. Other laborers scurried about on the wharf, rolling and muscling the cargo into place.

Mangy dogs and scrawny children chased one another through the throng of sailors and dockworkers. Stray chickens, blind in their quest for spilled grain or seed, bobbed across the footpaths and were kicked aside to flutter and squawk in the dust. Groups of men Emma recognized from the ship had just set foot on the soil of British East Africa—a land they had come to colonize. The Englishmen stood stiffly among scampering natives who wore little more than a cloth tied about the waist.

Just then Emma's eyes were drawn to a frenzied movement near the cargo plank. A large wooden crate had broken loose from its ropes and was careening down the long ramp toward the pier. Gasping, she watched helplessly as dockworkers attempted to slow the runaway box. Gaining momentum, it threatened to tip and fall into the sea. But it righted again and continued its downward plunge. Shouts echoed across the harbor as men fled before the hurtling crate.

"Oh!" Emma cried out just as the box collided with two men, knocking them into the water. On impact, the crate began to break apart—jagged, splintered boards seesawing this way and that. As it tumbled the final few feet toward the pier, Emma spotted a child—oblivious to the commotion around him—spinning a tin hoop directly into the crate's path.

"No, stop!" Horrified, she pressed her palms on the glass.

The ragged boy's brown eyes darted up and his face transformed to terror. His brown sparrow legs froze, rooted to the dusty pier. Just as the splintered box slid off the gangway, a black horse thundered through the crowd of petrified onlookers. A dark figure swept the child into the air. The crate slammed onto the wharf and split into a hundred fragments. Boxes of tea, chairs, iron barrels spilled out. Emma glimpsed a man in a black hat cradling the frightened boy in his arms, and then the crowd swarmed them.

Bolting from the window, she ran for the cabin door. Her heart in her throat, she could barely choke out the words. "Cissy, come quickly! An accident. People are hurt."

"Emma, what do you think you're doing? We're not to go ashore yet!" Cissy grabbed her parasol and rushed into the hallway after her sister. "What has happened?"

"A crate broke loose. There was a child. Hurry, Cissy!"

Emma lifted her skirts and sprinted up the stairs from the first-class cabins onto the deck. As she emerged, bright sunshine broke over her and she sucked in a great gulp of fresh sea air. The certain knowledge that she was needed propelled her toward the gangway. Racing past the row of Englishmen lining the ship's guardrail, she started down the sodden wood ramp.

Nearing the bottom, she assessed the situation. One of the African laborers knocked into the water had been rescued. He lay motionless on the pier. Pushing through a circle of agitated onlookers,

Emma knelt beside the unconscious man. Her mind hastily reviewed the nursing instructions she had learned under the tutelage of Miss Florence Nightingale and Mrs. Sarah Wardroper, matron of St. Thomas's Hospital.

Sound and ready observation, Emma recalled Miss Nightingale repeating. *Sound and ready observation.* The first and most important tool for a good nurse.

Stripping off her lavender kid gloves, Emma laid a hand on the man's chest. He was breathing.

"Thank God," she whispered.

Never let a patient be waked out of his first sleep, Miss Nightingale had instructed. But this man was not asleep. He had collapsed and was utterly insensible. What to do in such an emergency?

And now Emma realized she had left her instruction manual in the cabin. Without Miss Nightingale's *Notes on Nursing* to guide her, would she pass this first true test of her skills?

Emma was no doctor and such a dire situation called for a physician. Aware of the crowd pressing around her, she ran her hands along the African's limbs to check for distortion. He was dripping wet but not bleeding, insensible but whole. Yet, how to rouse him? How to restore him to consciousness?

Miss Nightingale's words flickered through her mind. *Accurate observation. A certainty of perception.*

Emma's fingers traveled swiftly across his skull and she noted a swelling near his ear. Yes, he had taken a blow—a serious one. As she watched the man breathe, her fear turned to resolve. At the least, she would do something to ease his suffering.

She mentally cataloged the essentials for a patient's comfort and healing. Pure water. Cleanliness. Light. Warmth. Effects of the loss of vital heat must be guarded against—especially in cases of collapse such as this.

First and foremost, he needed fresh air.

"Stand back," Emma ordered the crowd jostling around them. "Please, someone fetch a pail of clean water. Cissy?"

Before she could speak again, a pair of well-muscled arms slid beneath the man and lifted him from the ground.

"Let's get him out of the sun," a deep voice rumbled.

Emma glanced up in surprise to find the injured dockworker supported against the broad expanse of a leather-vested chest. Eyes the color of a rain-washed sky looked down at her from a face that might have been carved from oak. Although young, it had been worn into striking planes and hollows. The sun had burned it to a buckskin brown. A shock of black hair fell across the forehead and brushed the dark brows.

Recognizing him as the man she had seen on the horse, Emma nodded. "He should be in the shade. But he needs fresh air, and we must keep him warm."

"Yes, ma'am." The tall man turned from her, and the crowd parted as he strode toward a grove of palm trees.

Her patient momentarily out of her care, Emma stared after the stranger. Clad as no man she had ever known, he wore trousers of a blue that might have been indigo once but had long since faded into a soft, light shade. They molded to his long legs as if almost a part of him. His thick brown leather boots were nothing like the soft leather spats and buttoned footgear her father sported. These had odd chunky heels, squared-off toes and silver spurs that spun when he walked.

Her petticoats causing some difficulty, Emma stood from the wharf. As she started toward the palm grove, she noted that the stranger's shirt was clean and white—brilliant in the afternoon sun—but it didn't do the things a shirt was meant to do. It had somehow lost its stiffness, the collar hanging loose at his neck and the sleeves rolled to his elbows.

Oddest of all was the man's hat. Not a derby, a top hat or even a straw hat, this was made of jet-black felt, and it bore a wide, curling brim with a black leather band. The crown rose above his head, then dipped into a valley at the center.

As Emma approached, she saw him place the injured African on a patch of cool white sand near his horse. Then he slid a wool blanket from behind the black saddle.

"Emma, come quickly!" Cissy's voice drew her attention. "They've taken the other one out of the water. No one will touch him."

Whirling away, Emma followed Cissy through the crowd to the second African, who lay among the debris of the shattered crate. His body, clothed only in a fabric of native weave tied at the waist, glistened with water. He was awake but bleeding from a deep slash across his arm.

"Oh, Cissy, you know I'm not a surgeon," Emma exclaimed, kneeling. "But we can't wait for one. We must bind this wound without a moment's delay."

She glanced up to find her sister's normally rosy cheeks pale, eyes wide with trepidation. Realizing Cissy would be no help, Emma turned her attention to the injured man. With effort, she lifted his trembling shoulders into her lap.

"I am here for you now," she murmured. "With God's help, I shall put you to rights."

Miss Nightingale abhorred the practice of cheering the sick by making light of their danger or by exaggerating their probabilities of recovery. A good nurse must be concise and decisive, she instructed her pupils. Any doubt or hesitation should be kept to oneself and never communicated to the patient. Yet, Emma believed kind words could never hurt.

"Now, let me have a look at your arm," she said gently. The man probably could make little sense of her English language, yet she prayed her tone and touch would suffice. As she lifted his wounded limb, he flinched and tried to pull away. The gash was deep.

"I must bind your arm. I need a clean bandage. Can someone fetch a—"

Observing the sea of dark faces surrounding her, Emma understood at once that she was alone in this effort. The crowd hung paralyzed, every eye focused on her.

"What would Miss Nightingale say now?" she mused. In such a place as this, everything necessary to good patient care was unavailable. Shaking her head, Emma lifted the hem of her lavender skirt, grasped her cotton petticoat and tore off a wide strip. It would have to do. She wrapped the fabric around the man's arm and tied the ends into a neat knot.

"You must go home and wash this wound, sir. Use soap and hot water. Put on a clean bandage and then . . ." She paused and looked up again. Cissy had vanished, and the row of silent faces gaped at her. "Does anyone here speak English?"

"I'll talk to him for you, ma'am." The oddly dressed gentleman shouldered his way through the crowd and knelt in the dust beside her. "Touching a dead man is against these folks' religion. They're afraid both fellows are going to die."

"Not if I can help it. Will you please tell this man something for me?"

"If he knows Swahili."

"You're American, aren't you? I can tell by your manner of speech." Emma looked up into the brilliant blue eyes. "At first I thought you might be Italian."

"Italian?" The man's mouth curved into a slow grin. "Born and raised in Texas. But I've lived here long enough to get by in the language."

"I'm glad to hear it." She made a desperate attempt to calm her fluttering stomach. "Please tell this man he must find a doctor as soon as he can. A surgeon if at all possible."

"I'm afraid that's not going to happen, ma'am. He won't be able to afford the treatment."

"He should have stitches." Dismayed, she shook her head. "Please tell him to wash the wound in fresh water. And keep it wrapped in cloths—clean ones, mind you."

The stranger listened intently, then turned his focus from her and addressed the wide-eyed patient in a string of incomprehensible syllables.

"What did you tell him?" Emma asked.

"What you said, but he won't do it. He'll visit the *mganga*—the local medicine man—and get some homemade remedies. He'll be all right."

"Medicine man? You mean a witch doctor? But that's dreadful—"

"Emmaline Ann Pickering, what do you think

you're doing?" A familiar voice growled overhead. Hard fingers clamped around Emma's shoulders.

She cried out as she was jerked to her feet. The wounded man's head slid from her lap to the ground as Emma confronted a pair of hard gray eyes.

"Father."

Godfrey Pickering scanned his daughter from head to toe. "Explain yourself, girl."

"I was helping . . ." Suddenly faint, she realized her serious lapse in judgment. Any effort to justify her actions would fall on deaf ears, but she must try. "This poor man was badly hurt and—"

"Emmaline, look at yourself," Pickering ordered.

She glanced down at her silk skirt, now dusty and spotted with blood. Her puffed sleeves had collapsed, all the air gone out of them like a pair of burst bubbles. A wisp of hair had slipped from beneath her velvet hat to curl down her arm. Attempting to find a pin and tuck up the stray tress, Emma focused on her father's red face.

"How do you do, sir?" she murmured, dipping a slight curtsy. She had no choice but to play the demure daughter. "I hope I find you well."

Her father's portly chest rose in an annoyed sigh. "Emmaline, do attempt to conduct yourself in the manner to which you were raised. I should like you to meet the assistant director of the East Africa Railway, Mr. Nicholas Bond. Mr. Bond, my elder daughter, Miss Pickering."

A gentleman with brown hair, hazel eyes and a pleasant face stepped forward to extend a gloved hand. "Delighted to meet you, Miss Pickering."

Emma knitted her bare fingers for a moment, then held out her hand. "Mr. Bond, my pleasure. Do forgive me—I seem to have misplaced my gloves."

"Not at all." His lips brushed the back of her hand. "I'm dreadfully sorry you've had such a rude introduction to the protectorate."

"A rude introduction?" Emma turned her eyes to the injured man again. He was sitting up, picking at the cotton bandage. "Such a mishap could hardly have been predicted, sir."

The American gentleman who had assisted Emma earlier now stood and removed his black hat. He glanced at Mr. Bond as if expecting an introduction. When he received no response, he shrugged and thrust out his hand.

"I'm Adam King, ma'am. Pleased to meet you."

Emma placed her hand in the large warm grasp. She studied his blue eyes, assessing and finding them sincere. "Emmaline Pickering. Thank you for your assistance."

"Any time." He continued to hold her hand. "You're a nurse."

"No, she is not a nurse," Emma's father broke in, taking her hand and setting it on his arm. "She is my daughter."

"Mr. Pickering, may I speak plainly?" Nicholas

Bond asked. "This man is unworthy of your acquaintance. Adam King is a troublemaker. He has been most unwelcome in Queen Victoria's protectorate."

"As bad as that, are you?" Mr. Pickering surveyed the American. "Perhaps I should know more about such an adversary."

"Adam King. Rancher." He held out his bare hand to the heavy-jowled man.

"Godfrey Pickering, director of the British Railway." After a moment's hesitation, he shook the extended hand. "Your name is familiar, Mr. King. Is your family occupied in a transportation industry, sir? Railway, perhaps, or shipping?"

Nicholas's eyes darkened as he inserted his own answer. "I assure you, sir, this man is involved in no enterprise so honorable. His closest associates are uneducated farmers. He consorts with the native population—with savages of the lowest form."

A flicker of anger briefly transformed the taller man's features, but he made no reply. As the two men stared at each other in silence, Emma feared the confrontation would come to blows.

But Mr. Bond turned away with a nod. "If you will accompany me, Mr. Pickering, we shall make our way back to the ship and see that your baggage is sent directly to government quarters. Miss Pickering will be eager to prepare for tonight's reception in honor of her father. Indeed, I should be honored to escort you myself. May I have the pleasure?"

Taken aback by Nicholas's cutting remarks about the American who had been of such help to her, Emma nonetheless put on a smile. "How kind, Mr. Bond. I had no idea there was to be a reception."

"It's not every day the protectorate is graced with a dignitary of your father's rank. We rarely have such charming company as you and your sister."

With that he crooked his elbow for her to take. Reluctant to leave Adam King so abruptly, Emma nevertheless slipped her hand around the railway director's arm. But as she lifted her skirt, she turned back to the Texan. Nicholas had no choice but to pause.

"Mr. King," she said quietly. "Again, I thank you for your assistance."

The rancher nodded.

"Will the two men be all right, Mr. King?"

Adam's eyes met hers. "They will, Miss Pickering. I'll make sure of it."

"And the child—the one you lifted onto your horse?" For some reason, she wanted him to know she had seen him save the boy.

He tipped his head in acknowledgment. "He's with his mother."

"Your actions belie your reputation, sir," she said. "I'm glad. Good day, Mr. King."

Without meeting his disturbing gaze again, Emma allowed herself to be led up the gangway

26

and back onto the ship. Spotting Cissy at the rail, she disengaged herself from Mr. Bond, who was eager to accompany her father toward the myriad trunks and hatboxes emerging from below deck.

Joining Cissy, Emma noted her sister's damp cheeks. "What is it, dearest? Are you ill again?"

Clutching her hankie tightly in one fist, the younger woman gripped the railing with the other. "Dirk. He's leaving and I shall never see him again."

Emma spotted the contingent of German soldiers marching down the pier, beginning their long journey toward the border post. Dirk Bauer kept the formation. But as the brigade turned inland, he glanced back for an instant, his eyes locking on Cissy. Then he rounded a corner and was gone.

Cissy stifled a sob with her handkerchief. "I love him, Emma," she said softly. "Truly, I do."

"I know, dearest. Your heart is broken."

"Don't mock me, Emma! The pain is so great I can hardly bear it."

"I'm not making light of it. I understand your suffering."

"Impossible. Romance is as foreign to you as this sweltering continent is to me. You've never known real love."

I don't suppose I have, Emma mused, placing her hand over Cissy's. *But then, I've never cared a fig about men.*

Emma would not fall in love—of that she was

confident. Certainly she would never marry. God intended her to labor for Him as a nurse. He had called her into that glorious service, just as certainly as He had called Miss Nightingale.

Even as Emma recited the assurance she had held in her heart these two long years, her focus wandered to the pier below. Amid the dispersing crowd, the tall rancher stood watching her. He clutched his hat in one hand and hooked the thumb of the other over his belt. His weight rested on one leg, while his broad shoulders slanted in an easy slouch.

Unlike her father and the other Englishmen of her acquaintance, this American looked comfortable, perfectly at home in his body. She had never been allowed to feel so at ease with herself. Corsets, laces and petticoats were tangible reminders of the strictures that bound her.

What would such a man as Adam King be like alone, away from the crowds? Hadn't the warmth of his hand on hers made her shiver? Hadn't it conveyed a promise of strength and security she had never felt in her life?

"Emma, who are you staring at?" Cissy's voice broke into her thoughts. "It's that man on the pier, isn't it? The one in the strange hat. Who is he?"

"His name is Adam King," Emma murmured. "He's an American."

He had begun speaking with the ship's purser now, a much shorter man with a protruding belly.

As Emma made to turn her sister away from the rail, she saw the rancher lean forward, his index finger punctuating his words with regular jabs at the other man's chest. Clearly furious, he edged the ship's officer backward step by step.

"What could the purser have done to anger him so?" Cissy asked.

"I can hardly imagine," Emma replied. The American looked so different now—all his dark strength surged upward into black fury. She gripped the iron rail, conscious of her heart beating in heightened rhythm with the rancher's advance. Just as the purser backed into a low wooden box and could go no farther, Adam stopped. He appeared on the verge of throwing the hefty adversary into the harbor, when the purser whisked a long white envelope from behind his back.

The American snatched the envelope, and the purser scampered up the gangway like a hare eluding a fox. Tearing open the envelope, Adam took out a letter and scanned its contents.

Emma craned forward, anticipating the reaction. Suddenly lifting his head, Adam raised his eyes to the sky. For a moment the man stood frozen—a great tower of pulsing strength, barely leashed by rigid muscles. Then, as if a cord had been severed, the bonds broke and he snapped back to life. Ripping the letter in two, he hurled it to the ground and spun on his spurred heel.

He strode to the grove of palm trees, took his

horse's reins and mounted. The animal reared, hooves churning, then it turned away from the ship to gallop along the harbor and out of sight.

"Heavens," Cissy exclaimed. "I should like to know what was in that letter. Shall I go down and fetch it?"

"No, Cissy." Emma caught her sister's arm. "That man's business is not our affair."

"But haven't you the least bit of curiosity? After all, it's not every day one sees a cowboy."

"A cowboy?" Emma frowned. "Mr. King introduced himself as a rancher."

"He's American, isn't he? With those boots and spurs, what else could he be?"

Emma watched the dust settling along the path the horse had taken. A cowboy . . . the sort of character she had only read about in books. Cowboys led wagon trains across the prairies and drove herds of longhorn cattle down dusty trails. What could such a man be doing in Africa?

"I hope we see him again," Cissy said. "I should like to tell my friends at home that I talked to a real cowboy."

"We won't see him again," Emma told her sister. "Mr. King must have come to Mombasa for that letter and he certainly wasn't pleased with its news."

"He *was* in a great hurry to be off." Cissy tilted her head. "Emma, are you all right?"

Stiffening, Emma realized she was still staring

after the man. "I'm fine, of course. Look, Cissy, our father's new acquaintance is moving our way. He'll expect an introduction."

His top hat a burnished black in the late sunlight, Nicholas Bond held his shoulders straight and his chin up as he approached. Nothing about him echoed the casual slouch of the cowboy rancher. A sudden thought brightened Emma's spirits. Perhaps Mr. Bond might capture her sister's fancy and draw Cissy's attention from poor Dirk Bauer.

"I should like you to meet Mr. Nicholas Bond," Emma said as the man presented himself. "He's the assistant director of the railway. Mr. Bond, my sister, Miss Priscilla Pickering."

"Delighted to make your acquaintance, Miss Pickering." He smiled, swept off his top hat and pressed his lips to Cissy's hand. "And now your father awaits. May I direct you ladies from the ship?"

With a polished clip in his step, he escorted the sisters down the gangway behind their father.

"Your trunks are safely stowed," Bond announced, clapping his hands to summon a trolley. As a pair of young African men pulled the wheeled vehicle to a halt, he turned to the women.

"Miss Priscilla," he said, holding out a hand. "Take care, please. This is no English carriage."

Cissy dipped her head in polite acknowledgment. As Nicholas and her father helped Cissy up the squeaky stair into the covered trolley, a flutter of white caught Emma's eye. Half of Adam King's letter tumbled toward her in the gentle breeze. After a moment's hesitation, she snatched it up.

Roses the color of blood and wine bloomed in a tangle of green vines across the top of the paper. Watercolor florals, done in an elegant hand. The scent of perfume, heady and evocative, clung to the letter as Emma began to read.

My darling. The words swam out in flowing blue ink. *How I've longed to be in your arms! How I've missed you—*

The torn page stopped the words. Emma glanced up to see the men busily tucking Cissy's skirts into the trolley. She read on.

As you know, I had planned to arrive in January, but unfortunately—

Another stop. Emma rushed to the next line.

—the governor's inauguration on the twenty-fifth, and I do wish you could—

—such a long trip, but I know it will be worth it to see you—

—I understand how lonely you've been and how much you want someone to—

—and so after a great deal of careful deliberation as well as many conversations with—

"Emmaline?"

Her father's tone froze Emma's eyes on the final words: *I remain forever, your faithful wife—*

—Clarissa

The torn paper cut through her like a razor's edge.

Dropping the letter, Emma saw the breeze catch it and whip it across the pier, whisk it high into the air and send it fluttering into the turquoise sea.

"Emmaline!"

Her father's voice left no room for longing.

Chapter Two

Emma adjusted her crinolines on the narrow trolley seat as Nicholas Bond sat down beside her. She would have preferred to sit by Cissy, but the layers of petticoats lining their skirts prevented that possibility. As a result, she was forced to ride back-to-back with her sister. The space was cramped, and Emma found herself pressed awkwardly against Nicholas as the trolley jerked to life.

The air smelled of the sea. Emma lifted her face to the sunshine. The turquoise ocean mirrored the sky. Long rippling clouds paralleled an endless white-sand beach. Between shore and sky, seagulls fluttered, calling raucously above the crash of waves and the shouts of dockworkers.

"Mombasa town is on an island," Nicholas explained over the rattle of the trolley. "Actually the coastal strip belongs to the sultan of Zanzibar, while we English control the inland region all the way to Lake Victoria. As you're well aware, Mr. Pickering, we're in dispute with the Germans over control of the Uganda territory to the west."

"Why do you think I've come, young man?" Godfrey Pickering retorted. "It is imperative that our railway reach the lake before theirs does. I don't mean to leave until I'm certain we shall win that race."

The younger man nodded. "I am glad to hear it, sir. My own dream is to see the protectorate become a full-fledged colony of the Crown."

Aware the conversation was little more than bluster, Emma gazed out across the landscape. Huts with thatched roofs graced the shade of stately palm trees. Chickens wandered across the road, oblivious to the trolley. In this populated area, the air was thick with the smells of salted fish and smoke.

Emma had longed for this moment, dreaming of the day she would see Africa. Lying awake at night on board the steamship, she had pictured a land, animals and people known only from sketches in books. Here at last, she could hardly keep her focus. Rather than the white-rimmed waters and the fishing boats, her eyes saw a dark man rising into the sky on a black stallion. Her ears heard not the sounds of clattering trolley wheels, but a deep voice with a strange, lazy accent like a long, slow river winding to the sea. Her ungloved hands felt the touch of a man's fingers—worn and callused yet gentle, too. Even the strong sea scent faded beneath a memory of leather and dusty denim.

Emma wondered what her Aunt Prudence would

have thought of Adam King. She smiled, knowing that her beloved mentor would find the man intriguing. Her thoughts slipped back in time to Aunt Prue's large house in London where she and Cissy had spent the years after their mother's death. Before Mrs. Pickering's calamitous visit to the continent, the family had enjoyed happier seasons at their country estate. But after she died, their father's business and his failing health had forced Emma and Cissy to the city.

Emma redirected her thoughts from her father to the memory of her clandestine ventures to the Nightingale Training School for nurses at St. Thomas's Hospital. In a year's time, she had attended all the required lectures and worked with patients under the supervision of the ward sister. Like the other new nurses, she enjoyed the culminating event of her training—an invitation to take tea with Florence Nightingale herself.

Miss Nightingale had told Emma that at age seventeen, while in the gardens of her home in Embley, she had experienced a call from God. Emma felt a similar divine urging. She intended to imitate Miss Nightingale who had never married, preferring to spend her time writing books and overseeing the nursing school.

When Godfrey Pickering's daughters learned his business was to take him to Africa, they had pleaded to go along. Cissy was eager for the adventure. Emma viewed the journey as God's open door to escape her father and find a mission hospital.

"And how is the railway progressing, Mr. Bond?" Pickering's voice broke into Emma's thoughts.

"Quite well, despite a few setbacks." Nicholas hesitated a moment. "Did you receive the letter about the lions?"

"Lions? No, what about them?"

"We've had a bit of trouble, sir. Farther north, in the Tsavo area . . ." Nicholas glanced at Cissy. "Perhaps we should discuss it later."

Emma sat up straight. What was this about lions? The Englishman's classic profile, pale against the black trolley hood, revealed a subtle tension.

"Do speak frankly, Mr. Bond," Emma told him. "My sister and I are familiar with railway business."

Nicholas cleared his throat. "It appears . . . it is quite clear, that lions have taken to . . . to raiding the workers' camps."

"Raiding?" Cissy spoke up. Her eyes darted from Emma to Nicholas. "Whatever can you mean, Mr. Bond?"

His cheeks suffused an awkward pink color. "The lions . . . two of them . . . have become man-eaters."

Cissy gasped and covered her mouth with her hand. Emma touched the foreman's arm. "Mr. Bond, are you telling us that lions have been killing . . . and eating rail workers?"

"Do let us discuss this later, sir," Pickering cut in. "Your first instinct was correct. Such conversation has no place in the company of ladies."

"I quite agree, sir." A thin line of perspiration trickled from Nicholas Bond's sideburn. "The situation is righting itself even as we speak. Lieutenant Colonel Patterson has tackled the problem head on. Your daughters have nothing to fear, I assure you."

"Have you need for additional personnel or munitions? I can telegraph for the funds from England if need be."

"No, no." Nicholas shook his head. "It is under control."

Emma heard her father give a brief harrumph. This lion business was no small thing. With laborers huddling in fear of their lives, work should be stopped. But her father would never halt the race against the Germans toward Lake Victoria. Surrender was not an option.

Looking out again, she saw that the trolley had taken them into the narrow, cobblestone streets of Mombasa town. Flat-roofed two-story houses sagged upon one another as if weary of standing in the blazing heat. Corroded iron balconies thrust out over the street. Wooden doors, carved in geometric shapes and studded with brass, stood open to let in air.

"This is the business sector," Nicholas said, his voice stronger now. "Luxurious wares arrive from the Far East on *dhows*—the small trading ships you saw in the harbor. They sail the monsoon winds up and down the coast. Ah, here we are . . ."

The trolley rolled up to an iron gate, and the four passengers descended. The grounds of the compound were a sea of lush grass dotted with islands of orange and blue birds of paradise, deep purple bougainvilleas and green philodendrons.

The men deposited their hats with white-gloved servants and walked ahead into the shadows of the wide verandah.

"Emma," Cissy whispered, catching her sister's arm. "Do you think there's danger here? From those lions?"

"No, Cissy," Emma assured her. "There's a fence all around. And guards. We're quite safe."

"I feel at odds with everything here. It's dreadfully hot, and the talk about man-eating lions gave me a fright. Oh, Emma, I'm not suited to this sort of place."

Emma squeezed Cissy's hand and led her up the stairs into the cool depths of the verandah. "Perhaps you are and you just don't know it yet."

"Emmaline, Priscilla, do come here." Their father stood beside a handsome couple. A tailored tea dress identified the woman as a lady. Her husband's refined face with its aquiline nose was a study in classic grace.

"Lord and Lady Delamere," Pickering said. "I present my elder daughter, Miss Emmaline Pickering. Her sister, Miss Priscilla Pickering.

Ladies, this is Hugh Cholmondeley, third Baron Delamere of Vale Royal in Cheshire, and his wife, Lady Delamere."

"Such formality!" Lady Delamere laughed. "I'm Florence, and everyone in the protectorate calls my husband 'D.' You must do the same."

"You have a lovely home," Emma spoke up.

"Oh, this is not our home! It belongs to Sir Charles Eliot, Her Majesty's commissioner in East Africa. He's on leave in England. Hugh and I live up country at Njoro. But you both must be exhausted. Shall I have tea sent to your rooms?"

"Yes, thank you." Emma looked ruefully at her blood-spattered gown and dusty hem. "I must apologize for my appearance today."

"Take no trouble over it, Miss Pickering," Lord Delamere said. "You'll learn one can't be terribly proper here—though we try to keep up a good show."

"Thank you, sir. You see—"

"Never mind, Emmaline," Pickering interrupted. "Get on with you now. I shall see you at dinner."

Biting her tongue at being summarily dismissed, Emma watched her father step into the house with Lord Delamere. His wife led the young women into the house. The grand home might have been in England for all the lace antimacassars and porcelain figurines scattered throughout. Only the zebra skin on the hall floor reminded Emma that she was in Africa.

Left alone at last in their suite, Emma and Cissy hurried to the settee and dropped onto the soft cushions. "I could do with a bath to calm my nerves."

"Nothing better," Emma agreed. Then she frowned. Actually, things could be better. But a bath would have to do.

With a warm soak and a cup of tea to rejuvenate her, Emma set her sights on the evening ahead. As Cissy laced the corset over her sister's chemise, Emma worked out her strategy.

She would not allow the evening to go to waste. Nicholas Bond had lived in the protectorate for some time. She must make him tell her everything she wanted to know—locations of hospitals, the need for nurses and all the other questions that clamored to be asked.

Once she had answers, Emma could map out a plan. The sooner she set that plan into motion, the less time her father would have to think up other options for her future.

When the sisters were dressed at last, they descended the stairs to dinner. Cissy floated in a cloud of blue silk and feathers. A pair of nervous African ladies' maids had managed to arrange her golden hair around an artificial bluebird, and she did look stunning.

Emma felt as awkward as she always did beside her glowing sister. Although her green gown had a silk sash and was trimmed in soft pink roses, she could never compare with the dainty treasure at her side. Her sleeveless shoulders were just as creamy and her waist as narrow, but she knew she would never look as enchanting as Cissy did. Such trivialities had long ago ceased to matter. Neither men nor fashion were the objects of her dreams.

Cissy placed a gloved hand on Emma's arm and leaned close. "Do I look all right?"

Emma smiled. "You'll turn all the men's heads."

Cissy's face did not brighten. "I miss Dirk. I miss him dreadfully."

Stifling the sigh that threatened to escape at the hundredth mention of Cissy's German soldier, Emma directed her sister's attention to the opposite side of the room, where their father stood. "You must not speak of Dirk to Father, Cissy. You know how he feels about that sort of thing."

"I know how he feels about our future husbands," Cissy replied. "Well, I won't marry without love. I assure you that."

The dinner bell rang, and the young women made their way to the dining room. It might have been an evening at Aunt Prue's house in London for all Emma could tell. Course followed course down the long table with its spotless white cloth. The gentlemen and ladies attending behaved as though they were visiting Queen Victoria herself. Even the conversation revolved around the empire.

After dinner, Emma rose with the others and left the dining room. She stepped into the center of the ballroom, her eyes on the tall figure standing beside the fireplace. Nicholas turned, and for an instant Emma felt as if she were in the presence of her father. Something in the set of the man's shoulders and the look in his eyes evoked the dark, uncompromising demeanor of Godfrey Pickering.

But the moment passed as Nicholas smiled and made a gallant bow. "How lovely you look, Miss Pickering. I'm delighted to be your escort this evening."

Emma saw that Lord Delamere had ascended the platform to stand before the military band. He was addressing the hushed crowd.

"I have known Mr. Godfrey Pickering only a few hours, yet I assure you, he is as fine a representative of our Queen as I have ever had the privilege to meet. Mr. Pickering is a man who believes—as do we all—in the supremacy of our beloved isle and the God-given directive to expand her empire. It is with pleasure that I give you the director of the East African Railway, Mr. Godfrey Pickering."

Emma clapped with the others as her father stepped to Lord Delamere's side. She should be proud, but as he lauded England and his part in her glories, she saw nothing but a hollow man. For all his wealth and power, Godfrey Pickering was a bitter person who expected the world and the lives of those around him to conform to his exacting expectations. He had demanded that of her mother, and look what had happened.

"Your father is the sort of gentleman who has made England what she is today," Nicholas murmured, surprising Emma as he took her into his arms and turned her onto the dance floor. Lost in memory, she had not heard her father stop speaking nor the music start. She stumbled a little as she strove to match her step with that of her escort.

"You were brave this afternoon at the harbor, Miss Pickering," he murmured, his mouth a little too close to her ear. "I don't wonder that your father was concerned. This is not England. You must be careful."

Emma recognized her chance and seized it. "I assist others as the need for my skills arises, Mr. Bond. I am a nurse."

"A nurse?" The flicker of a frown crossed his face. "Nursing is an unusual pastime for a woman of your standing, is it not, Miss Pickering?"

"Pastime? Nursing is my vocation, Mr. Bond."

"Strong words for a strong belief. I like conviction in a woman."

Emma glanced up at him in surprise. Although Nicholas seemed sincere, she wondered whether he spoke the truth. If so, he was a rare man, indeed.

A disturbance in the hall drew his attention, and he paused in the dance. Emma took the opportunity to study this railway officer who so admired her father.

Nicholas Bond wore a finely tailored black suit with a tailcoat and white gloves, and his stiff white collar stood fashionably high. Not a bad looking fellow at all. Just the sort to turn Cissy's thoughts from her German soldier.

As for her own feelings about the man, Emma had only one mission in mind. "Mr. Bond," she ventured. "Can you tell me where I might find a hospital in the protectorate? I'm hoping to—"

"Excuse me, Miss Pickering." He released her and took a step toward the door, his eyes on something at a distance.

Emma followed his gaze across the room. As the dancers ceased moving and all attention turned to the hallway, the musicians broke off in awkward discord. Voices, arguing and growing louder, carried into the ballroom. A group of agitated men surrounded a figure who rose head and shoulders above them.

Emma caught her breath as she recognized Adam King. The American. The cowboy. His blue eyes surveyed the crowd until they met hers. His focus unwavering, he took off his black hat and started across the room in her direction. Instantly the commotion began again.

"What is the meaning of this?" Lord Delamere's voice rose over the hubbub.

"Sir, this man insists on entering the consulate without invitation," a servant explained apologetically.

"Adam King?" Lord Delamere blinked in confusion. "I had no idea you were in Mombasa."

The taller man halted. "I'm here, D. Mind if I join you?"

"Not at all, sir. Do come in." Lord Delamere smiled and shook his guest's hand. He turned back to the musicians. "Carry on, carry on!"

As the violins sounded again, the dancers drew their eyes away from the tall rancher. Lord Delamere rejoined his colleagues at the fireplace. Emma decided it was time to find her sister and retire. But Nicholas gripped her elbow as Adam King made his way through the swirling skirts.

"Good evening, Miss Pickering." The American's blue eyes fixed on Emma's as he acknowledged her companion with a nod. "Bond."

"Good evening, Mr. King." Emma extended her hand, and this time he lifted it to his lips. His thick hair, glossy in the lamplight, shone a blue-black.

"What do you want, King?" Nicholas's tone was hostile. "You can have no good purpose in joining our company."

"But I do. I came to return these." Adam reached into the pocket of his black trousers and pulled out Emma's lavender gloves.

Her cheeks grew warm as she took them. "My goodness—I thought I would never see these again. Thank you so much, Mr. King. How kind of you."

"Yes, well done, sir," Nicholas said. "Now if you'll excuse us—"

"Mr. Bond, would you be so good as to see to my

sister's welfare?" Emma heard herself ask. "Cissy was greatly fatigued this afternoon."

Nicholas stared at her.

"I believe I owe Mr. King the next dance," she went on. "In gratitude for returning my gloves."

He opened his mouth to protest, then obviously thought better of it. "Of course, Miss Pickering," he consented. "I am happy to oblige."

As he stepped away, Emma noted Adam's amused expression. "Perhaps I spoke out of turn, sir," she said. "Normally I am not so bold."

"Aren't you? You were mighty bold this afternoon on the pier." His mouth curved into a warm smile. "You took control of the situation without stopping to think about consequences. That's good. A woman needs courage in this country."

"Thank you. I have been trained as a nurse, you see."

He searched her eyes. "But your father said—"

"My father disapproves. Nevertheless, I have undertaken rigorous instruction at Miss Nightingale's school in St. Thomas's Hospital."

"I don't know who Miss Nightingale is, but I'm sure she has a fine school." He stood before her, making no move to dance. "Miss Pickering, do you—"

The music stopped and Adam's question with it. Clutching her lavender gloves, Emma peered around his broad shoulder to see Nicholas striding across the room toward them. She looked back at

Adam. Now strains of the "Blue Danube" waltz began to swell in the warm air.

"Mr. Bond has completed his mission, I see," she said. "Thank you once again for returning my gloves, Mr. King."

Nicholas slipped his arm beneath Emma's. But as he moved to lead her away, Adam stepped in front of him. "Just a minute, Bond. I believe I was promised a dance with this young lady."

"Mr. King." Nicholas spoke the name in a steely voice. "Miss Pickering offered you the last dance. Now I've returned. If you will excuse us, please."

"No, I won't excuse you." Adam loomed over the Englishman. "But I will thank you to take your hands off the lady until I've had my dance."

Nicholas's eyes blazed. "And I'll thank you to hold your tongue. I am Miss Pickering's escort this evening. Have you no manners, sir?"

"Don't talk to me about manners, Bond. I was invited to dance by this young woman and I am accepting."

"Gentlemen, please," Emma interjected. She must end this nonsense quickly. "Mr. Bond, I did offer to dance with your friend. And then I must declare my dance card full for the evening. Mr. King?"

She looked up at him, but Adam made no move toward her. His focus had narrowed on the other man, and for a moment Emma feared Nicholas's disdainful expression would be shattered by a blow from the American's fist. Instead, Adam set his hat on his head, swept Emma into his arms and spun her out onto the floor.

"Mr. King!" Her eyes flew open as he whirled her around the room, barely avoiding collisions with more genteel dancers who stared at them in alarm.

An unfamiliar thrill coursed through Emma at the realization that the American had come back into her life . . . had sought her out . . . was holding her, even now, in his strong arms. Her feet barely touched the floor as the music soared through the room. Releasing Adam's shoulder, she clutched at the spray of pink roses pinned to her hair for fear of losing it. She might have twirled away entirely, but one of his hands held her waist while the other wove through her fingers.

"I'm not much of a high-toned dancer, to tell you the truth, ma'am," he said, spinning Emma toward the musicians at such a speed that her dress billowed up around her calves.

"Sir, this is a bit—" She caught her breath as he flung her away from him, then whipped her back against his chest in a crushing hold. "A bit different!"

He threw back his head in a hearty laugh, then looked down at her with shining eyes. "This is the way we dance in Texas. Those musicians just need a few lessons in fiddling, and then they'd do this tune up right."

Emma spotted Cissy gawking at her in astonishment. "But I do believe this is the way Mr. Strauss intended it played," she told Adam.

"Dull, don't you think?" He grinned at the glowering Nicholas as they passed him in a mad whirl.

Emma gave up on her hair and tossed her head, letting the curls pull out and tumble down her back. Catching his shoulder once again, she felt a ripple of shock at the hard muscle beneath his white linen shirt. His black tie fluttered at his neck and his hair bounced loosely, falling over his ears and down his forehead. He was all movement, all liveliness and rhythm—nothing like the stiff gentlemen who held her as though she were made of porcelain.

As she and Adam danced, Emma felt her body loosen and sway against his, melting into his easy whirl. And then the music slowed. Adam guided her toward the wide French doors that opened onto a long verandah.

"Something you said today intrigued me," he spoke against her ear. "I came here this evening because I wanted to talk to you. Would you like to take a walk, Miss Pickering?"

Her heart warned her not to be foolish. Hadn't Nicholas said this man was untrustworthy? And he was married, after all. Married. Somewhere his wife waited for him, wanting and missing and loving him.

"Mr. King, I—" Before she could answer, he eased her out onto a dimly lit walkway.

• • •

The last strains of the waltz faded. Adam glanced back into the crowd and caught sight of Nicholas Bond searching for them.

"I really should go back in, you know," Emma protested.

But as she looked into his eyes, Adam knew she would not return. He held out his arm. She hesitated, then slipped her hand around it. "Let's take a stroll," he suggested. "I never have liked crowds."

"What is it you wish to discuss, Mr. King?"

"You, mostly." He could see the toes of her slippers beneath the hem of skirt as they walked along a gravel path. Away from the stuffy air of the ballroom, he caught the scent of her perfume. Jasmine and roses.

He drew her closer. Somehow—against every shred of sense and determination he possessed—he'd let this strange, willful woman affect him. All he could do was stare down at her and feel things he shouldn't feel. Her flushed cheeks and shining green eyes mesmerized him. Her full rosy lips, barely parted, were tilted slightly upward. He bent toward her.

Just then, she stopped walking and touched her forehead. "Oh, my."

"Miss Pickering? Are you all right?"

"Out of breath. Perhaps it was the dancing."

Or maybe not. He was having a little trouble breathing right himself. "Would you like to sit down?" he asked. "I saw some chairs at the other end of the porch."

"No, I'm fine. Truly I am." She took her hand from his arm and wove her fingers together. "You wanted to speak with me?"

"Yes, I do." He straightened, forcing away the discomfort she'd given him. He couldn't let himself think about the fact that she was beautiful and brave . . . and completely a woman.

Emma Pickering could be useful to him, that was all, and he might as well lay the cards on the table. "I want to know more about your nursing skills."

Her eyes widened in surprise. "Nursing?"

"How much practical experience have you had?"

"Not enough to satisfy me." She shook her head. "Miss Nightingale does not permit nurses to learn pure medicine. I've always longed to know as much as any doctor, but such a course is not possible. I have looked after patients at St. Thomas's Hospital, many of them gravely ill, but that is the extent of my training."

Adam started forward again. "Can you do surgical kinds of things?" he asked as she hurried to match his pace. He took her hand and set it on his arm again. "Can you sew people up and set bones?"

"I've watched those procedures being done. But I have neither the tools nor the skills to do them myself. Mr. King, why are you asking me these questions?"

He couldn't tell her everything, but she was too

smart to keep completely in the dark. He would have to lead her around until he had learned what he wanted to know.

"I understand that doctors have ways to make people unconscious," he said. "Know anything about that?"

"Ether. I've seen it used. Why?"

"Do you know much about drugs? Medicines?"

"Morphia, quinine, cocaine, laudanum and others—I've dispensed them all."

"But do you know what they're used for? Do you know what can help pain—constant pain?"

"Laudanum is best, I believe—although one must be careful. Its use can become a habit. Morphia is similar."

"Miss Pickering?" Nicholas Bond's voice rang out down the long verandah and startled Emma into silence. The Englishman stood silhouetted in the light from the ballroom, his long coattails fluttering in the night breeze.

"Yes, Mr. Bond," she spoke up. "I'm just here on the path."

"Your father is concerned for your safety, Miss Pickering."

"The lady's fine, Bond." Adam escorted her onto the verandah and into a square of yellow light that fell from the French doors.

"Miss Pickering?"

"Indeed, I'm perfectly well, Mr. Bond. This garden is lovely."

Adam knew it was time to let Nicholas take the woman back to the ballroom. Good manners demanded it. He had been wrong to lead her outside unaccompanied in the first place. But when he began to remove her hand, she tightened her fingers around his arm.

"Mr. King mentioned his unusual dancing style," she told Nicholas as they approached. She gave a little laugh. "It's American, you know. I'm sure you must agree it's my duty as an Englishwoman to teach him a proper waltz. You won't mind, will you?"

Nicholas frowned, his lips tightening into a grim line. "Miss Pickering, I—"

"Dear Mr. Bond, it does seem the right thing to do under the circumstances. It would hardly show the English to good advantage if we let this poor man continue in his ignorance."

Bond flipped back his coattails and set his fists at his hips. He started to speak, paused, then turned abruptly and left. Even though the two men were not friendly, Adam could hardly blame Bond for his displeasure. Emma had rebuffed him.

"Come, Mr. King," she said. "With one dance you will know all I have to teach. And I shall understand why you asked me such questions just now."

She crossed to the French doors, and Adam pushed them open. Laying her lavender gloves on a side table, she gave him a little curtsy.

"Shall we dance?" she asked.

• • •

Adam made no move. Emma looked into his blue eyes and watched them gazing back at her. They had gone dark now, with black rims that matched the lashes framing them. He set his right hand at her waist and drew her close. Without taking his eyes from hers, he spread her slender fingers with his left hand and squeezed them gently.

The music barely filtered into her ears, even though she knew it was there—for as they drifted out onto the floor, Emma's sense of the world around her seemed to vanish. All she heard was the heavy throb of her heartbeat and the quiet jingle of Adam's spurs as his boot heels tapped the wooden floor. She was aware of her skirt, floating behind her on its stiff crinolines—meant to keep the dancers apart, but failing tonight. He held her close, too close for this dance. Yet she could not stop him, could not make herself say the proper words, the polite things, the gracious empty syllables.

"Emma . . ." The name floated from his lips in his strange, beguiling accent. His breath warmed her ear.

Her mind told her to pull back from him, warned her—he was treacherous, he was foreign. He was married.

Yet he lifted her feet from the floor, and her cheek brushed against his shoulder. The scent of leather and the plains filled her nostrils . . . and her mind reeled away with all its doubts and warnings.

Her eyes met his again, deep pools in which she thought she might drown. "Mr. King," she whispered, trying to prevent herself from falling into them.

"Call me Adam," he said.

They moved into the shadows of an alcove, and he stopped, still holding her close in his arms. The music died and the other dancers separated, sweeping into bows and curtsies and polite applause.

"Emma." He lifted her chin with a finger. "Thank you."

Aching to speak, she found it impossible to form words. She glanced toward the crowd as the music started and yet another dance began. Cissy stood in one corner surrounded by a cluster of attentive men. Their father was speaking with Lord Delamere.

And now she saw Nicholas approaching. He made a small bow. "You may leave now, Mr. King," he said. "I advise you to keep your attentions from Miss Pickering in the future. Her father is not pleased."

Adam's eyes flashed with an anger that twisted Emma's stomach into a knot. "I decide who gets my attention, Bond," he growled. "If you've got a problem with that, let's step outside and settle this."

"Do you challenge me, sir? I hope not. I may be

forced to speak with Lord Delamere and Commissioner Eliot about the sort of men scratching out a living on the queen's protectorate. Traitors to the Crown."

"Talk to anyone you want, Bond. I'm not budging from my ranch—not even for the queen herself. Excuse me, Miss Pickering. I have business to take care of."

Adam doffed his black hat and strode through the whirling dancers toward the verandah, his heavy footsteps echoing across the floor. Nicholas's neck was red above his white collar as he faced Emma.

"I must apologize, Miss Pickering. You can see the man has no respect for our queen or her empire. Adam King is a schemer and a liar. Not a word of truth escapes his lips. You must not trust the man for a moment. I beg you to keep yourself under guard if you chance to meet him again. His forward behavior with you this evening was inexcusable."

"Emma," Cissy cried, hurrying across the room and taking her sister's hand. "May I speak with you for a moment in private? Do you mind dreadfully if I take my sister away, Mr. Bond?"

Emma glanced at the young railway man. Even though he tried to maintain his genteel poise, irritation showed on his face. She spoke softly. "I'll just be a moment, Mr. Bond."

"Of course, Miss Pickering."

Cissy slipped her arm around Emma's and hurried across the room toward the verandah.

"What have you done, sister?" Cissy's voice was a shrill whisper. "You let that man—that cowboy—take you outside without a chaperone! Father is livid. Honestly, Emma, what were you thinking?"

"Father saw us?" She'd had no idea.

"Of course he did. You're meant to be dancing with Mr. Bond. He's your escort."

"Adam asked about my nursing."

"Adam? You call him Adam?"

But Emma did not hear her sister's words. She was gazing at the gloves on the side table beside the door. Lifting her eyes to the window, she looked out into the moonlit night.

A movement caught her attention and she focused on the long gravel drive lined with flowering trees. Down its silvery path galloped a dark shadow of a horse. As the rider urged his mount through the gate and turned onto the street, Emma gingerly lifted her gloves from the table.

Chapter Three

"Emmaline."

At the deep voice, Emma turned from the ballroom window to face her father. Lips rimmed in white, he stared at her.

"Yes, Father?" She heard the tremble in her voice.

"Come with me, Emmaline."

Emma glanced at Cissy, whose face had paled to

ash. With a quick squeeze of her sister's hand, Cissy nudged Emma toward their father. Godfrey Pickering turned on his heel and strode across the room toward the hallway.

Hurrying after him, Emma swallowed at the fear of what was to come, a scene father and daughter so often had played out. Knowing what to expect did nothing to calm the thundering of her heart. She ventured a look at Nicholas. He had risen from the sofa, his eyes narrowed in curiosity.

"Father, what is it?" Emma called after the man, though she knew her offense too well.

He opened the door to a study some distance from the ballroom. "Emmaline, sit down."

She perched on the edge of a long, overstuffed couch and knotted her hands together in her lap. Standing in front of a heavily curtained window, Pickering gazed at his daughter. He placed the tips of his fingers on the back of an armchair.

"Emmaline, did my eyes deceive me just now?"

She studied her fingers. "What did you see, Father?"

"I believe I saw you walking outside with a man. The American."

"Sir, Mr. King wished to speak to me about a matter of some import. Truly, you saw nothing untoward."

She stopped speaking, eyes on her father. Was he angry enough to strike her? It would not be the first time.

"Must I defend my actions on every occasion,

Father?" she asked him. "You insist that I marry, and the sooner the better. Why should it trouble you where I place my attentions?"

Pickering's eyes blazed. "Of course I want you to marry. I expect you to marry, and you will—as every woman should. But your husband must be suitable, Emmaline. A man like Nicholas Bond."

"I have no interest in Mr. Bond." Emma stood. "Nor do I want Adam King, for that matter. If I have my way, I shall never marry."

"Emmaline, lower your voice," Godfrey ordered. "Our words can be heard in the hall."

"I'm sorry, Father," she said with a sigh. "Forgive me."

His eyes narrowed. "Sit down, Emmaline."

"Father, I am twenty-two years old. Please speak to me as an adult."

"I might consider it if you would act like one. But you insist on disobedience—as though your own feelings and desires are all that matter to your future."

"What else can be of any significance to me?"

"The right and proper thing to do! Emmaline, you will one day be a woman of immense wealth."

She had heard this speech so often she could almost recite her father's words.

"You must see to it that your inheritance is not squandered," he continued. "My money can only be entrusted to a man with a good head for business."

"Do you wish you could take every tuppence

with you when you die, Father?" She tried to hold her tongue. "I'm nothing more than a bank to you. If I marry the right man, your wealth will increase—and that's all you care about. My feelings don't matter. My future happiness makes no difference. My only purpose is to ensure that your precious holdings continue to grow so that your name may be remembered with admiration."

"How dare you speak to me in this way?" Pickering's voice quivered with rage. He walked toward Emma as he spoke. "You are my daughter and you will obey me. You must marry, or you will never have a farthing to your name. And you will marry the man I select."

"I shall not." Emma took a step backward. She had never spoken her thoughts so freely, but something inside her had changed. "I don't care if I never see tuppence from you. I shall do what I'm meant to do, and you cannot stop me."

"I can stop you and I will stop you." Her father loomed before her now, his nostrils flaring as one hand gripped his chest over his heart.

Emma trembled as she faced him. "You can do nothing to me, sir. Nothing—ever again."

As her words registered, his hand shot out and caught her across the cheek in a stinging blow. Her head jerked backward. The ceiling spun and went dark. Then she was on the floor, clutching her burning face.

Her father took a step and set his foot on her

skirt, crushing the soft pink roses. "I am telling you now that you will marry the man I select," he hissed. "You will have nothing more to do with Miss Nightingale or her nursing school or any other harebrained scheme of yours. Never forget your mother's wickedness. I shall not allow you to disgrace me as she did. Do you understand?"

"Yes, Father." Her head felt as if it had burst and she licked at the blood on her lip.

"Your behavior tonight was unfortunate, indeed. You embarrassed me, Emmaline."

Nodding, she closed her eyes. "I'm so sorry, sir."

She had always tried to do as he asked. These many years she had taken the place of her mother in restraining Cissy, in managing the household, in acting as hostess to her father's associates. She had done all in her power to prevent his ire.

Cissy had no idea how often Emma had protected her from their father by blocking the advances of unsuitable would-be beaux. And yet when Cissy fell in love . . . and she often did . . . her father lightly reproved her, then hugged and pampered his younger daughter. Emma, who looked and acted so much like her mother, bore the brunt of his rage.

"Priscilla is in your charge," he reminded Emma. "You must set a worthy example for your sister. I expect you to take care of her and protect her. I cannot be both mother and father to my daughters. Is that clear?"

"Yes, Father."

"Then go to your room, Emmaline. I shall inform our hosts you were feeling tired."

Struggling to her feet, Emma tugged her hem from beneath her father's foot. At the door, she picked up the lavender gloves and held them to her lips. Her injuries would not look bad now, but she knew it could not be long until her face was blue and swollen.

As she stepped into her room, Emma shut the door behind her and ran to the window. Pushing back the curtain, she pressed her cheek against the cool glass and let the tears flow.

Her father was right, of course. She could never escape him. She must do as he said. Always.

Was it possible that her father was more powerful even than God? Although such a thought seemed blasphemous, Emma now knew without doubt that she would never be a nurse. The holy calling in her heart could not be answered. One day very soon she must marry the man of her father's choosing—a proper man, as her mother had done. She would bear children, her father's longed-for male heirs. She would live in a fine house in London during the season and spend the other months at a country estate.

She would do all the things she had been brought up to do. It would a fine life. A grand life. And somehow her father, a mere mortal, would overpower the will of God Almighty.

"Emma?" The door swung open and Cissy stepped into the darkened room.

"I'm here, Cissy." She drew away from the window.

"You must come quickly! It's Father's heart again. He's having a spell."

For an instant Emma hesitated. Her father had forbidden her to practice nursing. By rights she could refuse to go to him, letting him suffer or perhaps even—

"Where is he?" she asked, hurrying toward her sister.

"In the study. Mr. Bond found him collapsed on the floor."

"Did you use his smelling salts?"

"I forgot." Cissy clapped her hand over her mouth. "Oh, Emma, you know how useless I am in a panic!"

"It's all right. Come with me." Emma lifted her skirts and strode along the hall and down the steps.

The study was crowded with guests as she pushed her way toward the sofa where her father lay. Lady Delamere hovered over him while Nicholas placed a damp cloth on his pallid forehead.

"We must have fresh air," Emma said as she knelt on the carpet beside the settee. "Please clear the room, Mr. Bond."

She saw at once that her father's round stomach rose and fell evenly. His heart, though weak, still pulsed. Flipping back his lapel, she removed the bottle of salts from his pocket and held it under his nose. Instantly his eyes fluttered open and he began coughing.

"There, there," she murmured softly, as her mother always had. "All is well, sir. You must rest."

He caught her arm. "Emmaline, is my daughter—?"

"Calm yourself, Father." Emma anticipated the question that always formed itself upon his lips after an episode. "Priscilla is fine. You've given her a bit of a fright, but she's just outside the door waiting to see you. I shall send her to you in a moment."

Rising, she spoke with Lady Delamere, then she slipped out of the room. Cissy rushed to her sister's side. Her blue eyes swam with tears.

"Emma, did something happen in the study?" she whispered. "Did you quarrel?"

"We did have words."

As she turned away, Cissy gasped. "Oh, Emma! He's hit you again, hasn't he? Your cheek!"

"Shh, Cissy," Emma said. "Say nothing more."

Arm in arm, they left the others and returned to their suite. Cissy turned up the gas lamp so that the room was bathed in a golden glow. She turned toward her sister.

"Come with me, Emma. I want you to see something."

Emma allowed herself to be led to the mirror. When she gazed into it, she saw two figures staring back at her. One was just as she had been when they'd left the room earlier that evening. Cissy stood prim and soft in a powder-blue gown, her golden hair coiled around a bright bird, her eyes shining.

Emma hardly recognized herself. Her hair, no longer curled and pinned to the top of her head, hung wild about her shoulders from her dance with Adam. The pink stain of her father's handprint marred her cheek. Her mouth was swollen and bruised. Shaking her head, she touched the drop of dried blood on her lip.

"What has become of me?" she whispered. "Who am I?"

"You're my sister and I love you," Cissy said. "Do as he says, Emma. Please don't let him hurt you again. Please."

Emma folded her sister into her arms. "I love you, too, Cissy."

A loud thumping woke Emma from a tortured dream. Sitting up, she blinked in confusion at her surroundings.

"Oh, do come and look!" Cissy fluttered before the window in a long white nightgown.

Emma slid from her bed and padded across the room. "What is that noise? It can't be thunder—the sun is too bright."

"Just look!" Cissy clapped her hands in delight as Emma stepped out onto a small balcony and peered down at the tin roof of the wing below. A quartet of monkeys danced and cavorted across it—thin, wiry monkeys with gray fur and funny black faces.

Emma had to smile, but as she did her lip cracked painfully.

Cissy's brow furrowed at the sight. "Oh, dear. You look as though you've been to battle."

"I have been to battle." As she watched the monkeys, Emma dabbed at her lip. "We shall soon have our fill of wild creatures, you know. The train leaves at eight. What time is it now?"

"Six-thirty. The servants brought breakfast earlier, but I chose not to wake you. It's on the table."

Emma turned into the room, but her sister's next words brought her head around quickly.

"Emma, look! It's your cowboy."

The black horse she recognized from the previous day was trotting down the long drive. Adam tipped his hat to the window, a smile lighting the features of his handsome face. Emma shrank back, her hand over her bruised cheek.

"He saw you, Emma. He was looking for you." Cissy peeped out from behind the curtain. "Isn't he odd—and wonderful at the same time? Just look at that long riding coat. It's made of leather. Have you ever seen such a thing? And his boots. Aren't they rough?"

Emma couldn't resist peering over Cissy's

shoulder. Adam dismounted and looped the reins over the branch of a flowering tree. A gentle breeze ruffled his black hair.

"He's wearing those blue trousers again, isn't he?" Emma whispered. "They suit him. I do like that hat, although it certainly isn't anything one would see in London or Paris."

"Do you suppose he's come to call on you?"

"Call on me? Don't be silly, Cissy." Her heart fluttering, Emma left the balcony, drew the curtains and started for the breakfast table. "He has business with Lord Delamere, I'm sure. They know one another well."

"I think he likes you." Cissy eased herself into the chair across from her sister and picked up a slice of toast.

"Mr. King is married, Cissy." Emma swallowed a sip of tea. "He has a wife—in America."

"Oh." Cissy's voice was low.

"Do pass the jam." Emma blinked back the tears that inexplicably had filled her eyes. She took up a knife and buttered the toast. "I'm going to have to get married, Cissy. Father will choose the man."

Cissy's eyes clouded. "I'm not going to marry anyone. My heart belongs to Dirk Bauer. I hope he's safe. He promised to write me every day, but . . ."

Emma half listened to Cissy, whose conversation—as usual—focused on herself. Sounds in the hallway below were of greater interest at the moment. She wondered if Adam were now inside the house. What had he come for? What was his wife like? *Clarissa.* How long had they been married, and when would she arrive in the protectorate? Did they have children? He would wish to be near his children, she felt sure as she remembered the sight of him holding the small African boy he had rescued.

"I miss Dirk so much my insides ache with longing," Cissy was saying. "Every waking moment I think about him, Emma. I mourn him. He's probably at his post by now, standing guard against the enemy—us."

Emma took Cissy's delicate hand in hers. Of late, the German kaiser had been causing Queen Victoria no end of trouble. Safeguarding a claim to inland territory coveted by both the Germans and the British had led her father and his associates to build the railway. The ivory trade was essential to the realm.

"Oh, Emma," Cissy cried, "do you hate the kaiser because he wants to stop the spread of the empire? I don't! I can't make myself care about him at all. Dirk is a German, he's good and kind and he loves me."

"I know, Cissy, but you must do your best not to think about him. You and Dirk enjoyed three happy weeks together. Now you have your whole life ahead."

At a knock on the door, Emma took up her shawl and hurried across the room. In the hall, a servant held out a silver tray bearing a pen, an inkwell, and an envelope. She read the words written on it in a bold black hand:

Miss Emma Pickering

With a glance at Cissy, she took out the note and opened it. *Emma, please come down. I need to talk to you about the subject we discussed last night. Adam King*

She let out a breath. Of course she could never agree to see the man again. To preserve a fragile peace, she must obey her father.

"What is it, Emma?" Cissy called. "Am I wanted?"

"It's nothing," Emma replied. "I'll be with you in a moment."

She must send her polite regrets at once. It was one thing to disobey her father by following God's leading to become a nurse. It was quite another to pursue her own willful yearnings into the arms of a married man.

Picking up the pen, she dipped it into the inkwell on the silver tray and wrote on a clean sheet of paper.

Dear Mr. King,

I cannot speak with you again. Please forgive me. Emmaline Pickering

She blew on the ink to dry it, then she slipped the letter into the envelope and thanked the servant. The man nodded and set off down the hall toward the stairs.

"Was it from him?" Cissy rose from her chair. "Did Mr. King send up his calling card?"

"He asked to speak with me. I wrote that I couldn't go down."

Emma moved to the washstand and surveyed her reflection. Her cheek bore a pink bruise and her lips were still swollen. She poured cool water into the basin and splashed it on her face.

Why must she honor her father by complying with his wishes? Look what he had done to her. His mistreatment was insufferable. Yet suffer she would. The opportunity to ask Adam about a mission hospital had been lost. She would have to pry the information from Mr. Bond, even though he probably knew little beyond railroads and waltzing.

Praying for peace, Emma stepped to her trunk and took out a beige traveling skirt and a white blouse. Cissy helped Emma into her corset and began to lace it up the back.

"You ought to go down to him. Father has no right to tell us what we may and may not do."

"He is our father, Cissy."

"Yes, but we're grown women now. We must be allowed to make up our own minds."

Cissy tightened the laces, then Emma slipped on her chemise and pulled her tangled waves of hair through it. She fastened her petticoat and skirt at her waist, while Cissy began to dress. Emma was buttoning her blouse when a sharp ping sounded at the window.

"Whatever can that be? A monkey?" Cissy stepped to the window and gasped. "Upon my word, Emma! It's your cowboy. He's . . . he's . . ."

Emma hurried to her sister's side. As they crowded onto the balcony, they saw Adam on the grass below, spinning a looped rope over his head. His face was lit with the golden light of early morning, and Emma caught her breath at the glow in his blue eyes. Suddenly he released the rope, and both girls drew back as it sailed through the air, landed on the tin roof and slipped around a projecting drainpipe.

"Emma—oh, dear—he's climbing up here!" Cissy squealed, clutching her sister's arm.

Watching the rope pull taut against Adam's weight, Emma gripped the curtain as if the thin lace might somehow hide her. She could not let him see what her father had done.

"Cissy, what can we do?" she cried. "If Father sees Adam climbing up to our balcony, he'll have the poor man tossed in jail."

"I can't bear it. I'm going into the sitting room!"

"Wait, Cissy. Stay with me!" But it was too late. Her sister fled and Adam was halfway up the wall.

Adam hoisted himself onto the balcony, swinging one leg at a time over the rail. Not an easy task for a man with spurs on his boots and a six-shooter at his side. One thing he knew for sure—he hadn't been spotted by a compound guard.

The sight of Emma Pickering peering out from behind the curtain confirmed his decision to see her again. Her green eyes shone with a mixture of apprehension and joy. Her thick wavy hair gleamed like a field of wheat rippling in the wind. He had done the right thing.

"Good morning, Miss Pickering." He took off his hat and leaned against the white window frame.

"Mr. King, did you not receive my message?" She was almost breathless. "I cannot speak with you."

"I got your note, but I need to talk. Mind if I come inside?"

"Indeed, sir, you may not take another step!"

"Can we just talk for a minute or two?" he asked.

"Mr. King, I have already told you I'm unavailable. Now please let yourself down by that . . . that rope thing, and—"

"My lasso?" He began coiling his lariat.

"Sir, this is unseemly."

Adam studied the intriguing eyes peering at him around the curtain. Emma was edgy this morning. Almost frightened. Different from the bold young woman he had met yesterday.

He couldn't let that concern him, he decided as he tucked away the end of the rope. Last night after he left the consulate, he had made up his mind to keep things strictly business with Emma Pickering.

"I'll leave after I've had my say," he told her. "This is important."

"Speak quickly, sir. My father must not find you here."

"With all due respect, Emma, do you think I'm concerned about what your father thinks?"

"You may not care, but I do. What do you want from me?"

"I need a nurse."

Her face suffused with surprise. "A nurse? Are you ill?"

"Not for me. I have a friend—at my ranch."

"Your wife is surely tending to this friend in your absence." She paused a moment. "You are married, are you not?"

"Not the last time I looked."

"Really? Well, then . . ." Her eyes deepened in concern as she let the curtain drop a little. "What sort of illness does your friend have? Can you describe it?"

Adam looked away, his attention skirting across the tops of the palm trees. How could he explain the situation without scaring her off?

"It's not an illness. It's more like . . ." Searching for the right words, he turned back to Emma. But at the first full sight of her face, he reached through the open window and pulled the curtain out of her hands.

"Emma, what happened to you?" He caught her arm and drew her toward him. "Who did this?"

She raised her hand in a vain effort to cover her cheek and eye. "It's nothing," she protested, trying to back away. "Please, Mr. King, you must not . . . not . . ."

Even as she tried to speak, he stepped through the balcony door and gathered her into his arms. Brushing back the hair from her cheek, he noted the swelling and the darkening stain around it.

"Emma," he growled. "Who did this to you?"

She fell motionless, silent in his embrace as he stroked her tender skin with his fingertips. No wonder she had shied like a scared colt. She hadn't wanted him to know. The sight of a drop of dried blood on her lip stopped him cold.

"Bond," he snarled, his voice hardening in anger. "He did this to you, didn't he? I swear, if I see that lousy—"

"No!" Emma's eyes flew open as she backed out of his embrace. "No, it wasn't Mr. Bond. He never touched me. Please . . . please, Adam, just go away now."

"Emma, you have to tell me . . ." Realization flooded through him. The pompous, nattily dressed English railroad tycoon had struck his own daughter.

Without stopping to weigh consequences, Adam drew his six-shooter from the holster and pressed it into her hands.

"Take this, Emma," he told her. He squeezed her hands around the pistol. "This country is wild. It's filled with animals and people who prey on others."

"No." Emma held the gun awkwardly, as if it were a dead thing. "Take this weapon and leave me, I beg you. Our train leaves at eight, and you have no place here." She set the weapon on a table. "Please, sir. You must go."

"I want you to come with me," he told her. "I need your help. Emma, I'll take care of you."

"I don't need anyone to take care of me," she shot back. "I have my own plans, and God is watching over me."

"Emma!" Both turned toward the open door where Emma's sister stood, eyes wide.

"What is it, Cissy?"

"Emma, go with him!" Cissy crossed the room toward them. "Run away with him, Emma. It's your chance to escape—to become a nurse, as you've always wanted. You'll be safe at last and you can have your dream."

Cissy stopped halfway across the floor, her arms held wide in a pleading gesture. Emma turned back to Adam.

"Come on," he urged her. "Let's get moving."

"Do it, Emma!" Cissy insisted. "I shan't tell Father where you've gone. I'll say I woke to find you missing."

A loud banging rattled the door. Adam reached for his gun and found it missing.

"Emmaline!"

Cissy gasped. "It's Father! Emma, you must leave at once. Go with Mr. King."

Emma glanced at him and shook her head. "No. I can't go with you, Adam."

"Emmaline, Priscilla—open this door at once."

"Adam, get out of here!" Emma flew at him, pushing toward the window. "Don't you see? I must stay with Cissy—and it will only be worse for us if he finds you here."

Adam hesitated for an instant, an attempt to decipher the expression on Emma's face. Her green eyes were filled with fear, but he saw determination there as well. He had to leave her alone to face her tormenter. Before he could change his mind, Adam stepped out onto the balcony and swung over the side.

"Emmaline?" Godfrey Pickering strode into the suite, barking an order to the man behind him. "Wait in the hall, Bond. I may need your assistance."

As the door swung shut, Emma spotted the younger man brandishing a revolver. She faced her father as he advanced.

"Where is he?" Godfrey demanded, his voice hard. "Where's King?"

"Adam King?" Emma struggled to feign surprise. She stepped back toward the curtains and her fingertips grazed the gun on the table behind her. "Whatever would make you think we know where Mr. King is?"

"Honestly, Father." Cissy put on her best pout.

"We've just been eating our breakfast and dressing for the train."

"Priscilla, do not lie to me." Pickering strode across the room and flung open the wardrobe doors. "Adam King was here—at the consulate. We know that."

"He did send a note," Cissy ran on. "He wanted to speak with Emma, but she refused him."

Pickering glowered at Emma. She brushed a hand over her swollen cheek. "Cissy is telling the truth, Father."

"Emmaline, if I learn you have lied to me, you will never know the end of my anger." Her father pulled a derringer from his coat pocket before calling out again. "If you're in here, King, I shall see you dead before I rest."

As their father stormed out of the room, both girls turned to the window. The gravel road was empty, only a faint cloud of dust in a thin trail above it.

"You should have gone with him, Emma." Cissy's arm stole around her sister's shoulder. "He swore to protect you and he has an ill friend in great need of your help."

Remembering the letter she had read the day before, Emma wondered who this *friend* could be. A woman? A mistress? Surely not. Or could that be the sort of evil Nicholas Bond had been referring to?

Adam had told her he was not married. But

Nicholas had branded him a liar. Which man had spoken the truth?

Emma closed her eyes and breathed out a sigh. As she inhaled, she drank in the morning—the fresh air and the lingering scent of leather.

Chapter Four

Emma leaned her head against the railcar window and gazed out at the placid blue ocean. The train had pulled out of the station not long ago, and now it chugged across the three-quarter-mile Salisbury Bridge. Cissy sat on the seat across from Emma, a French novel lying unattended in her lap as she stared down at her hands. No doubt her sister was dwelling on Dirk, Emma supposed.

As the train rolled onto the mainland from Mombasa island, Emma drew her focus from her sister. At last—the protectorate in all its raw majesty. The train's twelve-mile-an-hour pace provided a constantly changing panorama. It pulled away from the palm trees and mango and banana groves. Into view came huge gray baobabs, lush green acacias and verdant underbrush.

Emma scanned the terrain for signs of wild game. Although her gaze was fixed on the landscape, she could not help overhearing an urgent conversation in the berth behind her.

"Patterson had been at Tsavo only two or three

days when the first coolie was dragged off." Nicholas Bond was making an effort to whisper, but he was forced to speak loudly enough to be heard above the rattle of the car.

"How long ago was this?" Emma's father asked, his voice tense.

"Two months, sir. Since that time the killings have escalated. Patterson's been after the lions nearly every night, but so far they've eluded him."

"And how many lions are there?"

"Two. That's for certain—only two. One would think we could bag them, but they are clever. And of course the workers' camps are spread so far along the rail line that the lions have quite a feeding ground, so to speak."

"Has Patterson tried poison?"

Nicholas hesitated a moment. "The lions have acquired a taste for human flesh, sir. They much prefer a live coolie to a poisoned dead donkey."

At this Godfrey Pickering gave a loud snort. "This is unconscionable, man. Can the workers not build fences?"

"They've erected large hedges of dry thorn brush around the tents, but the lions are able to jump over or go through every barrier. These two beasts are incredibly large and crafty, sir. The coolies call them *shaitani*—devils."

A knot of fear twisted in the pit of Emma's stomach. She shifted the heavy white pith helmet in her lap. Adam's gun lay hidden in the cloth chatelaine bag beside her. It comforted her . . . not so much for the protection it offered, but for memories it stirred of the man who had held her with such tenderness.

Thankful her path would never cross Adam King's again on this vast continent, Emma repented her thoughts about him. Married or not, the American was certainly not part of God's plan for her life. She had heard His voice and seen her path of service stretch out before her. Nowhere had she glimpsed a handsome cowboy on a black horse.

Forcing her thoughts away from Adam, she wondered where she and Cissy would sleep. Would they be safe from the marauding lions? Emma had never fired a weapon in her life and she could not imagine defending herself against a hungry beast.

Eager to stretch her legs, she stood and lifted the glass window. A gust of clean, cool breeze blew into the stuffy car and tugged a lock of hair from her chignon. Golden in the late morning sunlight, the wisp danced about her chin as she propped her hands on the sill and leaned out the window.

There! Beneath an enormous baobab tree in the far distance stood a great red-gray elephant. With tiny eyes it squinted at the train, then lifted a long wrinkled trunk to test the air. Emma drew in a deep breath, but as she took in the scenery, an unexpected sight startled her into a loud gasp. Could it be?

Leaning farther out, she saw spurred boots, one crossed casually over the other, protruding from a window several cars forward. Her fingers tightened on the sill and she let out a small cry as she drew in her head.

"What is it?" Cissy rose. "Do you see a lion? Let me have a look." She pushed her sister to one side and peered out. In an instant she was back in the railcar and pulling Emma onto the berth beside her.

"It's your cowboy!" she whispered. Her eyes were wide with excitement. "He followed you onto the train, Emma. You must go and speak with him."

"I can't talk to Adam King. Think what would happen if I were discovered."

Cissy's eyes darted to her sister's bruised cheek and puffy lip. Then she shook her head. "He needs you. He told you that. And he promised to protect you, Emma. I'm certain he will. He's that sort of man. Like Dirk."

Emma looked out the window at the tangle of shrubbery brushing past. Adam King did seem that sort of man. But why should she trust someone she knew so little about? Nicholas had vilified him. His behavior had hardly proven him a gentleman. Yet there was something about him . . .

Her thoughts slipped back to her first view of the man. He had been no more than a dark form on a black horse, yet he had cradled a child so gently.

"If opportunity presents itself, I shall speak to him," Emma said with quiet determination. "Yet

I'm certain he is not on this train because of me. He didn't even know I'd be here."

"But he did! I heard you tell him we were leaving on the eight o'clock train. Emma, he's following you, protecting you even without your permission. He saw what Father did."

Cissy glanced over the back of the berth to where her father and Nicholas Bond were still deep in conversation. Then she tucked her arm through her sister's.

"I know men," Cissy whispered, "and I can see that the cowboy has taken a fancy to you."

"You know far less than you claim, believe me." Annoyed, Emma shoved the wisp of hair back into her chignon. Even though he had denied it, he must be married. Emma had seen the letter. She felt sure that somewhere in America his wife was preparing for a governor's inauguration—and waiting for the husband who would accompany her. If Adam wanted to talk with Emma, it was only because she was a nurse. His ill friend must need one badly.

Her cheeks hot, Emma leaned back on the leather seat and shut her eyes. To imagine that there could be any hope for true love with such a man was impossible. Yet without success, she tried to resist the unbidden memory of his arms holding her close as they danced around the ballroom.

Rising suddenly, she grabbed the iron handles and slammed the window shut.

• • •

Lunch arrived and went away again—steaming cream soup with lobster soufflé, hardly in keeping with the sweltering heat inside the railcar and the increasing herds of game outside. Afterward, Nicholas chose to settle himself beside Emma and expound on his dreams for the railway. She made an effort to listen, but her attention slipped away to the changing landscape outside the window.

After crossing the Rabai Hills, the train descended to the wide expanse of the Taru Desert. Thin scrub thorn brush and stunted trees dotted the arid wilderness, so different from the wooded lands nearer the coast. Layers of fine red dust carpeted everything, sifting into the train so that Cissy rose again and again to shake out her white linen skirt.

Late in the afternoon, the train stopped at a station labeled in proud black letters, *Voi*. A major stop along the line, Voi boasted a crisp white-washed station building and several stone houses. Nicholas accompanied Godfrey Pickering off the train, leaving the two young women alone in the silent car. Cissy locked eyes with her sister for a moment, then she rose to peer out the window.

"He's there, on the platform." Her voice quivered with excitement. "He's standing with some other men—railway workers, I imagine. He's walking down the platform toward us now. He's—oh, Emma!—he's looking this way."

Cissy drew back from the window. Fingertips

covering her mouth, she focused on her sister. Emma stared back for a moment. Then, heart hammering, she slid across the seat and spotted the tall figure.

Adam leaned a shoulder against the blue wooden post of the station. He had one thumb hooked on his pocket, and a revolver rested in a holster tied to his thigh. His eyes, though in shadow beneath the wide brim of his black hat, were fastened on her window.

An odd curling sensation slid through Emma's stomach as she met his gaze. He lifted his hand and pushed back the brim of his hat with one tanned finger. Then, slowly, he brought the hand down and crooked the finger at her, beckoning.

Emma turned to her sister. "He wants me to go to him, Cissy. But Father will see me there. It's too great a risk."

"He wants you, Emma!" Cissy cried. "Oh, if he were Dirk, I'd go to him at once. I wouldn't hesitate another moment."

Emma looked outside again. Their father stood a few paces from Adam, talking with Nicholas and the stationmaster.

"I can't." She mouthed the words as she shook her head at Adam.

He frowned. Then he trained his focus on the railcar he had been riding in earlier. Turning to Emma again, he nodded in that direction.

She slid back against the leather seat and tried to

think clearly. Adam wanted to talk to her. But her father would know at once.

The train whistle blew, and Emma tilted her head to the window. Adam was striding back across the platform, his silver spurs spinning in the afternoon sun.

"Did you not wish to take a turn about the station, Miss Pickering?" Nicholas asked, resuming his place beside her. His eyes held a warm light as he smiled at her. "It's more than thirty miles to Tsavo."

Emma returned his smile as the train jerked to life and began its swaying rhythm down the track. "I'm fine, thank you, Mr. Bond. How far did we travel to reach Voi?"

"A little more than a hundred miles. It will be dark before we arrive at Tsavo. The sun sets promptly at six on the equator."

Turning away to the window, Emma saw that the flat, dry terrain had begun to change back to thick woods. Tea arrived then, and Emma poured Nicholas a cup. As he sipped, he made another effort at conversation.

"Has your father told you about our plans for the Nairobi station?"

"Do tell us, Mr. Bond," Cissy said.

"Nairobi is to be headquarters for the railway administration," he told them. "The site is a high plain, more than three hundred miles from Mombasa. We mean to build roads, bridges, houses, workshops and turntables. We'll lay in a water supply as well."

"Will there be shops?" Cissy asked.

"We'll have a regular bazaar, like the one in Mombasa. With new colonists arriving from England, I believe Nairobi may become a real town someday. And when the protectorate is made a colony of the Crown . . ."

As he spoke, Emma's eyes wandered to the pink-tipped foliage and the golden clouds lining the horizon. The sun hung above it, a giant orange ball. Sounds of gentle snoring drifted over the seat. Her father's snoring.

"Will you excuse me?" she blurted, rising to her feet and nearly upsetting the tea tray. "I believe I shall take a walk after all."

Cissy gave her sister a knowing look, but Emma said nothing as she slid past Nicholas out into the aisle.

"Miss Pickering, shall I accompany you?" Nicholas stood. "The train's swaying can be treacherous."

"Thank you, Mr. Bond, but I'm quite accustomed to trains. Please carry on with your report on . . . what was the town you've planned?"

"Nairobi," Cissy interjected, taking Nicholas by the arm and pulling him back onto the seat. "Yes, do tell me more of your plans for Nairobi. Such clever ideas."

Emma gave her sister a grateful smile and hurried down the aisle. She glanced back once, but all she could see was Cissy's bobbing ostrich plumes and her father's top hat.

Pushing open the door to the outside of the railcar, she stepped onto a shuddering platform. A firm grip on the iron railing helped her balance as she worked her way between the cars. She held her breath against the soot-filled air, opened the second door and stepped inside.

Far more shabbily outfitted than the other car, this one was filled with cargo. Boxes and crates cluttered the seats and partially blocked the aisle, making her path difficult. She picked her way past bales of cloth, chests carved from camphor wood, folded cots, rickety chairs and rough-hewn tables. These must be the new colonists' possessions. It would not be easy to live in this land, she thought as she reached the far end of the car, turned the door handle and stepped outside onto the next platform.

Again steadying herself against the iron railing, she tugged open the door to the next car. The sight that met her eyes forced out a sharp gasp. Foggy with tobacco smoke, the car was a jumble of broken bottles, top hats lying askew on the floor, button boots, umbrellas and morning coats. Sleeping men of every description sprawled on the seats. Others sat in groups, tossing playing cards onto tables. Over all, the smell of stale cigars and liquor filled the car while a strange plinking music drifted through the air.

Emma searched the car until she spotted Adam King perched on the tall back of a berth, a guitar resting on one thigh. He gazed out the window, his expression distant. Now and then he strummed the instrument, humming along with the chords.

"I say, sir!" One of the men lifted a glass of ale into the air. "Have a drink and see if you can find something a bit more lively in that box of yours."

"Don't you cowboy chaps know any spirited songs?" another called out.

Adam waved off the proffered drink. "I reckon this is about all I'm good for this evening."

As he spoke, his eye fell on Emma. His expression brightened at once. Standing, he quickly covered the space between them. Emma stepped back onto the outside platform and Adam shut the door behind them.

"I'm glad you came," he said over the clatter of the wheels beneath them. He still held his guitar, and the platform allowed barely enough space for them to stand.

The setting sun filtered through the sooty air, and Emma sensed a raw, animal strength in the man who towered before her. He had rolled his sleeves to the elbow and loosened the buttons at his collar.

"Shall we go into the baggage car?" she shouted, motioning behind her.

For a moment, Adam said nothing. Emma feared—and hoped—he might take her in his arms again, holding her close as he had done before. Her breath shortened as she looked into his indigo eyes. He reached across her shoulder, his hand grazing the soft fabric of her sleeve, and pushed open the door.

Heat creeping into her cheeks, Emma slipped into the baggage car. Adam set his guitar on a wooden bench and turned to her. Before she had time to protest, his hands circled her waist and he lifted her gently onto a crate. He eased his large frame up beside her.

"Where's your father?" he asked in a low voice.

"Asleep. Only a nap, I'm sure."

"Your determination conquered your fear. I like that in you, Emma."

Trying to still her fluttering heart, she smoothed the folds of her skirt before answering. "You must know it's quite irregular, sir."

The corner of his mouth turned up. "Are you always this proper, Miss Pickering?"

She looked away, doubting for the first time all the careful instruction in etiquette her governesses had imparted. "I am as proper as I can be, Mr. King. I was taught to be courteous to everyone. Especially to gentlemen who are my briefest acquaintances."

"I see." Adam tried without success to suppress a chuckle. "All right, ma'am, I need to talk to you about two things."

"Two?"

"This morning when I went to the consulate I only had one. Now I have two."

At that, Emma covered her cheek with her palm and turned away. But Adam's hand closed around hers to draw her focus back to him. He ran his fingertips down her cheek and over her lower lip, and she closed her eyes, shivering at the sensation that raced through her stomach.

"Emma, look at me," he said.

She opened her eyes as he cupped the curve of her jaw in his palm and stroked her cheek with his thumb.

"This morning, I'd have stayed with you." His eyes blazed with a blue fire. "If you say the word, I'll put him in his place. He'll never touch you again. I swear it."

"Please, you mustn't do anything." Emma knotted her fingers. "Two years ago, I heard the voice of God and I knew what I was meant to do with my life. My father disapproves. He's trying to control my wayward behavior."

"By hitting you? What do you want to do that's so awful—be a nurse?"

"I'm already a nurse. I've completed my training at St. Thomas's Hospital and now I've come to Africa." The words came out in a rush. "I must find a hospital here. Do you know of any?"

"There's a camp hospital with the railway. They've got a couple of doctors—Dr. McCulloch, and another one. Dr. Brock, I think. I'm sure they'd welcome your help."

"It can't be with the railway. It must be a place

where my father has no influence. What about a mission hospital?"

"Nothing near the rail stations. Farther into the interior, I think." Adam took a deep breath before continuing. "That's what I need to talk to you about, Emma. I need a nurse for my friend. Please come to my ranch and help me out."

"Impossible."

"If you'll do it, I'll take you to the interior. After you look in on my friend, we'll find a mission hospital where you can be a nurse."

"If I go away with you, Mr. King, my father will know where I am. He'll come after me. I can't risk it. I must go straight to the hospital and seek sanctuary. Then—when my father and sister have returned to England—I'll gladly go and look after your friend."

"No, it—" Adam looked away, his jaw clenched. "I think my friend is dying."

"Then you must go to the railway hospital. Let the doctors do what they can."

"I've had trouble with the railway. With one man in particular."

"Miss Pickering?" Nicholas Bond's voice echoed through the railcar. Emma sat up and Adam grabbed her hand, his strong fingers weaving through hers.

"Over here, Bond," he called.

Nicholas squinted in the dusk. "King, is that you? Is Miss Pickering there?"

"Yes, Mr. Bond, I'm here," Emma spoke up. "While walking, I crossed paths with Mr. King. How odd you should find us here, for we were just speaking about the railway."

Nicholas picked his way down the crate-littered aisle. "Your father is awake, Miss Pickering. He is asking for you."

"But you won't tell him what she's been doing." With a final squeeze of her hand, Adam jumped down from the crate and lifted Emma to the floor. "If you're half as smart as a bunkhouse rat, you'll keep your mouth shut."

"Or?" Nicholas halted before Adam.

"Let me tell you something, Bond." Adam lowered his voice. "I'm not going to interfere between the lady and her father. But I won't hesitate to interfere with you if you give me half a reason."

"Do you threaten me, King? You've seen what I can do when I'm crossed."

"I've seen your honorable way of handling things, you yellow-bellied—"

Nicholas's fist shot out and caught Adam on the jaw. The rancher's head snapped back, sending his black hat to the floor. Adam righted himself and set Emma to one side. Stumbling against Adam's guitar, she saw Nicholas swing again. Adam blocked the blow with one arm while his other fist found its mark in his opponent's abdomen.

Nicholas doubled over, and Emma cried out, "Stop it at once, both of you!"

But the Englishman's face was a mask of fury in the dim light as he charged at Adam. Emma grabbed the guitar and tried to shove it between them. Nicholas ducked and the instrument slammed into a barrel with a discordant crack. Adam seized the momentary distraction to step backward and hoist himself onto a crate.

"Mr. Bond, please!" Emma watched in dismay as the two men faced off. None of the three in the railcar could afford her father's disapproval. She grasped Nicholas's arm. "Truly, sir, you must stop this nonsense at once."

He clenched his fist, struggling to restrain himself. "This is not over, King. I assure you of that."

"Of course not." Adam's voice dripped venom. "One way or another, you're going to pay for everything you did."

Lifting her skirts, Emma pushed past Nicholas and hurried down the aisle. This was why she must have nothing to do with their ilk. This was why she must have nothing to do with men.

"Emma." Adam's deep voice drew her, but she did not stop. "Emma, remember what I told you."

"As if such a woman would remember you," Nicholas taunted as Emma shut the door on them.

The sun had set when the train squealed to a hissing halt. Nicholas had left the baggage car shortly after Emma. Saying little, he sat beside her father for the remainder of the journey.

"Tsavo station," he announced at last. "End of the line."

Emma stepped down from the train onto the lantern-lit platform. She put on her white pith helmet and shook out her khaki skirt. Eyes questioning, Cissy came to her, but Emma held her tongue.

The platform was a bustle of activity as colonists and railway workers poured out of cars carrying boxes, chests, crates and other belongings. Coolies from India, working fast to earn a coin or two, streamed back and forth lugging loads of goods. For a moment Emma thought she would not see Adam again, but then she caught sight of his hat in the crowd.

"Emmaline, Priscilla," Godfrey said, drawing his daughters' attention. "I should like you to meet our railway physician, Dr. McCulloch." The stocky doctor's strong handshake and warm smile encouraged Emma. She would talk to him later.

She ventured a glance at Adam. He had led his black horse down from a car and was strapping on a leather saddlebag.

"We deem it safest for your daughters to stay the night in the train, sir," Nicholas Bond was saying. "There's a sleeping car not far down the line."

Emma tried to listen as she watched Adam shove a long rifle into a leather scabbard on his saddle.

"That will be suitable, will it not, Emmaline?" Nicholas asked. "Emmaline?"

94

Her head jerked around. "Yes, of course. We'll feel quite safe in the sleeping car."

Nicholas favored Godfrey with a slight bow. "I shall escort your daughters, Mr. Pickering. It will give you the opportunity to speak with Dr. McCulloch about the lion situation."

"Thank you very much, Mr. Bond." Godfrey began to walk away, but stopped. "Emmaline, I shall visit your quarters later this evening. We have matters to discuss."

"Have we, Father?"

His gray eyes went hard. "Good evening, Emmaline."

"Good evening, Father." Setting her jaw, she hurried after Cissy and Nicholas.

The platform was nearly empty of travelers now. The black horse had vanished and with it Adam. A sense of emptiness descended over Emma as she stepped into the car.

"This car has rarely been used," Nicholas explained, holding up a kerosene lantern as they started down the narrow aisle beside the windows. He opened a door and showed them into a compartment with two narrow beds. Hanging the lantern on a hook by the door, he stepped back. "When the railway route is long enough, there will be night journeys. We keep this car on a side track for our guests. Dinner will be brought to you within the hour."

Emma placed her chatelaine bag with the gun in

it on the cot's rough gray blanket. "Thank you, Mr. Bond. You are most kind."

"Miss Pickering, may I speak with you for a moment?"

She glanced at Cissy. "You may say whatever you like in front of my sister, sir."

"I beg your forbearance, Miss Pickering. Please step this way."

Emma hesitated, then accompanied him into the aisle. As Cissy shut the door, they were plunged into darkness.

Nicholas took one of her hands in his. "May I call you Emmaline?"

Emma leaned against the paneled wall beside her. She had learned to hate the name—her father used it so often in anger. Yet she saw no point in continuing formalities. "You may call me Emmaline if you like."

"Dearest Emmaline, I must apologize for my behavior this evening in the baggage car. I was inexplicably rude."

"Inexplicably? On the contrary, sir, I'm certain you can explain the enmity between you and Mr. King."

He answered in a low voice. "I beg you not to think me rude again, but that is a private matter. A matter better left buried."

"It is hardly buried, sir. Your last encounter erupted into violence."

"The situation is complicated. Mr. King is an American, you see."

"I believe it is not a crime."

"In Adam King's case one cannot be certain. He does not have the empire at heart. His concern is for his own interests—his ranch and his laborers. He will do anything to advance himself. The man has no scruples."

Emma tilted her head away, annoyed. She had no interest in half truths and evasions. Something serious had happened between the two men.

"Where is Mr. King's ranch?" she asked.

"Not far. He purchased acreage along the route of the railway."

"Does he have an ill person on his property?"

At that, his fingers stiffened, tightening on her hand. "Why do you ask?"

"He said someone was ill. Perhaps you know who it is."

Falling silent, Nicholas dropped her hand and moved to the window. Pale moonlight silhouetted his nose and mouth. Even though the night was cool, a trickle of sweat ran from his sideburn. Brushing it away, he turned to face her.

"Mr. King is thought to be a slaver," he said. "The market for slaves is enormous in the Orient and Arabia. There's an active trade from the African interior."

"But the queen—" Emma paused, a lump in her throat blocking the words.

"Queen Victoria is opposed to slavery. The

Americans abolished it years ago. But Mr. King is from a Southern state, I believe."

"Texas," Emma murmured.

"His conscience—if he has one—is overruled by the money slaves can bring. He transports them from the Uganda territory. The ill person he mentioned might be a favored slave—a woman, perhaps."

But he's married, Emma's heart cried out. Yet what difference would a female slave, a concubine, make to a man who bought and sold human flesh? Adam had denied a marriage, but his letter revealed the truth. If he had no scruples about slavery, why should he bother to remain faithful to an absent wife?

"Emmaline, I tried to warn you. The man is a liar and a conspirator. You cannot believe anything he tells you."

Nicholas placed his hand at Emma's waist and drew her closer. "I beg you to stay away from him. Indeed, I must make clear my growing affection for you. You cannot be unaware of my feelings."

She lifted her eyes to his. "Your attentions have not escaped my notice. But—"

"Say no more," he cut in. "You have two months in the protectorate. Time enough to prove my loyal, kind and generous nature. Give me opportunity to demonstrate the falseness of other men, Emmaline."

She had heard such words of avowal many times.

Men were always in pursuit of an unmarried heiress, she had learned. Two months of Nicholas Bond's persistent courting—the thought was enough to turn her dreams to dust.

She stepped away from him. "Surely you can find another woman more willing, sir. Nursing—not marriage—is my life's goal. Now if you will excuse me."

"Wait." He caught her hand again. "I must have you know that a guard will be posted outside your window tonight. But do not leave the railcar under any circumstance. The lions are not to be taken lightly."

He lifted Emma's face to the moonlight and pressed his lips to her mouth. The kiss was hard and possessive. Emma stiffened as a sense of panic rose in her throat.

When he drew away, his eyes wore a dark pleasure. "Good evening, Emmaline."

"Good night, Mr. Bond."

Her mouth dry, Emma stood aside as he brushed past her. When the car door clanged shut, she closed her eyes and leaned back against the paneled wall.

Dear God, she lifted in silent prayer. *Why have You led me into this? What am I to do?*

Her eyes burned with unshed tears. Brushing her cheek with the heel of her hand, Emma hurried back to her compartment. She pushed the door open to find Cissy at the open window, her soft white nightgown ruffling in the cool breeze.

"Sister, what are you doing?" Flying across the room, Emma pushed the younger woman aside and slammed the window. "Have you forgotten the lions?"

Cissy's face was a mask of pale shock. Her bright blue eyes blinked as she lifted her hand to her mouth.

Alarmed, Emma grasped her sister's shoulder. "Cissy, what's wrong? You look as if you'd seen a ghost."

"I heard him," Cissy whispered. "I heard him, Emma."

"Heard who?"

"Dirk." Cissy turned back to the window. "He was calling my name."

Chapter Five

"Dirk?" Emma shook her head.

"I know it sounds mad," Cissy acknowledged. "But it was his voice. He was calling me. I heard him say, *Cissy, Cissy.*"

"Impossible. By now Dirk is at his post on the border, miles and miles from here." Emma tried to pull her sister away, but Cissy lifted the window again and leaned over the sash.

"Be quiet and listen, Emma. I beg you." Golden hair dancing in the breeze, Cissy stared into the blackness. Dismayed, Emma sat on the bed. She was powerless to dispel her sister's imaginings. Powerless to disperse her own confusion.

"There!" Cissy jerked back inside. "Just listen, Emma. Dirk is calling me."

"It cannot be him." Emma crossed to Cissy's side. She could hear nothing but a cacophony of chirping crickets and buzzing insects. Drawn to the light of the lamplight, moths and pebble-sized beetles whizzed through the window and smacked into walls. A lone African guard manned his station some distance away, his rifle resting against his shoulder. When a big scarab alit in Emma's hair, she jumped back from the window.

"Cissy, do be sensible." She tried again to drag her sister inside. "We must shut the window. The compartment will fill with insects and we shan't get a moment's sleep."

"Shh! There he is again."

Against her better judgment, Emma returned to the window. This time she heard a distinctive sound. It was not a young man calling his lady, but rather a low, stomach-deep grunting. Heart stumbling, she focused on the noise. Yes, there was something outside. A sniffing, searching grumble. She reached for her chatelaine bag.

Then she heard it.

"Cissy! Cissy!"

Or was it the wind? Was it the grass whisking beneath a lion's tawny underbelly?

"Cissy . . . Cissy . . ."

"Oh, Emma!" Cissy threw her arms around her sister for an instant, then she ran from the cabin. "Dirk! Dirk, I'm coming."

"No, Cissy!" Struggling to free the gun from her bag, Emma grabbed at her skirt, yanked the lamp from the wall, and followed her sister down the dark passageway. "Cissy, stop! The lion—there's a lion. *Dear God, please help us.*"

Just ahead, Emma heard the iron railcar door clang open and shut. Throwing herself against it, she fumbled with the latch. "Cissy, stop, I beg you. It's not Dirk."

When the heavy door swung open, Emma stumbled down the dark stairs in pursuit of her sister. An earsplitting roar shattered the night, stopping her cold. Close on its heels came the sound of anguished screams. Emma held the lantern high. Before her on the grass stood an enormous lion, its powerful jaws clamped on the throat of the railway guard. He lay limp, his long legs and arms hanging on the ground like a rag doll's.

The huge cat eyed Emma.

Slowly she lifted her pistol, pointed it at the creature's head, and squeezed the trigger. But as the gun exploded in a blinding flash, the lion bolted into the night with the dead man.

"What's happening? What's going on here?"

The area around the railcar filled with running figures—Godfrey Pickering in his bathrobe, Dr.

McCulloch with a rifle at his shoulder, Nicholas with a lantern in hand.

"Emmaline, where is your sister?" Pickering took her arm and shook it roughly. "Where is Priscilla?"

Emma sagged. "She ran off—the lion . . ."

He clutched his chest. "A lion?"

"Look!" Dr. McCulloch shouted. "Blood on the grass. A lion attacked here. Miss Pickering, did you see what happened?"

"Did you fire that shot?" Nicholas dashed to Emma's side. "Where's the guard?"

Emma pushed away from the men, feeling faint. Her healing skills could not save the poor man now. As she sank down in the grass, she heard a shout.

Adam King rode his horse into the clearing, his pistol drawn. A short, barrel-chested young man followed on a smaller chestnut horse. Dismounting, Adam knelt in the grass beside Emma.

"Are you all right?" His voice was almost a whisper. "Where's your sister?"

Drawn to Adam's deep eyes, Emma saw his concern. The younger man crouched nearby. His shock of yellow hair bobbed as he spoke in the same slow tongue as his companion.

"You okay, ma'am? We heard a—"

An air-splitting roar stopped his words. Emma stiffened. Clutching the pistol in her cold fingers, she stood.

Cissy. The word formed on Emma's lips, but the sound never reached her ears. She had to find Cissy. Somewhere in the night, her sister wandered alone and unarmed. One of the two man-eaters had not yet made a kill.

A second roar sundered the night. Emma ran toward the sound, lamp in one hand, pistol in the other. Shouts rang out behind her, but nothing could stop her now. She had seen what the lion could do. She could not allow that to happen to Cissy. Her sister was still alive. She had to be!

As she ran through the dark brush, she nearly collided with the chestnut horse. Emma set the lamp on the ground and caught the leather reins. Pushing the pistol into her pocket, she jerked her skirts above her knees, set her foot in a stirrup and heaved herself onto the saddle.

"Wait—that's my horse! Hey, Red!" The shout sent the chestnut skittering sideways as Emma grabbed its long mane.

"Emma!" Adam's voice was far away as she rode into the night breeze. "Emma, come back! Soapy, where'd she go?"

"Emmaline. Emmaline!"

The black sky melted into a purple glow, and still Emma rode, calling her sister's name. As the hours wore on, visions of the guard's limp body and Cissy's pale face kept her focused.

Her sister had to be alive. Emma must find her.

She rode much of the night with eyes closed against thorny branches that tore at her sleeves and skirt. But as the sun peeked over the distant escarpment, she lifted her head to a sky streaked with orange, pink and lavender.

Only then did Emma give in to the sorrow that threatened to engulf her. Cissy, her beloved, beautiful sister was so childlike, so trusting. Even now, that perfect body might be lying torn to shreds by a killer lion.

As the horse ambled along, Emma wiped her cheek. Where was she now? She had come so far, searching through the night, for nothing. Peering across the tall grass, she felt a tremor of shock. This was the African bush country. And she was alone. As lost as Cissy.

In the distance, zebras tugged mouthfuls of grass, oblivious to the woman in a tattered white shirt, wet suede button boots and a khaki skirt damp to the knees from the long dewy grass. Rolling grasslands studded with scrub thorn trees stretched away on every side. Against the sunrise a grove of bright green thorn trees wound like a snake toward the horizon. A stream ran among them, Emma surmised.

Far to the south she discerned a great mountain like a cloud of purple smoke on the horizon. A sudden squeak turned Emma toward a gray squirrel peering at her from a rocky perch. The sharp-faced creature had no tail, but it sat upright as it crunched a beetle and dropped iridescent blue shells onto the stone. The satisfied munching reminded Emma of her own hunger.

The horse plodded onward, and as the sun climbed in the cloudless blue sky, Emma grew hotter. She had no idea where the Tsavo railway camp lay, but a river might lead to people. People meant civilization. At least in England they did. She shook her head as she thought of herself in the heart of Africa.

As the tired mare picked her way through the grass, Emma patted the damp neck. Riding had been a rare pastime on the country estate. Her father thought it unladylike. True, her legs ached from the chafing saddle and her back protested the unaccustomed posture, but Emma was relieved to find she could control the horse by tugging the reins as she had seen carriage drivers do.

By now the sun was well above the horizon. The plains animals vanished in search of shade. The grove of thorn trees still seemed miles away, and Emma wondered if she would reach it that day. Her body begged her to stop and rest, but she was too frightened to consider it.

As the hours wore on, her thirst grew unbearable. Black spots darted before her eyes. Vultures circled overhead. The mare began to falter and stumble.

As she floated through mists that sifted across her vision, Emma's mind wandered. She was walking with Cissy beside the Thames as boaters plied the green water. Now they were having tea with Aunt Prue. Cissy giggled in her bright pink organdy gown. They were children, running ring-o-roses around their mother's skirts as she strolled beneath oak trees at the country estate. And they sang a favorite song.

"Lavender's blue dilly dilly," Emma murmured through parched lips. "Lavender's green. When you are king, dilly dilly, I shall be queen."

Her mother's skirt transformed into a shady thorn tree. Beneath it, a pride of lions feasted on a carcass. Emma caught her breath and pulled on the reins.

One lion licked its lips. Four striped legs lay splayed on the ground. A zebra.

As Emma stared, the limbs became human legs and arms. The head no longer bore stripes, but a thick mane of golden hair around a pale, blue-eyed face.

Screaming at the gruesome vision, Emma dug her heels into the mare's sides. As she did, a lion bounded to its feet with a roar. Averting her eyes from certain death, she rode head down. The mare stumbled along until suddenly her hooves disappeared beneath her. Emma tumbled onto the grass. Knives of pain thrust through her sides and ripped into her stomach. A black fog gathered before her eyes, and she was lifted up into a silent emptiness.

A throbbing heartbeat in her ears brought Emma to the threshold of consciousness. A black curtain hung before her eyes. And there was a smell—a pungent smoky smell that caught at her stomach and twisted it into contortions of agony.

But it was the touch of a bare human palm on her cheek that made her sit up screaming. Coming fully awake, Emma struggled to stand, pushing away the hands.

An urgent voice murmured something as strong arms captured her. Still she fought them, unable to see even though her eyes were wide open.

"Emma." The voice was one she knew, and she twisted around to see countless pinpricks of light sparkling in a band across the inky sky. She began to distinguish a man—firm jaw, strong nose, tall hat.

"Adam?"

"I'm here, Emma. Thank God I found you. I've been looking since last night." The dark face turned in profile. "Some friends of mine found you here beside Soapy's horse. Old Red stayed with you, although she's in pretty bad shape herself."

Adam reached across to stroke the horse's velvet cheek. Nearby, a fire crackled, and Emma noted dark shapes reclining around it. With a start, she remembered her search, her frantic journey across the wilderness.

"Cissy!" she cried out. "Have you found my sister?"

"Not before I left. Don't fret, Emma. They've sent out four big search parties. Everyone's looking for her."

She nodded. Cissy was not dead. Something in

Emma's heart reassured her. Somewhere, somehow, her sister was safe.

"Sit with me now. You need to rest." Adam helped her onto a blanket on the grass. He wrapped his arms around her and stroked her hair.

Emma longed to tell him about Cissy's quest, about the lion and the guard, but all she could to do was relax against Adam's broad chest. Lulled by his gentle fingers, she closed her eyes as the tension drained out of her.

"Thank you for searching all night for me," she murmured. "Now we must find Cissy and take her to Tsavo."

"Emma, your sister is gone." Adam ran his hand down her arm. "You have to accept that she may be dead. I need to take you back to the railway."

"No." Emma shook her head. "Cissy's not dead. She ran away after Dirk called her, and then the lion came."

"The lion—you saw the blood on the grass?"

"It was a guard. I came out of the train after Cissy, and . . ." Emma faltered. "The lion had the poor man by the throat."

"The night watchman? Are you sure?"

"It wasn't Cissy. My sister is alive. She may be with Dirk."

"Who's he?"

"Dirk Bauer. Her suitor. He's a German soldier. Cissy insisted Dirk was outside the railcar calling her name."

"Did you hear him? Was the fellow really there?"

Emma looked down. "I'm not sure. I heard something. It sounded like a man calling, but it might have been the wind. Dirk should be at the border with his contingent."

"Emma." Adam's voice was so low she could barely hear it. "There's something I have to tell you. Before I do, I want you to take heart about your sister. It's rough in the wild, but she could have lasted this long. You survived, didn't you?"

"Barely."

"What I need to tell you is about your father." Adam laid his hand on her shoulder. "When you and your sister left, your father went down. He collapsed. And then he . . . then the doctors carried him into the railcar."

"He's dead, isn't he," she said flatly—a statement of fact, not a question. "Father saw the blood on the grass and thought it was Cissy. He believed the lion had killed her. I didn't stay to explain. And now he's dead."

"It wasn't like that, Emma," Adam told her. "Your father was worried about you. He didn't want to lose you."

"You're wrong." She shivered as a chill wind blew over her. "My father loved Cissy."

She left Adam's arms to stand alone in the darkness. Her father was dead. How many times had she thought she would welcome those words? And now? Now she felt cold and empty. She felt nothing—not even the presence of God, who had sustained her through so many years of disappointment and pain. Her once-shining path to the future had vanished in a mist of confusion, dread, sorrow.

A movement from the fire drew her attention. Emma glanced over at the cluster of men. Or were they women? Light danced on elaborate braids and long, pierced earlobes.

They conversed in a rhythmic language as one rose and nodded at Adam. Emma knew by the ropy biceps and sinewed legs that this was a man. He wore a beaded leather sheet fastened at one shoulder and carried a spear with a leaf-shaped blade.

The rancher spoke several words to the warrior, who turned to offer Emma a long dry gourd. She accepted it, and Adam removed a leather cap from its neck end.

"Take a drink, Emma. It's not water, but it will do you good."

She lifted the gourd to her lips. A sour, nauseating odor filled her nostrils as a liquid that tasted of curdled, salty milk slid onto her tongue. Suppressing a gag, she managed to swallow. Once the concoction was down, her stomach began to unknot and grow warmer.

"Thank you." She told the African man as she pulled a handkerchief from her pocket and wiped her mouth. "Most unusual."

Adam's grin softened his somber features. "It's a mixture of cow's blood and milk."

Emma felt her face drain, but she kept her voice steady. "Milk and blood. I see. And who are these gentlemen—your slaves?"

He frowned. "They're not exactly gentlemen, and I don't have slaves. These are warriors from the Maasai tribe. Kiriswa shared his calabash with you."

The warrior said a few words to Adam, who translated for Emma. "They want to take us to their village for the night. It's not far."

As he spoke, the men doused the campfire with dirt. In the sudden blackness, Emma knew a wave of fear. But a warm arm circled her shoulders.

"I hope you're good for a little more riding tonight." Adam said. "I'll protect you now."

He mounted the black horse, then bent over to lift Emma up behind him. She said nothing as she slipped her arms around his chest and felt the horse begin its rhythmic stride.

As night closed around them, Adam found it hard to keep his attention on the ride. Emma had rested her cheek on his back and her soft hair brushed his neck. There was something about the way she molded against him, her arms wrapped tightly and her hands warm on his chest.

Any man would be interested in a woman like Emma. What he didn't like to admit was the growing certainty that she was more than just another woman. He had begun to care what happened to her. Snapping off the thought as though it were poison, he returned his focus to the trail and the line of tall men walking in silence ahead of the horse.

"You're wearing the same shirt and vest you had on earlier," Emma said, her voice drowsy. "Did you look for me a full day without stopping?"

"I wanted to get you safely back to Tsavo. I knew you'd want to be there—the situation with your father. You feeling all right, Emma?"

"I feel . . . odd." She was crying, he realized. Where her cheek rested on his back, his shirt was damp. "I can't imagine my father dead. I hardly know what to think. Life has always been the same. I hoped and planned, but I doubted it could be different. I should mourn my father, yet I can only think of Cissy."

She fell silent, and Adam covered her hands with his. "Try to believe your sister is alive," he said.

"I do believe it and I must find her. I shall need help doing it."

Before he could think of a response, he saw the warriors break into a lope. A fire glowed red in the distance. One man began a low chant, echoed by the others.

As they neared the light, Adam distinguished the outlines of low earthen mounds surrounded by a high fence of piled dead thorn brush. The group entered single file through a narrow opening to find the trampled area inside almost deserted.

The warriors melted into the darkness, leaving Emma and Adam alone with Kiriswa. Adam kicked a leg over his saddle horn and slid down. He lifted Emma to the ground, set her on her feet and braced her to be sure she could stand. Then he spotted a gnarled old man sauntering into the clearing.

"Entasupai," the Maasai growled the familiar greeting and spat into his hand.

Adam grasped it without hesitation and gave the response. *"Hepa."*

He took a moment to explain the situation, his effort at speaking the Maa language stumbling over the description of the railway, the missing sister and the dead father. Then he introduced Emma.

"Sendeyo." The man slapped his hand across his chest.

Adam smiled. "That's his name—Sendeyo. He's the chief elder of the tribe."

Emma gave a polite nod. "So pleased to meet you, sir."

"Sendeyo asked if you'd like to sleep in one of his wives' huts," Adam told her. "Frankly, I'd recommend—"

"No." She caught his sleeve. "I can't sleep now. There's no time. I must speak to you at once."

"You need to rest, Emma." Frowning, he looked down at her. Starlight silvered her soft shoulders, and the breeze played with her hair.

"Adam, please." She took his hand in hers. "I have a business proposal for you."

"In the middle of the night?"

"I cannot delay. My sister's life depends on it. I've been weighing this since you found me and it is the only solution. I have a proposal for you. Strictly a business proposal, you understand. We must marry."

Adam's mouth fell open. He stepped back and took off his hat. Flustered, he turned on his heel and took two long strides. He glanced back, disbelief washing through him.

Finally he managed to croak, "Marry?"

"I need your help to find my sister. I believe Cissy may have truly heard Dirk. To learn if he's missing from his post requires a journey to the border. Then I must go into the bush in search of them. Cissy needs me. She hasn't a clue how to survive on her own. Or with a man she barely knows."

"You barely know me. What does a marriage between us have to do with finding your sister?"

"You know the protectorate, Adam. How to speak to the people and find your way about." Emma's green eyes blazed hotter than the fire. "And you need money for your ranch. I need money, too—but unless I'm married, I cannot touch my inheritance. If you agree to the partnership, I shall pay you the sum of two thousand pounds. We'll take the train back to Mombasa and make a draw from the bank on my affidavit of marriage. That will provide the funds I need to finance my search for Cissy. We must have supplies, horses, tents."

He was trying to think of a response when Emma spoke again. "After two months, whether we have found Cissy or not . . ." She looked away, her face drawn. "No matter what, we'll dissolve the partnership, and I shall pay you what I promised."

"But we'd be . . . married." He shook his head. "For two months, you'd be my wife."

"Only the bank in Mombasa and its affiliate in England will know. You'll soon be free of me."

"And you'll be free, too."

"To find a hospital that needs my service, yes."

"Emma, I can't—"

"But you can! Think of it—two thousand pounds. For your ranch. Think what you could do with that much money. And all you would have to do is help me find Cissy. Please, sir, just help me."

Adam studied the brim of his hat in silence. He straightened the braided leather band and slid his hand through the crown's center crease.

The woman was crazy. Why would he even consider her half-cocked scheme? He'd be loco to haul a citified Englishwoman around the countryside searching for a sister who was probably dead.

But Emma did have guts, and Adam was ripe for a challenge—if he could get what he wanted from her.

He looked up. "I'll do it on one condition. You

come to my ranch and tend to my friend after our visit to the border."

"Impossible! If I stop even for a day, something might happen to Cissy. You cannot ask that of me."

He shrugged. "I'm not crazy about the idea anyway. Marriage isn't much my style."

Shucking his hat onto the back of his head, he gave her a long look before turning toward his horse.

"Wait!" Emma caught his arm. "All right, I'll do it. I'll see your friend. But I won't stay long, Adam. You don't know Cissy as I do. If she's still alive, she'll be frantic. She can't do anything without help. She can't fix her hair or lace her corset or—"

"If she's out in the bush with a runaway German soldier, she's going to have a lot more to worry about than lacing her corset."

"Just as I'm trying to tell you. Can't you see?" Emma brushed a hot tear from her cheek.

"Okay." Adam took her hand and pulled her closer. "Okay, I'll help you find your sister."

Her green eyes shimmered. "Thank you. We'll find a church in Mombasa. I promise, you won't regret it."

"Now hold on." Adam took a step backward. "You never said anything about a church. I'm not going to do this thing in front of a preacher."

"God knows I would never make light of the sacrament of marriage, but we must have the union witnessed. The bank in England will require signed documents. We can't marry out here in the middle of the bush with no one to see but these savages."

"Sendeyo and his family are not savages, Emma. They're people, with pride and a culture as good as yours. Better, probably. They marry and raise families and take care of each other. We'll get old Sendeyo over there to do the honors."

Adam tipped his head at the two men who had stood watching in silence. Sendeyo smiled back, as if he already knew that something interesting was afoot.

Adam related the scheme to the elder, who listened with bowed head. Then Sendeyo began to respond, his deep voice lilting over phrases almost as though he were singing. At last he stopped and leaned on his spear.

Adam turned to Emma. "He won't do it."

"But why not?"

"He says it's not their way. We have to observe the proper waiting time, and it's not even calving season. You don't have a hut, there's no cow to slaughter for the feast and we aren't even betrothed."

"Preposterous. Surely they don't get betrothed."

"It's called the *esirata*—the picking of one girl from many."

Emma's eyes flicked to the old man. He was staring at the stars. "Tell him I shall pay him well. I'll give him fifty pounds."

"Fifty pounds? Why not fifty thousand? Sendeyo

wouldn't know what to do with one shilling. The Maasai way of life is based on the cow."

"Then I shall send him a cow. Ten cows."

Adam laughed. "He's not going to do it, but I'll try again."

He spoke to Sendeyo, stressing the urgency of the missing sister and the German who had stolen her away. Then he mentioned the cows. Sendeyo made a brief answer and prodded Adam with his cattle stick until he was facing Emma again.

"All right," he said. "He'll do it."

She let out a breath of relief. "Thank you, Mr. Sendeyo. I shall see that you have as many cows as you like."

"He doesn't want cows, Emma. He wants me to pay the bride price."

"Bride price? What is that?" she asked, her desperation growing.

"Payment—for you. And since there are no parents to negotiate, he says I'm to give the bride price to you. Wait here."

He walked to his horse, slipped a knife from his boot and sliced into a leather strap on one of the saddlebags. It was one of four that held the bag closed with brass rings.

"Here's the bride price," he told Emma.

Unwilling to meet those green eyes, he took her hand and slid the ring onto the finger of her left hand. Sendeyo held aloft a knobbed stick. As he lowered it, he spoke in a raspy voice.

"I'm to take care of you," Adam translated. "I'm to give you many children and a hut and lots of cattle. You're to take care of the children and the cattle and the hut. I can't divorce you unless you're barren, or you practice witchcraft, become a thief, desert me, behave badly, or refuse me conjugal rights."

He glanced up but she was not smiling. "You can't divorce me unless I commit the same evils you're supposed to avoid," Adam went on. "You can leave me if I get drunk or treat you badly."

Sendeyo set the stick on the ground. His next words were firm, uncompromising. Adam turned to Emma.

"As God has willed it," he told her. "We're married."

"I see." Emma looked down at her finger. The brass ring glinted in the firelight.

"I'll get Sendeyo to sign something in the morning."

"Morning, but . . . ?"

"I'm not going back to the train tonight, Emma. The horses are too tired, and so are we."

She sighed in resignation as Adam thanked the two men and watched them melt away into the shadows.

"Sendeyo says we can have the hut by the gate," he told her. "It's empty."

Her eyes went wide. "But we can't stay in the same place. It isn't right."

"I'll sleep outside in the grass beside the horses." He stepped closer and took her hands, suddenly unwilling to let her go. "You know what's not right? This wedding."

"I know, but it's only—"

"Marriage vows ought to be sealed with a kiss."

Before she could protest, he bent and brushed his lips across hers. To his surprise, she leaned against him. Her arms slid around his waist. Her head settled on his shoulder.

"Oh, this is not in the plan," she murmured as she lifted her eyes to his. "This is a partnership. Nothing more."

"A deal," he affirmed, kissing her again. But as she moved her hand to his cheek, the brass ring flashed.

Emma stepped back with a gasp. "I'm so sorry. It's not real. The marriage. The ring. None of it."

"I need you and you need me. That's real."

Emma bit her lower lip and shook her head. "Good night, Adam."

Chapter Six

———◦•◦•◦———

Emma felt his eyes following her across the clearing, but she could not bring herself to look back. Adam's kiss had burned her lips and seared her conscience. She had entered into a sacred union with a stranger, a man who was probably already married. If God had permitted confusion and obstacles in her life before, what would He do to her now?

With shaking hands, she reached for the chestnut mare and untied the bedroll from behind the saddle. She listened for the jingle of Adam's spurs but heard only the chirp of a cricket. Clutching the blanket, she could feel the ring on her finger. A brass ring.

Even though Adam had said he wasn't married, his heart was pledged to another woman. Clarissa. Emma had read her letter, and such passionate words could not be ignored or denied. Nicholas had called Adam a liar and a troublemaker. And now Emma had joined her life to such a man.

"Where will you sleep?" Adam's voice broke into her thoughts.

She turned to find him silhouetted against the fire, a towering figure, his face obscured in the shadow of his hat. Without answering, she pointed to the long dry grass just inside the thorn hedge. She should sleep in the hut for safety, but the grass would be soft . . . and he would be near.

He nodded and ambled across the clearing, his boots sending up puffs of powdery dust as he led the horses away from the fire. "Still have my gun?"

"It's in my pocket."

The leaves of a nearby bush shone silver in the starlight. Emma spread her blanket across the grass beside it and settled there to begin unpinning her hair. As she worked, she watched Adam place his bedroll on the ground a short distance away. He flipped his hat onto the pallet he had made, and the stars lit his black hair, dusting it with a shimmery powder.

Emma lay down on her blanket and looked up. Like a trail of spilled sugar, stars glittered across the African sky. Never had she seen so many stars nor a sky so velvety and deep. She closed her eyes, wanting the sleep that her body demanded, but her mind refused to rest.

Her father was dead. Cissy missing. Emma married. Each unreality piled on the next. She clasped her hands together, determined to pray.

The cricket chorus rose, and she realized once again this was no English countryside. The dark continent had come to life. Insects fluttered by, soft wings fanning the air above her ear. Deep grunts echoed across the plains as swishing noises whispered from the grass.

Her heart pounding harder with every new sound, Emma drew the pistol from her pocket. Clutching it in both hands, she stared into the darkness trying to remember the prayer her mother had taught her. *Now I lay me down to sleep . . . now I lay . . .*

A shriek of high-pitched laughter split the air, and she sat up in fright, brandishing the gun. As the laughter wound down into a low growl, she swallowed against the dry lump in her throat and lay down again. What could it have been . . . that inhuman hilarity?

I pray the Lord my soul to keep . . . and if I die before I wake—

An earsplitting roar sent her to her knees, the gun barely controlled in her trembling fingers. Struggling to her feet amid the tangle of her skirts, she looked for Adam. He lay beneath the thorn tree, hat over his eyes and booted feet crossed at the ankles. In the silence that followed the roar, Emma focused on the hut Sendeyo had offered. Jerking the blanket into her arms, she tossed it over one shoulder and started forward, pointing the gun before her.

"Emma." The soft voice from behind her startled her, and she whirled around, pulling the trigger. A blaze of fire shot from the barrel. The deafening report sent her staggering backward.

"Emma! Confound it, woman." Adam materialized in the darkness, wrapped his arm around her waist and wrested the gun from her fingers. "Give me that thing. You're going to get one of us killed."

"Oh, Adam, I'm sorry." Emma sagged, relieved she hadn't shot him. "I heard the roar and I thought of the lion . . . and the guard . . . and Cissy."

He laid a finger on her lips. "Why didn't you tell me you were afraid? Come with me."

He turned her toward his blanket, but she drew back.

"No, please. Let me go to the hut."

"That hut is full of fleas, cockroaches and lice,

and tomorrow you'll be a lot more miserable than you are right now. Sit with me under the tree, and I'll teach you about the African night. Then you won't be afraid."

Deciding she feared the night more than she feared Adam, Emma allowed him to walk her through the grass to the tree.

"The roar was a lion," Adam said, seating Emma on the blanket beside him. "They're prowling this time of night."

"And that laughing sound?"

"Hyenas. They mostly steer clear of people."

As he spoke, he brushed a tendril of hair from her shoulder. She caught her breath at the touch.

"I've been thinking," he said. "The ceremony tonight. You . . . my wife."

"But I'm not your wife."

"The first time I kissed you, Emma, something happened to me. You're beautiful and strong—like no woman I've ever known."

He leaped to his feet like something had stung him. "I'm getting tangled up here."

As he walked away, Emma looked into the sky, fighting unexpected tears. Stars hung in the branches of the thorn trees. The pale outline of the moon dropped toward the horizon.

Adam could neither desire nor expect anything of her. Nor could she hope for anything from him. He had promised himself to another woman. He belonged in her arms, not Emma's.

Their sham marriage ceremony had changed nothing. She had her plans, and Adam King had no place in them. She turned the brass ring on her finger. It was only a monetary partnership, this arrangement they had made. No doubt God abhorred her mockery of His holy sacrament.

"Adam, please don't think twice about tonight," Emma called to the man who stood a few paces away. She rose. "The old man's words? They were simply that—words. A means to an end. I must find Cissy. You have your ranch. All I really want in life is a hospital where I can work. I can't afford misunderstandings or complications any more than you."

"Emma, listen to me." He caught her hand and pulled her near. "It's not that simple."

"Adam, please." She removed her hand. "We're partners in a pact designed to benefit each of us. I expect nothing from you other than help in finding my sister. You ask nothing more of me than to keep my end of our agreement."

"Is that what you really want?"

Words of denial dancing on her tongue, Emma moved away and again shook out her bedroll. "Good night, sir," she called over her shoulder. "I really must sleep. It's almost dawn."

But sleep had hardly come when the horses stamped and snorted, and the first herd of cattle headed out of the village toward a new day on the burning grasslands.

• • •

Adam studied the woman curled against the sun-warmed mud wall of the hut. He felt sympathy for the fatigue etched in her face.

When he touched her soft shoulder, the green eyes flew open. With a gasp, she sat up, one hand clutching the collar of her white blouse.

"Oh, Mr. King," she murmured, absently combing fingers through waves of tangled golden hair. "You startled me."

"Sendeyo's senior wife has offered breakfast in her hut," Adam told her. "It won't be much, but we have a long day ahead of us."

"Yes, of course." She made an effort to smooth out her rumpled skirt as he helped her to rise. "We must ask Sendeyo to sign an affidavit as well."

"I already wrote it and got his signature. Take a look."

Emma read the document and returned the certificate with a nod. Her silence didn't surprise him. There was nothing to say. The previous night he had been rash, and she was right to spurn him. The written record of his marriage to Emma would go the way of Clarissa's last letter. An avowal that meant nothing and would soon crumble to dust.

As he escorted Emma through the dewy grass, they stepped aside to let a dozen scrawny goats file past. The naked child who scampered behind them stopped in astonishment at the sight of the tall man and the golden-haired woman.

Adam watched Emma assessing the boy's sparrow-thin legs, his protruding stomach and the flies crusting his eyes. The child held the woman's stare before breaking free to race after his goats.

"The boy is so thin," Emma remarked. "Is he well?"

"As healthy as a child can be with almost no water or food. Flies get their moisture where they can find it."

Emma shook her head. "Why don't they dig wells and grow gardens? Can't they wash? Is it too much—"

Her words halted as she became aware of a gathering crowd of curious villagers. Adam knew the sight was a first for both parties. The African women wore layers of bright beaded necklaces with earrings hanging from lobes stretched nearly to their shoulders. Men in leather loincloths leaned on their spears to balance on one leg.

"The Maasai are nomads," Adam told the woman at his side. "They follow the green grass and pray for rain. Doesn't do much good to dig a well when there's no water underground."

An elderly woman elbowed through the group. Rheumy eyes glittered through narrow slits as she stood before Adam and Emma, her bare feet crooked and gnarled in the dust.

He took off his hat and dipped his head low. "*Takwenya,* Endebelai," he addressed her in the traditional greeting of respect.

"Iko," she returned with a smile, showing a single tooth.

Adam took Emma's elbow. "This is Endebelai. She's Sendeyo's senior wife. Say *Takwenya.* It's a form of greeting."

"Takwenya." Emma dipped a curtsy.

"Iko." The old woman cackled aloud over the white woman's unexpected bow.

At her merriment, the crowd surged forward to surround Emma. Their hands reached to stroke her skirt and fondle her hair. One little girl lifted her hem and peered in amazement at the white petticoat beneath it.

Emma stiffened at the attention, and Adam wondered if she would back away in distaste. The people smelled pungent, a mix of wood smoke, perspiration and odors so familiar he hardly noticed them. Their fingers were crusted with dirt. Flies swarmed. But as he stepped forward to rescue Emma, she held up a hand.

To his surprise, she dropped to her knees among the children, touching their faces and running her hands down their thin arms just as they had hers. A little girl's arm bore an angry, blistered burn. Emma stroked her fingertips over the raw skin. A boy showed her a festering black thorn embedded in his leg.

"Oh, Adam!" Lips trembling, Emma stood. "Have they no hospital? Can they not see a doctor?"

"They have a *laibon,* a traditional healer."

"But the thorn in the boy's leg . . . Adam, he could die. We need hot water and clean cloths and—"

"Emma." Adam set his hand on her shoulder. "Emma, the protectorate is filled with villages like this. People live with disease and death."

"But I must do something. You don't understand."

"I do understand, Emma. I want you to help these people, and you will. But your sister comes first. The Maasai will be here when you come back. They'll need you in two weeks as much as they do now."

Before Emma could respond, Endebelai took her arm and urged her to the hut. Adam followed, noting how the old woman's fingers read the bumps and hollows of the mud wall. At the doorway, Endebelai ran her hands around the opening before bending and slipping inside.

Emma turned to Adam, her face pale. "She's blind."

He nodded. "Go on in. She's waiting for us."

Smoke flooded his nostrils as he followed the women into the hut. As his eyes adjusted to the darkness, he saw Emma seated against a wall. Endebelai poked at the fire until a breath of air fanned the embers into flame, then she set a pot of milk atop it.

Coughing, Emma blinked at the small vent in the low ceiling. "Has she no chimney?"

"Smoke keeps the bugs down," Adam told her.

Endebelai passed small gourds of milk to her guests. Adam spoke to her in the singsong language of the Maasai. Sipping warm milk beside him, Emma seemed to relax.

"Comfortable?" he asked.

"Oddly enough, I am. Your friend is as warm as any English mother. May I ask what you're discussing?"

"Her son." Adam stretched out his long legs. "He's a friend of mine."

"He lives here, then?"

"No." Adam took a sip of milk. "I've told Endebelai about your sister. She'll ask Sendeyo to send out warriors to search for her."

"Please thank her," Emma exclaimed. "I'm sure no one knows this country better."

Adam relayed the words of gratitude. Endebelai nodded and began to speak.

"What is she saying?" Emma whispered.

Adam shook his head. "She says your sister is dead and will not return. But look outside tonight and you will see the moon."

Chapter Seven

"No!" Emma cried out. "Cissy is not dead. The soldier came for her. Please—it must be so."

"Whoa, now." Adam pulled her close. "It's just a feeling she has."

131

"But Cissy is not dead." She shrugged out of his arms. "Tell her I'm going to find my sister."

Adam transmitted the message, and the old woman whispered a reply. "She offers the Maasai farewell. I pray to God that you meet nobody but blind people who will not harm you."

Emma gazed down at the woman whose own eyes saw nothing. "Please tell her I shall return soon. Perhaps I can bring a doctor. There must be some way to help."

Adam spoke in a low voice as he ushered Emma out of the hut. "It's not good to offer too much hope," he told her when they stood in the sunshine once again. "I gave Endebelai the guest's farewell: May you lie down with honey and milk. She was satisfied with that."

Her eyes caught the light and flashed a deep olive green. "You've been in Africa a long time. You know the people well."

He settled his hat on his head. "I know this clan. They're my family."

"How can that be? Their lives are so different."

"Are they?" he asked. "The Maasai have a religion. They marry and love their children. They have their own ritual greetings, traditions, legends. They take care of their homes and look after their animals."

Her face had softened. "Perhaps you're right."

"Let's move out." He motioned toward the horses. "The sooner we get to Tsavo and find out if anyone's seen your sister, the better. And don't forget your hat."

"Hat?"

He winked and gestured at the white pith helmet lying beneath a bush. A crowd of curious children encircled her headgear. One held a stick and prodded it. When the helmet suddenly rolled onto one side, the children shrieked and scurried backward.

Adam spoke to one of the older boys, who hooked the helmet with the end of his cattle stick and carried it to Emma. She thanked him and settled it on her head, much to the children's amusement.

Adam noted that her efforts to pin up her hair had failed. Long golden waves covered her shoulders and tumbled down her back. The urge to touch was palpable.

He and Emma mounted their horses and rode from the village. They spent the morning crossing trackless yellow grasslands. Dust coated their clothing and made Emma cough. Even though she called for Cissy and Adam fired his gun into the air, they saw no sign of human life.

But they were not alone. Herds of gazelle, antelope, zebra and giraffe grazed on the savannah. Adam pointed out a circle of vultures gliding over a lion's kill on the horizon. Emma shuddered and wondered aloud if it might be Cissy. But they rode near and saw that the slain animal was a young hartebeest.

Adam enjoyed sharing the mystery and majesty of this land with the young Englishwoman. He had no doubt the Master Creator had arranged the order of nature so it blended and harmonized. He had learned about God as a boy in church, but he had lost interest in religion amid his rebellion against his parents.

Lately, though, he had taken to praying again. In fact, he talked to God more or less throughout the day. At night by lantern light, he often read the Bible his mother had packed in his trunk before he left for Africa. He took comfort in the words of forgiveness, peace and hope.

Reflecting on his past, Adam thought about his decision to follow his own path, refusing his father's order to stay in Texas and run the family businesses. His parents had angrily yielded to his stubbornness. Years passed without contact. He had written to his mother once but his father had readdressed the envelope and sent it back unopened. Then one day he had learned it was too late ever to make amends.

He saw that hardened part of himself in Emma, the way she erected walls and refused to give up her dream. Now her father had died, and Adam lifted a petition heavenward that she would not have to live as he did—haunted forever by the unresolved pain of a broken bond.

"Your mother stayed behind in England?" he ventured to ask as they traversed a dry gully.

"My mother?" Emma appeared startled by the question. "No, she died some time ago."

Adam bent to stroke his horse's neck. "Are you anything like her?"

Her expression sobered as her attention drifted across the landscape. "My mother and I were identical in spirit. When I was a girl, we walked through the countryside together, and she urged me to notice everything."

"Observation—like your Miss Nightingale taught."

She glanced at him in surprise. "You remembered," she murmured. "Yes, I learned to look carefully. My mother wanted me to understand more than painting and beading. She took me along when she visited orphan workhouses and hospitals. My father opposed such ventures. Perhaps he was right. My mother's spirit of determination and independence caused her to wander astray. Her willfulness, Father always said, led to her death."

Adam considered this, aware there was much Emma had not told him. "You should know they've buried your father by now. It's not easy to manage funerals out here."

"He'd be pleased to be buried near a railroad."

Adam could not find more to say, so they traveled in silence. The sapphire sky was a giant bowl that dwarfed the grassy hills. The sun beat down like a golden hammer. He worried about Emma's pale English complexion. Beneath that silly hat, her cheeks were a bright pink.

"You're burning," he told her. "Here. Wear this."

She blinked in surprise as he leaned over, lifted off the pith helmet and replaced it with his hat. "But you'll cook," she protested.

"My skin is leather already. Besides, you look good in that hat. Beautiful."

"Nonsense." Her cheeks flushed a vivid crimson as she reached up to touch the wide brim. "Are we far from Tsavo?"

He eyed the sun. "I'd say another hour. Are you thirsty?"

"And hungry. I feel as if I haven't eaten for days."

He handed her the canteen with its remaining swallows of water. "When we get to Tsavo, we'll eat. You can rest on the trip back to the coast. You're going to need your strength for the search."

"Do you think it will take long to transfer the money? I can't bear to wait. Cissy's life hangs in the balance."

"Emma . . ." Adam said her name gently, the urge to protect her was stronger than he had expected. "Emma, you know it's not likely that Cissy—"

"I shall never believe she's not alive," Emma cut in. "Until I've searched every inch of the protectorate, I must believe Cissy is somewhere out there. I shall know when my sister dies."

"How will you know?"

"My heart will tell me. It may sound odd, but I believe that."

"When a person you love is hurting, you feel it, too."

"Do you love someone in such a way?" she asked, her eyes searching his face. "I can see that you do. Your souls are bound, as mine is to Cissy's."

Adam chose not to answer. At this moment, he was sure of only one thing. He must never let this woman close to him again. She was too dangerous to his plans and his future. More important, she was too dangerous to his heart.

The sun had started to dip when Adam and Emma rode into Tsavo railhead camp. At first sight of them, a cry rose from the workers, and men poured out of the corrugated tin buildings to hail the arrivals.

"Miss Pickering!" Nicholas Bond dashed through the station doorway and ran down the steps. His dark coattails fluttered in the breeze as he hurried toward her, top hat in hand. "You're alive. Thank heaven."

Emma slid down from her horse. Her wrinkled skirt hung heavy with dust. She removed Adam's hat and pushed her damp hair back from her forehead.

"Cissy?" she asked Nicholas. "Have you news of my sister, Mr. Bond? Is she here?"

"No trace of her." He caught her hand and pressed it to his lips. "Dearest Emma, I thought I had lost you. You should never have left the station. We were all frantic, and your father . . ." He caught himself. "My deepest condolences on your loss."

"I have no doubt my father would want me to find my sister." She pushed away from him. "Excuse me, for I haven't a moment to lose."

"But it's impossible she could still be alive." He took Emma's shoulders, forcing her to meet his eyes. "There's little water and nothing to eat. Lions and wild dogs are savage hunters."

"Enough of that, Bond." Adam stepped up beside Emma. "People do survive alone in the bush. I did, in case you've forgotten. There's a chance the girl may be with someone. Right now, I need to get this woman something to eat and drink."

"I shall see to her needs, Mr. King," Nicholas informed him. "The Crown appreciates your service, but now Miss Pickering is under my protection."

"I beg your pardon," Adam countered. "The lady and I struck a bargain. She's under *my* protection."

Nicholas's lips tightened. Emma brushed a hand across her forehead. "Adam, please. Mr. Bond, I can explain."

"Adam! Adam, you ol' turkey buzzard!" A laughing voice carried across the heated air, and the three turned to see a short, compact young man striding toward them. He waved a white hat high as his head of bright yellow hair bobbed with each step. "Where'd you go? I been scoutin' this place high and low. You bring my horse back?"

"Soapy." Adam stepped around Nicholas to greet the younger man with a firm handshake. "Red's back, sound as ever. She's covered half the protectorate in the past few days."

"Hey there, Red." Soapy stroked the horse Emma had ridden. "Who's your lady friend, boss? She looks as limp as a worn-out fiddle string."

"Soapy, this is Emma." Adam set his hand on her back. "Emma, meet Soapy Potts. He's my right-hand man."

"I'm the ranch cook. Ain't nobody can make a batch of sourdough biscuits like me. Secret's in the starter dough."

As they shook hands, Emma could not help but return his smile. "So pleased to meet you, Mr. Potts."

"You ever ate anything the boss here cooked? Meat so tough you got to sharpen your knife just to cut the gravy."

A wry grin creased Adam's face. "Don't listen to Soapy. His coffee's thick enough to eat with a fork. How about getting these horses fed and watered, Soap? We're taking the first train back to the coast."

"One moment, Mr. King," Nicholas cut in. "I should like to know what's going on here."

"Please, sir." Emma laid her hand on the Englishman's arm. "I can explain everything. But first I beg your escort to a drawing room where I might sit down and take a cup of tea. I have little time to spare and must make the most of it."

"But of course." Nicholas cupped his palm around her elbow. "My office is as comfortable as any drawing room."

As he started to lead her away, Emma turned back to Adam. "Will you join us, sir? There will be maps in the office, and we must chart our course."

Adam's gaze swept over her face, then locked briefly on her lips before coming to rest on her eyes. "Thanks but I need to see to the horses." He turned to his companion. "Soapy, my friend, we have to get our hands on another nag for you to ride. Emma and old Red have hit it off pretty well."

"Now, wait just a minute, boss!" Soapy protested.

"I'll be back for you, Emma," Adam said. "And I'll have your trunks carried to the train."

"Thank you." Emma ached to say more. She felt a pang of regret that their time alone with each other had ended.

Then Adam turned on his spurred heel and strode across the station yard. Soapy's wide gray eyes ran up and down her once before he hurried after Adam. Emma watched them go, strange replicas of one another in their boots and denims. Soapy stood only as tall as Adam's shoulder, even in his hat.

Remembering, Emma studied Adam's black felt hat in her hand. She wondered how she must look with her hair astray and her skin ruddy from the sun.

"We must see that you have a proper helmet, Miss Pickering," Nicholas said.

"This one served me well, actually." She tucked the hat under her arm. She had no doubt her hair was a fright, but nothing could be done with it at the moment. "Now, sir. Do show me to your office."

Inside the whitewashed station building, Emma stepped into Nicholas Bond's office and took in the scrubbed wooden floor and bare walls. Heat radiated through the tin roof. Sparsely furnished with a wooden desk, two chairs and a settee, the office was stacked with imported goods. It smelled of ink, burlap and rust.

"A cushion," Emma said as she spread her skirts and settled on the settee. "Lovely."

Nicholas clasped his hands behind his back as he paced before the single window. "I can scarcely believe whose company you have been forced to endure, dear lady. But you must have been exhausted when he found you."

"Mr. King treated me well," Emma assured him. Nicholas's words bespoke tenderness and concern, but his tone revealed irritation. She felt the need to clarify. "I wanted to return to Tsavo station, but Mr. King would not hear of going before I had rested the night. Now I must begin to search in earnest for Cissy."

"You cannot be serious." Nicholas unclasped his hands and sat in the chair nearest his desk. "You expect to journey out once more on such a hopeless quest?"

She held her tongue when a young man stepped into the room bearing a tray of tea and a loaf of bread. He poured out two cups, and bowed low as he left. Emma gratefully lifted the sweet liquid to her lips.

"Miss Pickering . . . Emmaline," Nicholas said. "You have not asked me about your father."

"Mr. King told me everything." Her hand suddenly trembling, she set the cup on the saucer. "Is his grave nearby?"

"Behind the station—with the other workers who . . ."

"The lions' victims," she said. "Yes, I know."

She closed her eyes, searching for words to explain emotions she could hardly decipher. Her father was dead. Such relief she felt . . . and such sorrow.

She thought how others would respond to the news of his death. Those who had lost their lives to the lions would remain anonymous, but her father's death would be widely reported in England. The London papers would call him a martyr for the empire.

Emma stopped her thoughts. She must reconcile herself to her loss, to her father's passing, to the part she had played in it.

"I shall visit his grave before I go," she told Nicholas. "You must understand, sir. Had he lived, my father would have insisted on searching for his younger daughter. Now it is my responsibility to find her."

"I see you will not be dissuaded." He set his cup on the tray. "I sent search parties to look for you and your sister. The men returned not long before you did. To the best of our knowledge, Miss Priscilla is nowhere in the vicinity of the railhead. But I must caution you that the railway cannot afford to spare the men for long. A week at the most."

"A week is not enough." Emma ran her fingers over the brim of the hat in her lap. "I mean to search for Cissy until I find her. I shall transfer a portion of my funds to a bank in Mombasa, which will allow me to outfit an expedition. Mr. King has agreed to lead the mission."

"Mr. King?"

"We shall travel to the border first," Emma continued. "I hope to interview the German soldier who courted my sister. Better yet, I may learn that he is missing and doubtless in her company. From there, I shall search the country until Cissy is found. Mr. King is a capable guide."

"I daresay he is not." Nicholas stood. "Emmaline, have you any real knowledge of that man? Do you know his history, his associations, his dealings in the protectorate?"

"I understand all I need to about Adam King. He is well-traveled. He knows the tribal people. He speaks their language and can engage their support. Most important, he has agreed to take on the job."

"For a large fee, no doubt."

"He will be compensated."

"Have you such ready funds?"

"My inheritance." She picked up her teacup and took a sip for fortification. "Mr. King and I have an understanding, you see. According to my father's instructions, I must be married before I can receive my inheritance. I proposed such a partnership to the American, and he accepted. Having taken a husband, I can now collect my inheritance and pay for everything I need to find my sister."

Nicholas appeared fit to burst. "Are you joking, madam?" he sputtered. "You have actually agreed to marry Adam King?"

Emma shrank from his vehemence. "We are wed. A Maasai elder performed the ceremony last night. It is an odd contrivance, I admit, but I am assured the pact is legally binding."

"A pact? A contrivance? Madam, have you any idea what sort of man you have attached yourself to?"

Emma stood and crossed to the window, wishing she could escape. "I care nothing for my own comfort and well-being, Mr. Bond. My sister's life is my only concern."

Nicholas's voice was steely. "Adam King is a

money-grubbing agitator—a mercenary. Miss Pickering, I must speak bluntly. The Crown has reason to believe that Adam King is collaborating with the Germans to foment unrest in the protectorate."

"Surely this cannot be!"

"There is little doubt. Indeed, we seek only final proof before we expel him from the country."

"But what evidence do you have?"

"King receives regular shipments to Mombasa harbor. Do you know the contents of those crates?"

"No." The word choked from her throat.

"Guns. Ammunition."

"But—"

"He claims the crates contain farming implements. He imports equipment for his ranch—or so he tells the port authority when he presents the bills of lading. But we are certain he is trading in arms. His true name, by the way, is not Adam King. He is Adam Koenig, and a German by descent. If you doubt me, Emmaline, ask the man yourself. Believe me, if your sister was abducted by Germans, you can be certain your so-called protector knows about it."

Emma gripped Adam's felt hat, its brim warm in her fingers as she stood beside the window. Could this be true? He had seemed so honest, so forthright. Yet what did she truly know about the American?

"Are you saying that Adam King may know where Cissy is?" she asked.

"You say your sister was befriended by a German soldier. She supposed that man called her name in the night and she fled with him. If a German has taken your sister, Adam King will have had a hand in it."

"Taken my sister? No, you must be wrong. I met Dirk Bauer. I saw his eyes when he looked at Cissy. He truly loved her. Even if it were a ruse, why would the Germans capture a young Englishwoman? It makes no sense."

"It makes perfect sense. They've had no end of trouble building their railway to the Uganda territory, and now they lag behind us in the race to complete the track. England's relations with the kaiser are deteriorating. Should we charge the Germans with absconding with a British citizen—a woman, no less—the accusation will stir the pot further. Which is exactly what the kaiser wants."

Emma leaned against the window frame for support. There was logic in Bond's argument. His assessment of the political situation was accurate. Yet Dirk and Cissy had seemed truly in love. How could the courtship have been nothing more than a subterfuge?

"Why would Adam King import guns?" she challenged. "The Germans are well-armed."

"Ten years ago they faced a native uprising. Arabs had armed the Africans with breech-loading rifles. Now the Germans believe they can put guns into the hands of natives in the British Protectorate and create similar trouble for us. Adam King serves the kaiser. His assignment is to import weapons and arm the locals. As you have said yourself, he knows the tribes and speaks their languages."

Her heart racing with dread, Emma shook her head. "But you said he was a slaver."

"Emmaline, I fear this information may be too much for you." Nicholas's eyes were soft with sympathy. "You have suffered one shock upon another. Your alarm must be great, indeed."

"It will be greater still if you fail to reveal even the smallest shred of intelligence about Mr. King."

"Then let me make it simple. Adam King is a wicked man. Some years ago while in the Uganda territory buying slaves, he formed an alliance with the Germans. His human property is transported down the old slave trails to Bagamoyo and Dar es Salaam on the coast of the German territory. They turn their heads because they need his services against their enemies."

"The British."

Nicholas tipped his head. "It's quite simple—the tale of a mercenary. The empire is laced with such miscreants. We do not fear Adam King. We simply observe his actions and thwart him when we can."

As he finished speaking, Emma turned to the window again. Adam . . . a traitor, a mercenary, a slaver? Was it possible he knew Cissy's fate even now?

A movement near the track caught her attention.

Dressed in a clean white shirt and black hat, Adam was speaking earnestly to Soapy as they walked along the rail line. His black boots caught the sunlight, their silver spurs spinning. As she watched, he paused and looked to the window where she stood.

Disconcerted, she stepped backward—straight into Nicholas's arms.

"Forget him, Emmaline," he whispered. "Your agreement is easily broken. The word of a native will hold no weight in a British court. Your union with King is a sham, a folly."

With one finger, he tilted her chin so that she was compelled to look into his brown eyes. "My feelings for you are unchanged. Please believe I shall do all in my power to help you find your sister. I want nothing more than to make you happy. Transfer your attachment from Adam King to me, Emmaline. I beg you to consider me as the most beloved partner for your future life."

Nicholas's awkward proposal added to the tumult of emotion that Emma felt. His indictment of Adam was shocking in its detail. Should she trust Nicholas? Her father approved of him. Even Cissy liked the man. But rather than despising Adam as reason demanded, Emma knew she could not reject him until she had learned the truth for herself.

"If indeed Mr. King knows where Cissy is, I have all the more reason to continue our association," she said. "I shall study his movements and make every effort to intercept his communications. Perhaps I may learn enough about his treachery to help you put a stop to it."

"Emmaline, you cannot mean this," Nicholas exclaimed. "Do be reasonable."

"I am perfectly rational." She stepped toward the door. "Please wire ahead to Government House. Inform Lord Delamere I shall be arriving in Mombasa tomorrow."

As she stepped outside the office, he caught her arm. "By my honor, I will not let you go so easily. I love you, Emmaline. I shall come after you, I swear it."

She pulled free and turned away. "You must do as you see fit, Mr. Bond. I shall do the same."

Chapter Eight

Standing near the train, Adam faced down a small Englishman with wide gray eyes and a tremor in his lip.

"Mr. King, I have my orders," the man declared, his voice quaking. "My timetable is set."

Adam frowned. "Queen Victoria herself wrote out your little schedule? Is that what you're telling me?"

Catching sight of Emma striding toward them, he straightened. By the set of her jaw, he could see she was in no mood for nonsense.

"Is there a problem, Mr. King?" Emma asked.

"Seems the train isn't scheduled to leave Tsavo station until tomorrow morning. Mr. Perkins here is the engineer and he says he can't make a change without permission."

"Permission from whom?"

"Mr. Bond makes out the schedule." Perkins edged toward Emma. "We depart for the coast at eight in the morning."

"But I cannot wait until morning," she informed him. "In deference to my father, once commissioner of this railway, I beg you to set off at once. Every hour could mean the difference between my sister's life or death."

"Madam, with all due respect to your late father, we do not run the train at night." The little man gave Adam an uneasy glance. "Elephants and rhinos and other such beasts roam about the track. In the dark, it is quite impossible to spot even such a huge creature in time to stop the train."

"Who can think of elephants at a time like this?" Emma set Adam's hat on her head. "I order you to start this train, sir. At once."

"I beg your pardon, but I cannot." The engineer faced Emma. "Not in good conscience."

"Start the train, sir, or we shall be forced to start it ourselves."

"I'd listen to the lady if I were you." Adam took another step toward the engineer, prodding the

150

man's chest with his index finger. "You get that train started, hear?"

"As you wish, then." With a reproachful glance at Emma, he hurried toward the locomotive.

"I'll clear this up with Bond," Adam told her. "Don't worry about a thing."

Reading the dread in Emma's eyes, his grin faded. He saw at once what he had done—intimidating the engineer, physically forcing the man to relent. Emma would hate that in him.

"I shall speak with Mr. Bond myself," she said. "We have an understanding."

"Oh, you do?" He didn't like the sound of that.

Emma looked up at the verandah of the station building. Her expression told Adam who stood there.

"No more fighting," she said. "I've had a lifetime of conflict already. Please, sir. I just want to leave this place."

Adam met her pleading eyes. "Emma, sometimes a man has no choice but to grab trouble by the horns." He touched her arm. "Soapy's waiting for you in the passenger car. I said I'd take you to the coast tonight and I will."

He started toward the station building, then stopped and looked back. "It may take money."

"I shall pay it," she said. "Whatever the cost."

Emma set her hand on the iron rail near the door and stepped up into the car. She recalled the way

Nicholas had accused Adam of being a mercenary. A money-grubbing agitator. A traitor for hire. Was this the beginning, then? Would the American ask for money at every turn, trying to get as much from her as he could?

In the cool darkness of the railcar, Emma gazed at the berth where she had last sat with her father and Cissy. All the seats were empty now, save one. She saw a white hat up ahead and made her way down the aisle toward it.

"Mr. Potts?" she asked softly.

"Howdy, ma'am." The cowboy leaped to his feet and whisked the hat from his head, leaving his yellow hair standing on end. "Call me Soapy. Been my name since I was two days old and rolled into the washtub and nearly drowned."

His smile warmed her heart as she took the seat opposite him. "You're the cook?" she asked, her focus on the shuttered window.

"I give it my best when we're out on the range." Soapy's hand covered Emma's as she moved to raise the shade. "Let the boss handle him, ma'am. He can draw faster than you can spit and holler howdy."

"Draw?"

"Adam King was raised with a gun in one hand and a milk bottle in the other. He can take care of himself, sure enough. That fancy pants Englander ain't got a chance against the boss."

Now more determined, Emma pushed Soapy's

hand aside and lifted the shade. As she feared, the two men faced off on the verandah. Nicholas's hat lay in the dust and his fists were knotted in anger. His brown hair glimmered a burnished copper in the afternoon sunlight slanting across the stone floor.

Adam had pushed back his hat and rolled up his shirtsleeves. Emma noted the gun in its holster at his side. His right hand was poised over it, fingers spread wide.

"Dear heaven, Mr. Potts," Emma cried, rising to her feet. "Do they mean to kill one another?"

"Not hardly. Like I said, Bond don't stand a chance."

"But he has no weapon." Emma held her breath as Adam took a step toward the Englishman and began speaking. Nicholas shook his head. Adam jabbed the other man's chest with his finger, just as he had done to the ship's purser and the rail engineer. As he prodded, Nicholas stepped backward until he stood against the verandah railing.

Just as Emma felt sure he must surrender, Nicholas ducked under Adam's arm and spun around behind him. A revolver flashed in his hand and he leveled it at Adam's heart.

"No!" Emma bolted from the window, stumbling past Soapy into the aisle. Grabbing up her skirts, she ran between the seats toward the open door.

"Hold on now, Miss Pickering!" Soapy called, his boots pounding the metal floor of the car as he followed her.

Emma's mind filled with the image of Adam lying in a pool of blood. She would lose him, just as she had lost Cissy . . . her mother . . . her father . . .

"Emma?"

A cry broke from her as Adam's huge dark form loomed in the doorway, and she barreled headlong into him. His scent engulfed her as he lifted her lightly up and away from the open door. His boot flew out and caught the door, slamming it shut as the train lurched forward.

"Oh, Adam." The breath sighed out of Emma all at once. Then her body went rigid and she pushed away from him. "Mr. King, if you cannot refrain from provoking people to the point of using weapons, then I must disengage your services. Is that clear?"

Adam pushed his hat back with the tip of one finger. "You don't want to see any more fighting."

"*See* it? I don't want there to *be* any more fighting." Emma gripped the seatback as the train picked up speed. She needed to rest . . . to close her eyes and escape the truth that Cissy was missing and their father was dead. Now Emma was alone in the middle of Africa with two Americans—one accused of slaving and mercenary activities against the empire. Worse, all she really wanted to do was curl into that very man's arms, lay her head on his shoulder and fall asleep.

"Promise me, sir," she said with all the emphasis

she could muster. "Promise you'll never use a weapon against Nicholas Bond again."

"What makes you think he used his gun?" Soapy protested.

She turned to the smaller man. "I include you in the pact, Mr. Potts. No guns and no fists."

"But you can't take away a man's right to defend himself, ma'am."

"It's okay, Soapy." Adam laid a hand on his friend's shoulder. "I know better ways to handle Bond anyhow. No guns, Emma. Not while I'm working for you. Soapy neither. And now, you need to rest."

She preceded the two men down the aisle. Soapy took his former place. As if Adam had read her mind, he drew Emma down beside him, placed one arm around her and eased her head onto his shoulder. He propped his boots on the opposite seat and raised the window shade.

"Sunset in Africa. My favorite time of day." He spoke in a low voice and Emma could not resist the lull of it. "Unsaddle my horse and turn him out in the corral. Cattle rounded up for the night. My men gathered by the fire . . ."

Emma relaxed in Adam's embrace and gazed out at a golden sky streaked with pink. Thorn trees silhouetted in black spread gnarled branches across the horizon. A pair of giraffes emerged in the dusk, their long necks swaying in rhythm with the train as it slipped along the track.

Adam stroked his finger down Emma's cheek, and she shut her eyes. In a moment, she drifted off to sleep to the rattle of the train taking her back to Mombasa.

Adam looked down at the woman sleeping in his arms. Moonlight filtered through the window, silvering her skin. Dark lashes fanned her cheeks, pink from the heat of the sun. What was he to do with her? She snuggled close to him as if they belonged together. As if they really were married.

No.

He couldn't think that way. He couldn't want the woman anywhere near him. Emma Pickering was trouble. Strong-willed. Stubborn. She didn't know a thing about the real world. Her life had been little but tea, ostrich plume hats and fancy dancing. She could barely even ride a horse, although she had done pretty well with Red.

Her hand lay on his arm, and he could see the brass ring on her finger. She had said the marriage was all business, and it was. She wanted to be a nurse. That suited him just fine. He needed a nurse.

But he wanted more. He wanted Emma. Shutting his eyes, he willed away disturbing thoughts. He couldn't feel like this. Clarissa and his future should be all he thought about. She would be coming sometime. Those pale blue eyes would look up at him. He would kiss her lips . . . and think of Emma.

The Englishwoman in his arms was anything but

frail. She was soft, though. Her skin velvety and her hair a tumble of silky waves. Reaching up, he trailed his fingers through the golden strands. She stirred, let out a sigh and eased closer against him.

Adam groaned. He was starting to want things a man like him should never consider. The years in Africa had been an attempt to change his life, and he would not step off the straight road laid out before him. God had let him live, given him another chance. He couldn't cast that to the wind.

But there was something in Emma's heart that beckoned him. Her spirit matched his in fiery stubbornness and the determination to follow a dream. He liked being with her, talking to her, dancing with her, making plans. He was amused at the way she tossed her head and shot looks of insolence at him. He even admired her order not to use his guns. It took guts to tell a cowboy he couldn't use his gun. Emma had spunk. And she was beautiful. And he was in trouble . . . deep trouble.

He clenched his jaw and looked out the window. It was going to be a long night.

The sudden cessation of rhythmic rocking brought Emma out of the depths of sleep—a sleep so heavy she was unable to move or even think. Her focus fell first on a pair of worn black boots, crossed one over the other and resting on the train seat in front of her. She studied them for a moment, knowing whose they were, yet unable to make sense of what she saw. She had dreamed of those boots and the man who wore them. He had walked in them through her dreams.

"Emma?" His voice was deep, lulling, hypnotic. "Emma, are you awake?"

As reality intruded, a jolt ran through her and she sat up straight. Adam King's blue eyes shone like sapphires in the morning light.

"We're at the station," he told her. "Mombasa."

Still drowsy, she turned to the window. The early sun had bathed the whitewashed station buildings and the porters' uniforms in a pink hue. Only a few men stood on the platform, all wearing curious stares.

Humidity pressed in on Emma as the heavy weight of her mission reawakened. "I must go into town at once," she whispered, starting to rise.

"Wait, Emma." Adam caught her hand and pulled her back to his side. "Don't run off just yet. I've been thinking about things."

"Don't think. Just—"

"Mornin', ma'am." Soapy shuffled down the aisle as Emma stood.

"Good morning, Mr. Potts."

"Lord have mercy. You look as limp as a neck-wrung rooster." Yawning, he held out the hat Adam had given her to wear. "Let's rustle up some grub. You, too, boss."

"We'll head over to the bungalow, eat some breakfast and wash up."

"What?" Emma said, turning to Adam. "I cannot delay another moment. Mr. Bond telegraphed ahead. We're expected at the bank."

Leaving the men, she hurried down the aisle. The heat hit Emma like a lead weight when she stepped out. She ran a hand around the back of her damp neck. Adam was right. A bath and a change of clothing would help. A solid meal would be even better. But such luxuries must wait until she had set her plans in motion.

Mombasa town was coming to life as she stepped away from the station in search of a trolley. But Adam's hand on her shoulder stopped Emma.

"Now I want you to listen to me," he said. He took her hand and set it on his arm. "Soapy's right. We'll do better at the bank after some food and a change of clothes."

A glance down at her tattered skirt told Emma the truth. "But I cannot be long."

He walked her toward the row of waiting trolleys. "Emma, a few minutes more or less won't make a difference. Bond was right on one account. No one alone and unprotected can survive for long in the bush. Hold the hope that the Germans or the Maasai found your sister. But if not . . ."

Emma closed her eyes as he let the words go unspoken. She didn't want to hear it. Any of it.

"Keep praying for your sister," he continued. "I have faith we'll find her."

"Faith?" she sputtered, coming to a stop. "What

good is faith when God sets one stumbling block after another in my path? He called me to become a nurse. He sent me to Miss Nightingale's school at St. Thomas's Hospital. He told me to go to Africa. I've done everything He asked, and now just when I need Him most, He has gone silent."

"Emma, you're taking this too personally." He started walking again. "Sure, God made the world, but He doesn't pay it much heed now."

"Are you saying God doesn't care about Cissy? Do you doubt He called me to become a nurse?"

"He's God. Why would He pay attention to us?"

"Why wouldn't He? God created us. Before the dawn of time, He had laid out a plan for each of us. Jesus died on the cross for us. Everything God has done is for the purpose of uniting us to Himself."

A trolley wallah caught their attention. After seating them and getting directions, the man pulled his vehicle into the street. They passed a fisherman making his way to the shore, a heavy net draped over one shoulder. A shoe seller opened wooden shutters at the front of his shop, while his wife used a bundle of sea grass to sweep white sand from the doorway. Only a few days before, Emma had traveled this road with Cissy and her father. So short a time, yet everything was different.

She was different.

Adam was studying a row of palm trees in the distance. "You make it sound like God knows and cares about each separate person."

"Of course He does. Which is why I cannot believe so many confusing and dreadful things are happening. Cissy lost. My father dead. And you . . . you . . ."

Mortified, Emma realized she had started to cry. She tugged out a handkerchief and dabbed her eyes. "We didn't see anyone," she muttered, "not a single human during that whole day's journey back to Tsavo."

"No, but that doesn't mean they weren't out there. The Maasai know how to hide. They take note of everything that happens on their land. Besides, if what you say is true, God planned out this whole thing for a purpose. A good purpose. If He cares the way you say, then God is watching you right now. And me. And your sister."

"You believe it's possible Cissy may still be alive?"

"Anything's possible, Emma."

Adam held Emma's hand as the trolley took them along the narrow cobblestone streets of Mombasa. Shadowed alleys merged one after another between whitewashed houses crowded together. Men sold coffee from gleaming brass pots as women hurried by in black veils. Their kohl-lined eyes glanced at the strangers, then flicked away. A salty smell of fish and the sea and old baskets and leather lingered in the air.

But most of all there was Emma.

A loose tendril of golden hair brushed against Adam's neck. The warmth of her hand filled his heart with something inexplicably good.

Before long the cobblestone gave way to a track of white sand. The trolley took a path through a gate and down a long road between coconut palms planted in straight rows.

"Is this your land?" Emma asked.

"Seastar is my plantation. I planted the trees about eight years ago, and we've just harvested our first crop. In a few years I'll export copra, the oil that comes from the white meat inside the coconut. It's made into soap and candles. I'll sell the dried leaves for thatch and the fiber around the nuts for ropes."

"When I think of a plantation, I imagine a brick house with tall white columns. Fields of cotton. And slaves."

"Not many brick mansions on the coast of Africa," Adam remarked as they rounded the edge of the grove. A rambling, thatch-roofed bungalow stood at the end of the trail. Its verandah with blue-painted posts and blue doors circled the white-washed building. Wide windows faced the grove on one side. On the other an endless stretch of turquoise water was broken only by a line of white surf across a distant reef.

"Beautiful," Emma exclaimed. "After the voyage from England, I thought I never wanted to see the ocean again. But this is lovely."

As Adam dismounted and lifted her down, it was all he could do to keep from drawing her into an embrace, kissing her sweet lips and telling her that the most beautiful sight he'd seen in years was the woman in his arms.

But she stepped away to gaze out at the Indian ocean. "You are blessed indeed, Mr. King."

"I bought the land right after I got to Africa," he said after paying the trolley wallah. "Built the house a few years later. I stay here when I come to pick up shipments."

"Shipments?" Emma turned to him. "What shipments are those?"

"Farm machinery, mostly." He stepped onto the verandah. "Medicine sometimes. The day we met, I was expecting a crate of tools, but the purser had no record of it. While we're here, I'll see if it's come in on another ship. I'm planning to put in a railhead right over there."

"A what . . . ? Oh, a railhead. Of course."

Adam glanced at Emma and saw that her cheeks had drained of color. He took a step toward her. "Are you all right?"

"Sorry, yes. I was just thinking. Thinking of something I was told a few days ago."

He frowned, wondering what she had been told that could cause such a response. When she said nothing further, he went on. "I plan to ship coconuts into town. A factory is in the works. I've lined up some investors."

"You have quite the head for business." Emma lifted her skirt and stepped onto the verandah.

"I have plans." He studied the crashing breakers in the distance. "This country is where I'll make my dreams come true. All of them."

"What of your family in America? They must be proud indeed. Do they visit you?"

"No," he said. "They don't."

Taking off his hat, he tossed it onto a gazelle horn hat rack mounted by the door. He crossed the verandah to a wicker chair.

She took the chair beside his. "Surely they'll come from Texas to see you."

"My father wasn't happy with me for leaving home. He was buried three years ago."

"I'm sorry," she said. "Very sorry."

"Too late for that now."

"Is it? I think not. You'll reconcile with him one day, just as my father and I will finally understand each other."

He studied the earnest expression on her face. Emma believed she would be with her father again. In heaven. She thought God took a personal interest in her—so much that He had called her into nursing and sent her to Africa. That was the kind of faith he had seen in his mother's life. Simple trust. Unquestioning conviction.

"Why did you leave Texas?" Emma asked. "Could you not find work?"

"The frontier is gone. Texas is crowded. I heard

about opportunities in Africa, and right away I knew this was where I was supposed to start my empire."

"Your empire?"

"Ranching, farming, the railway." Adam leaned back in his chair, feeling easier now that the conversation had turned from religion. "This land is raw and untamed. Lawless. Free. Out here, a man can do what he wants."

"Has your family lived long in Texas?"

"My great-grandfather came over from Germany. The family name is Koenig. It's the German word for king."

"German?"

"I've got Irish blood in me, too. Even some Cherokee."

He started to tell her about the grandmother whose Cherokee blood had given him a head of black hair, but as he began, Soapy came running around the corner of the house.

"Boss!" His gray eyes were wide as his boots pounded along the wooden floor. "Boss, a feller from the warehouse caught up to me when I was on my way here with the horses. He said your shipments are in!"

Soapy stopped before Adam, his white hat in hand. "All five crates got here this morning. Everything made it safely past customs . . . nothing opened. They're all sealed up tight and stored at the warehouse. Shall I round up some fellers to go get 'em?"

Adam glanced over at Emma. "Why don't you head on inside?" he told her. "Your trunks should get here anytime. The lady who works for me will take you to your room. Just tell Miriam when you want to eat and she'll fix you something."

Standing, Adam started across the verandah. "I'd better go with you, Soapy. In case there's any trouble."

Chapter Nine

Emma started down the verandah after the two men. If they were going after the crates, she should follow. The scene she had witnessed from the ship's railing filled her thoughts when she heard Soapy's announcement. Had Adam been so angry with the purser over a missing shipment of tools?

Not likely. Only something very valuable could have caused such a heated response. Nicholas claimed that Adam was importing guns. No wonder the American had been edgy that day. With English customs officials roaming the dock, he would have been worried about discovery.

Accompanying Adam into town might be her only opportunity to learn the truth about him. He and Soapy would talk about the crates and perhaps even open them. Then she would know the sort of man he really was.

"Memsahib?" A voice called to her from inside

the house. "*Bwana* King say breakfast for you. Come inside."

Emma's spine prickled as a black-veiled figure glided out onto the verandah and began to circle her like a vulture. "Who are you?"

"Miriam." The woman edged around Emma, blocking her path of escape. "You stay. I cook fish now."

"Thank you, Miriam, but I must go into Mombasa." Emma tried to step around her. "To the bank."

"No, you stay here. *Bwana* King say."

Emma spotted Adam and Soapy riding away and she sighed. Clearly the man was determined that she remain at the house. Why hadn't she insisted on going? Hunger must be clouding her thinking.

She turned her attention to the woman whose black robe and veil concealed everything but a pair of bright brown eyes sparkling through a rectangular opening. Bare feet poked out from beneath the hem of the heavy garment.

"Are you a slave?" Emma asked.

The eyes blinked twice. "Slave?"

"Does Mr. King pay you a salary? Wages?"

"I live here, *memsahib*. Seastar my home."

"But are you paid for your work?"

Emma thought she heard a slight sniffle from beneath the folds of fabric. "My home here. My children here. My husband die."

Emma took a step toward the woman. "Do you have money?"

"No money!" The voice took on a higher pitch. "No money. I stay here with *Bwana* King."

Startled at the reaction, Emma drew back in confusion. If Miriam lived and worked at Seastar without pay, then what could she be but a slave? Yet why had she spoken of this place so fondly, calling it her home?

"Miriam." Emma reached out to the robed woman. "I did not mean to upset you. Please show me to my room."

"Come." An arm stacked with bangles grabbed Emma's wrist.

Miriam marched Emma through the open door and into a spacious room. "Sitting room," she announced. "Parlor here, kitchen outside, bathroom there. Here you stay."

Emma stepped into the large room and came to a halt—her surprise complete. A canopy of wispy white netting draped over a bed. A sunbeam from the curtained window sliced across the bed's white linens and onto the wooden floor. Seashells of every shape and color marched across the window sills.

"I bring food soon," Miriam said, her voice soft for the first time. "Now you rest." She spoke the words with finality before gliding out of the room and shutting the blue door behind her.

For several minutes Emma stared out the window at the turquoise sea with its line of white breakers. She was not in charge of her life at this moment.

God had seen to it that she could depend on no human, not even herself. Her faith must rest only in Him. God knew what lay ahead. He could protect Cissy. In silent submission, Emma placed her life in His hands.

She stepped to the wash stand, tipped the porcelain pitcher and let water flow over her tired fingers. When she tilted her face to the mirror, she caught her breath in shock at the reflected image. Her hair hung in tangled waves, stuck here and there with bits of grass and leaves, making her look like a half-blown dandelion pod. Once the proper shade of creamy ivory, her skin now gave off a ruddy glow that highlighted the olive green of her eyes.

She took a moment to assess the remainder of her appearance and found it just as bad. The sleeves of her blouse were ringed in dirt and her skirt was torn and dusty about the hem.

Scrubbing away the grime and grit, Emma had never enjoyed a wash so much. She lathered and rinsed her hair until it gleamed. Miriam returned several times to toss out the soapy water and refill the pitcher.

As she cleansed her body, Emma prayed for clarity of mind. God rewarded her reverence by calming her heart and filling her with a sense of serene confidence. It didn't matter where Adam had gone or what he was doing, she understood as she toweled her damp hair. She would dress in a lovely gown, place her most beautiful hat on her head and find some way to travel into town.

Indeed, it would be better if Adam weren't there to bungle her presentation at the bank by hesitating about the marriage. She would declare it to be so, present the affidavit that Sendeyo had signed and complete the necessary paperwork. Then she would find an outfitter and order the supplies needed for the long journey.

She paused a moment while puffing soft talcum powder on her skin. In truth, she had no idea how much food to order, nor did she know how many men she would need or how they would travel. But any good outfitter could be relied on to provide that information.

The trunks arrived—both hers and Cissy's. Emma tried to ignore memories that assailed her at the sight of their familiar baggage. With Miriam's assistance, she managed to dress in an emerald-green silk skirt and its matching jacket. She fastened the black toggles down her chest, then tugged a comb through her hair. Such impossible waves! Groaning in exasperation, she pinned up the offending tresses as well as she could. She slipped on her boots and buttoned them as quickly as her fingers would allow.

Rummaging through hatboxes, she found a green, ostrich-plumed flimsy and set it on her head. Glancing back into the room as she made her way to the door, she saw Adam's hat lying on the bed.

She was half tempted to toss aside the ridiculous green bonnet in favor of it. The hat was a part of the man—and despite everything she wanted him close to her.

Tugging on her gloves, she stepped through the door to find a tall figure silhouetted in the light of a hallway window.

"Well, well. What have we here?" Adam looked her up and down, his blue eyes taking in every detail from her green hat to her pointed emerald boots. Then his focus rose back to her face, and she saw the longing in his eyes.

Lest her own expression mirrored his, she spoke quickly. "I thought you had gone after the crates."

"Gone and back again." He took off his hat and ran his fingers through his dark hair. "Didn't want to stay away too long."

"I see." She shivered in spite of the heat. "If you please, then, I'll need a carriage to take me into town."

"Listen, Emma . . ." Adam reached out to touch her arm. "I need to tell you something."

"*Bwana* King!" Miriam's shrill cry echoed down the long corridor. "*Chakula tayari, sasa hivi!* Food ready now!"

Adam didn't move, and Emma couldn't. His presence seemed distilled to his very essence at this moment—his cotton shirt molded against his broad shoulders and his eyes as blue as the ocean. Her tension drained away and all she wanted was to feel his arms around her.

"*Bwana* King?" Miriam's voice ebbed as she wandered into another part of the house in search of them.

Adam took Emma's hand and pulled her close. "You smell like sunshine," he whispered. "I try to tell myself otherwise, but there's nothing I've wanted more than you. Emma, I—"

He bit off the word and straightened, now looking past her. "Coming, Miriam," he called. And then he was striding across the hall faster than Emma had ever seen him move before disappearing into the sitting room.

Clenching her fists, she struggled to regain the composure that had fled the moment Adam looked at her. She refused to let such a man play with her heart. Starting down the hall, she vowed to resist him. This was a dangerous man, she reminded herself for the thousandth time.

She would not succumb to Adam King every time he touched her. She would not let him touch her at all! Never again would she long for his embrace or imagine her fingers threading through his thick hair.

Furious with herself, she set her jaw and stepped into the dining room. He stood at the far end of the long table perusing a letter. Long and lean, he wore his strength with an easy grace. Emma halted for a moment, shoring herself up against emotions that crashed like waves within her.

"If you'll excuse me," she spoke up. "I should like to take a carriage to the bank. A horse will do, if you have no other form of transportation."

"I have a carriage." Adam pulled out a chair for her. "Take a seat. The bank closes at midday and opens again in the late afternoon. A tropical tradition. You'll like Miriam's fish. Fresh—caught offshore not far from the house."

Emma took the offered chair just as Soapy stepped into the room and took the seat across from her. Adam recited a perfunctory blessing. When Emma looked up, Soapy was grinning.

"Boy, howdy, Miss Pickering," he said. "You got all gussied up. You look mighty fine."

"Thank you, Mr. Potts." Emma smiled at the kind man staring at her with wide gray eyes. "This is my normal attire, actually. Cowboy hats and dusty stockings leave something to be desired."

"I like you in my hat." Adam stuck his fork into a piece of white fish, then punctuated the air with it as he talked. "I'll tell you what, Soapy. Despite those green ostrich feathers, I reckon we'll turn Emma into a bush woman yet."

"Sure thing, boss." Soapy chuckled. "But you got a lot of layers to get through first."

"I'll manage." Adam took a bite before looking up at Emma with a grin and a wink.

Mortified by their frank discussion of her attire, she turned her attention to lunch. Refraining from joining the casual banter of the two men, she ate her fish, which she found delicious.

How had she ever let Adam King matter so much to her? Emma wondered. She studied a wedge of white coconut on her plate. Why hadn't she listened to Nicholas Bond? It appeared she had made a grave mistake in hiring Adam to lead her search for Cissy. She would have to be near him constantly, and unless she barricaded her heart against the man, he could send it reeling with a glance.

She permitted herself a fleeting look. Just at that moment, he leaned back in his chair and laughed at something Soapy had said.

"Hey, Emma!" He leaned toward her. "What's wrong? Don't you like Soapy's stories?"

"I beg your pardon." She dabbed at her mouth with her napkin. "I was not listening."

"What do you say, Soap? Shall we tell her about the early days and the trouble I had trying to find my ranch? I was used to scorpions and rattlers and I could handle a herd of stampeding cattle. But when that rhino came after me—"

Both men burst into guffaws. Emma struggled to keep from joining their merriment. At this moment she wanted nothing more than to hear every detail of Adam's past. How would she ever manage to harden herself against the man?

Spotting Miriam standing near the doorway, Emma knew what she must do. She had to find out every horrible truth about Adam—the slavery, the gun smuggling, the treachery with the Germans and most of all, the truth about Clarissa. Everything. Not for Nicholas Bond. Not even for Queen and country. She must do this for herself. Once she knew everything about the man, her mind would never let her heart take control. She would be safe.

"Ah, Texas," Soapy was saying. "I sure miss her, boss."

"Texas longhorns are what I miss," Adam stated. "I wish I could put some longhorn breeding stock on my ranch."

"I wonder, Mr. King," Emma spoke up. "Did you have slaves in Texas?"

The room fell silent as both men turned to her. Soapy coughed and looked at Adam.

"Slaves?" Adam frowned. "Slavery was abolished a long time ago, Emma. During the War between the States. You know that, don't you?"

"I have heard," Emma said, folding her napkin, "that some places in the world still trade in human flesh. Do you know anything about that?"

"I've heard the rumors, but I don't see how anyone could get away with it these days."

"I suppose slave trading would be a lucrative business," Emma went on. "A way to make a great deal of money in a short time. Of course one would need protection. Weapons, I imagine, and connections within the government."

"If I didn't know better, ma'am," Soapy said,

"I'd think you was plannin' to start tradin' slaves yourself."

"Me? Of course not!"

Adam laughed and leaned back in his chair. "Well, I'm full. Thank you, Miriam. That was delicious."

The black-shrouded figure hurried out of the shadows and swept up Adam's plate. "*Asante sana, Bwana* King," she said, her eyes soft. Then she pronounced the translation in careful English. "Thank you very much."

Emma was not ready to abandon her line of questioning so soon. "Mr. King, Miriam tells me she has not earned wages while in your employ. I wonder how that can be."

While speaking, Emma observed the reactions of the other three in the room. Miriam stopped still, her hands frozen on the plates. Soapy's brow furrowed. Adam stood, his chair scuffing across the wooden floor.

"Emma, come with me." He stepped the two paces to her chair and took her hand.

"Release me, sir," she said as he guided her toward the door. "I am perfectly capable of walking—"

"Be quiet, Emma. Just settle down." Adam ushered her onto the verandah. "You don't know anything about me."

"I know all I need to know."

"Really? You need to get your particulars straight

before you say things people could take wrong."

"Can you deny the talk about you, sir?" When he gave no answer, she halted and pulled away. "I thought not. What are these particulars I need to get straight? Miriam works for you with no wages. How can you defend that?"

He gazed at the sea without speaking. His eyes reflected the cobalt ocean and sapphire sky. If he could not deny it, Emma reasoned, it must be true. The reality of his desperate wickedness brought unexpected tears.

"If you are a slaver," she went on, "then you had better tell me the truth. Confess your duplicity at once. For I shall not go off in search of my sister with a man whose actions are so far astray of all that is moral and right."

"Emma." Adam's voice was low, soft, as he turned to her. "Emma, listen to me."

"You listen to me for once," she ordered. "I am a respectable woman. Even though my errors have been many where you are concerned, now such blunders must cease."

Unwilling to speak further to such a man, she hurried down the verandah in the opposite direction. She rounded the corner of the house, grasped a blue-painted post and leaned her forehead on it. The wash of waves did little to soothe her heart.

"Miss Pickering?" The low voice startled her. Soapy stood nearby, hat in hand. "Are you all right, ma'am?"

"I am put off by Mr. King's ill manners—not to mention his illicit activities."

Soapy scratched his head. "I'm not sure what that means exactly, but the boss ain't done nothin' wrong to my way of thinkin'."

"To your way of thinking, perhaps not. But to most of civilization, trading in human flesh is both illegal and immoral."

"Ma'am, I don't know what you're talkin' 'bout. The boss wouldn't do nothin' like that."

Emma wrapped her arm around the verandah post and looked out at the sea. The tide had come in and waves were crashing just beyond the line of palm trees at the garden's edge. A movement caught her eye and she noticed Miriam wandering toward the beach with two children, one holding each of her hands.

"Why doesn't Adam pay Miriam?" Emma asked.

"She don't want him to." Soapy's voice was matter-of-fact. "Her dead husband was meaner than a rattlesnake on a hot skillet. His family tree ain't much better. The boss had him workin' on the coconuts when some enemy came along and pulled his picket pin. Miriam found the boss right after she buried her husband and asked him if she and her young 'uns could stay here and work. But she didn't want no pay. Said if she had money, her dead husband's kin would come after her tryin' to get it. All she wanted was to stay right here and cook and clean for the boss. He said okay and took in all them folks like they was family. Been here for nigh on two years, and—"

"Soapy, what yarns are you spinning now?" rumbled a familiar voice behind them. "Don't pay any attention to him, Emma. He's always airing his lungs."

"I was tellin' her about Miriam, boss."

Adam shrugged. "Pack of lies, no doubt. The cook here always tries to make me out a hero."

"Aw, boss." Soapy hung his head for a moment. "You're gonna get Miss Pickering all mixed up."

Adam turned to Emma as a servant drove a carriage up to the front of the verandah. He extended his arm to her. "Shall we visit the bank, Mrs. King?"

Chapter Ten

Emma clutched the green velvet chatelaine bag in her lap and focused on the long rows of palm trees as Adam set the horses in motion. Despite the carriage top, the afternoon sun beat down on them, and humidity curled the tendrils of hair around her neck.

Velvet and silk, Adam thought to himself, were not a practical choice for this outing. Khaki and cotton would have served her better. And a different hat.

"What have you got stuck on that hat, anyway?" he asked.

Emma kept her eyes averted and spoke in a clipped voice. "Two ostrich feathers, a rosette of purple taffeta and a rhinestone buckle."

"Fetching," he remarked.

Arching one eyebrow, she glanced at him. "Too bad if you don't like it. I purchased it at the finest milliner's in London. Cissy adored it, although our aunt thought it dreadful."

"Maybe you should have listened to your aunt."

Seated close beside Emma on the buggy bench, he felt her stiffen. He tried not to grin. Something about watching Emma get mad tickled him. Maybe it was that pretty shade of pink in her cheeks.

"Aunt Prue would go in search of Cissy without a second thought," Emma spoke up. "Nothing would stop her."

"She enjoyed a good adventure, then? Like her niece."

"My aunt had few opportunities for daring. She was married at seventeen to Uncle Theodore. Forced into the role society had predestined for her. She was beautiful and the daughter of a wealthy industrialist, you see."

"So she had no choice?"

"None whatsoever. But she slaked her thirst for intrigue by reading novels and attending lectures of the African Association. Aunt Prue would approve of my decisions."

Relief eased the tightness in Adam's chest as she spoke. Staying on safe subjects, he realized, would keep him out of trouble—the kind of trouble that made him want to take Emma into his arms.

"So, how do you like my buggy?" he asked. "I got her three months ago."

"Very nice," Emma replied, giving the carriage a perfunctory examination.

"It's a Stanhope. Made in Ohio."

"I see."

"It's got wrought-iron sill plates and full-length body loops." He was warming to the subject now, glad to fill the awkward silence between them. "I ordered the Sarven's patent wheels, although the shell band hub wheels would have been just as good. One of the things I like best about this particular carriage is the elliptic end springs."

"Elliptic end springs, did you say? Fancy that."

"I chose the Brewster-green color. Thought it might look better in the bush. And I knew the full-spring cushion and back would help out on these rough roads."

"How lovely."

"I considered a surrey, but you know, they can be tricky to handle in rough terrain. Probably should have gotten a mountain wagon. Costs about the same. I thought about it long and hard, but then—"

"We have a Stanhope in London." Emma was studying the narrow whitewashed buildings along streets that led to the Arab market in Mombasa. "I adore a Stanhope for calling. One hasn't the energy to climb in and out of a surrey all afternoon. So tiring."

"Dreadfully tiring." He awarded her a smirk and to his surprise, she giggled.

It felt good to be casual with Emma. Friendly. They had shared so many intense moments that he hardly knew what she was like in normal life. If they sat down to dinner, would she talk of bonnets and gloves and the latest fashions? He half hoped he would find her boring. That would make it so much easier to let go.

As he looked out toward the street again, his pleasure died. "Bond." He spat out the name. "That figures."

Nicholas Bond leaned against a pillar of the bank. He must have ridden a horse all night to catch up to them. Motivated, Adam thought.

"Miss Pickering!" Bond swept off his black top hat and descended three whitewashed steps to the dusty street. "How lovely to see you. May I say you look ravishing."

"Why, Mr. Bond, such a surprise to find you here." Emma extended her hand so he could help her down. "I imagined you still at Tsavo. Have you news of my sister?"

"None at all, I'm afraid." His expression solemn, Nicholas reached for her. "We've had another lion attack. An Indian railway worker."

"Step aside, Bond." Adam had left the carriage and come around it. He brushed the other man aside and lifted Emma to the ground. "The lady's with me."

"Emmaline?" Nicholas queried.

"It's quite all right," she said. "Mr. King did drive me to town. Have you an assignment at the bank, sir? Perhaps you might join us for a cup of tea after our business is complete."

"My business is to tend to your welfare, madam," Nicholas said. "I told you I would find you and I have. Under no circumstance can I stand by and allow you to be cheated out of your money by this man."

Before Adam could react, he saw Emma bristle. "I beg your pardon, Mr. Bond," she told the Englishman, "but what I choose to do with my money is my own affair. Lest you forget, Mr. King is now in my employ, while you are but the briefest of acquaintances."

Lifting her skirts, Emma slipped between the two men and hurried up the steps.

Gliding into the cool shadows of the bank, Emma let the heavy wooden door swing shut behind her. Despite its presumptuous name, the Bank of England at Mombasa contained nothing more than three old oak desks, behind which sat three weary-looking men. Each was engrossed in a ledger lit only by the green glow of a small lamp. No one looked up as Emma's heels clicked down the stone floor toward the first desk.

"Excuse me."

She tapped her finger on the ledger before the first man. His pale blue eyes focused on her.

"Yes, madam?" The man's Adam's apple rose and fell as he spoke. "Have we had the pleasure of meeting?"

"My name is Emmaline Pickering." She hesitated a moment. "Mrs. King is my married name. I should like to speak with your manager, please. I have urgent business."

"But of course. Do follow me." The clerk led her to the last desk. A portly man stood as she approached.

"Mr. Richards, sir, may I present . . ." The young man stammered for a moment, then forged ahead. "Mrs. King."

"Emmaline Pickering King," she clarified, grasping the clammy hand. "I see you are busy, Mr. Richards, and my time is limited as well. Allow me to set forward my request in the simplest terms."

"But of course, Mrs. King. How may I be of service?"

"I am in need of funds," Emma began. "I arrived in the protectorate not a fortnight ago and I have, in the meantime, lost my father and married a local landowner."

"Do accept both my condolences and my congratulations."

"Thank you." Emma hoped Adam would stay outside with Nicholas. The two men would complicate her request should they enter and begin arguing.

"My father's death and my recent marriage have made me the rightful heir to a considerable estate," she said. "Thus, I wish for you to please telegraph the Bank of England in London and request a transfer of money."

"I see." Mr. Richards shifted in his chair. "And how much do you wish to transfer?"

"Five thousand pounds."

Mr. Richards rocked back in his chair, his pale eyes widening. "Five . . . five thousand pounds? You mean to transfer five thousand pounds into this bank?"

"As I said. The transaction will benefit you, of course. You will act as my agent and keep the funds in your vault. You do have a vault?"

"Well, yes . . . but it is quite small." He ran a finger around his collar. "I should not like for anyone to know the sum involved."

"No one will know. Not even my husband."

"You will have difficulty spending so much money here in the protectorate. But of course, I should be delighted to handle the transaction."

"Howdy, John!" Adam's voice echoed the length of the stone room. "What's the holdup here? My wife giving you fits?"

"*Your* wife?"

Mr. Richards gaped as Adam strolled toward his desk. Nicholas entered the bank behind him, dusting off his top hat and hurrying forward.

"Emma King," Adam said. "Didn't she tell you we're married?"

"I see you already know my husband." Emma awarded Adam a sweet smile as she addressed the banker. "How nice to meet another of his good friends."

"Mr. Richards." Nicholas took the banker's arm and started to draw him to one side. "May I speak with you in private? Emmaline, come with us at once."

Adam's hand shot out and stopped him. "Let's talk this out right here, why don't we? The woman married me of her own free will. You have no choice but to get the money for her, John."

"But they are not legally married," Nicholas barked. "Not to mention that Adam King already has a—"

"Here's the affidavit that proves the marriage is legitimate." Adam took the document Sendeyo had signed from his pocket and shoved it into the man's hands. "Telegraph London right now, John. Get my wife her money."

By this time the other two men in the room had risen to their feet and were hovering by their desks with anxious faces.

Emma nodded. "Do as he says, please."

She studied Nicholas's flushed face as he watched the banker scribbling a quick note. Was the railway man right? Was she being duped by the American? She glanced at Adam, who towered over John Richards and watched every word the man wrote. He meant to see that she got the money. Fine. She had hired him to direct the search, and the search required money. But how much more of her inheritance did he intend to get his hands on?

And what could Nicholas Bond's motives be? She examined the tall Englishman with a critical eye. He certainly was not anxious to get his hands on her money. He didn't even want her to have it sent from England. Perhaps he truly did care for her, as he had professed.

Mr. Richards finished writing, removed his spectacles and held the slip of paper at arm's length to read it. "I believe that should do it," he said.

"Good." Adam pronounced the word as God might have when He first observed His creation. "Now send it."

Emma glared at him. Stepping over to Mr. Richards, she plucked the message from his fingers and read the words.

"This will do nicely," she said. "I shall expect to receive approval for transfer by tomorrow afternoon at the latest."

"But, Mrs. King," the banker replied, "that is a most unreasonable hope."

"Tomorrow afternoon. Mr. Fitz-Lloyd is a close friend of my family. I hope to be able to report to him on the fine service this bank provided me."

"Mr. Fitz-Lloyd?" Mr. Richards paled. "Do you

mean Mr. Fitz-Lloyd who is chairman of the board of directors of the Bank of England?"

"The very man." Emma tipped her head. "Good day, Mr. Richards."

Before he could respond, she turned on her heel and strode out of the bank. The warmth felt wonderful after the chill inside the bank. Surprised the hour had grown so late, Emma unpinned her hat, lifted it off and marched down the steps. She tossed it onto the carriage seat and climbed in.

"Find your own way home, Adam King," she muttered to herself. "Thus far you've managed to take care of all my affairs as well as your own."

Taking the reins, she flicked them across the horse's back as she had seen Adam do earlier. The mare shied, then jerked the carriage forward. Before Emma knew what was happening, the horse had started down a narrow alley and was thundering across an old wooden bridge.

Her heart hammering, Emma realized she had no idea how to control the animal. She let go of the reins and grabbed onto the carriage-top bows. As she did, the vehicle swayed into a wall, knocked off a chunk of plaster, then careened around a corner on two wheels.

At the sight of the skittish horse, ragged urchins shrieked and scampered into the shelter of arched doorways. Dogs barked from rooftops. Someone threw a stone. The horse whinnied in fear and reared as the pebble struck its flank.

"Stop!" Emma cried. She let go of the bows and grasped for the reins just as an axle began to crack. The rocking carriage rattled past a long row of houses and out onto the beach, its gyrations growing more pronounced by the second. Every time the carriage swung to one side, the horse bucked, and it was all Emma could do to stay seated.

Her bone-white fingers grasped the leather reins so tightly that they cut into her palms until she felt a strong hand close over hers.

"Whoa there, Poker!" Adam leaned from the saddle of Nicholas's galloping horse to grab the harness and pull the runaway carriage to a creaking halt.

The vehicle collapsed as the axle snapped, and Emma slid to the beach in a heap. Unable to catch her breath, she lay sprawled across the sand. Aware only of the purple-and-pink sky overhead and the quiet lapping of waves nearby, she wondered if she had died. Then Adam's face appeared above her, his eyes dark and his hair whipping in the wind.

"Emma!" The word choked from his lips. "Dear God, don't let this happen."

She coughed as air rushed into her chest.

"Emma?" Adam lifted her shoulders onto his lap. "Don't move. Here, let me help you."

"Leave me in peace, I beg you." Pushing him away, she rolled onto her knees and struggled to her feet. "Stay away from me, Adam King. I can take care of myself."

She grabbed up her skirts and stumbled away from him toward the waves. She couldn't need such a man. She didn't. Adam wasn't to be trusted, and she had erred in placing so much faith in a stranger. Now he had rescued her again from her blundering attempts to be free of him.

"Emma?" Adam stepped beside her and took her arm in his. "You could have been killed back there."

Her temper flared as she shook him off. "Well, I am not dead, am I? Stop interfering in my affairs. I can manage everything on my own."

"You managed to lose control of my horse and send my buggy tearing all over Mombasa town."

With a cry of exasperation, she hurried ahead of him down the beach, setting her eyes on a distant line of palm trees silhouetted against the pink sky. But in moments he was beside her again.

"Emma, be reasonable now."

"You are my employee and that is all," she told him. "I'm paying you to find my sister."

"You haven't paid me a dime yet." Adam stepped two paces ahead and stopped Emma in her tracks, his strong hands covering her shoulders. "What's got you so riled up, woman?"

"You're after my money, aren't you?" Emma searched for an answer in his eyes, but the sun had set so swiftly she could see only deep shadows.

"Emma, for Pete's sake." Adam's hands slid from her shoulders down her arms to her hands. He held them gently, his fingers pressing into her palms and his thumbs running along the slender bones on top.

"Is that what you think of me?" he asked. "You think I'm a gold-digger?"

She studied the distant reef. "Why not?" she asked him. "I have a large inheritance."

"I know that."

"You like money very much."

"I like what it can do." He laced his fingers through hers. "I don't know a man worth his salt who doesn't like money. I plan to make my fair share of it and more, if I can, before they plant me in the ground. But not off you."

Emma blinked again. A tear threatened, and she tried to lift her hand to brush it away before it could spill over. But Adam held her hands firmly in his.

"I've ruined your Stanhope." Her voice quavered and she fought to regain her poise. "I shall pay for it, of course."

"It'll need a new axle," he murmured, his lips close to her ear. "I'll send some of my fellows out after it tonight. And the horses."

"The horses." Emma swallowed. She could feel her control wavering again. Her mind warned her against him, but as his lips touched her cheek, she shivered. His hair smelled of sunshine and soap. Thick silky strands brushed her temple. But the sensation was enough to make her draw back, startled.

"What are you doing?" She pulled away from

him. "You must stop it, Adam. I'm paying you. You're in my employ."

"I'm not your servant." He caught her in his arms. "This feeling between us . . . I don't want to let it go. And neither do you."

"You're wrong. I'm perfectly fine without you." She set her attention on the moonlit waves. "I made my plans, and they do not include a wayward cowboy."

"Plans don't have anything to do with what I'm talking about." He pulled her closer. "I'm talking about right now . . . about how beautiful you are."

He kissed her cheek again, and she finally understood how impossible it was to deny the attraction between them. Despite every bad thing she had come to believe about this man, despite countless warnings against him, despite the call of God on her life, she could not make her heart reject him.

Yet she must continue to try.

"You make every effort to overpower me," she told him, pulling her hands away. "You barge into my affairs and impose your will on me. I despise that."

"Okay, Emma . . . okay." He stroked his fingers down her cheek. "This is about your father. I'm nothing like him."

"You're hoping I'll fail."

"Not at all. I submit to your leadership."

She shook her head, certain he was mocking her. "We must get back. Where is Seastar?"

Adam pointed to the nearest row of palm trees, and Emma realized they were just a short stroll from the clearing in front of his verandah. As the sun sank, she set off toward it, her boot heels sinking into the sand with each step.

"So, what are you going to do now that you're in charge?" Adam folded his arms across his chest as he strolled beside her. "Do you have a master plan?"

Emma stepped up onto the dark verandah and shook the sand from the hem of her skirt. She felt lost, unsure which direction to take. After waiting so long to experience freedom, she had discovered she was afraid of it.

"Miss Nightingale," she blurted out. "She knew the master plan. When I visited her in Mayfair, she told me about the Master's plan. Nursing requires careful observation, she said, and life demands the same. Just as a nurse must study her patients and be sensitive to their needs, so should a Christian study the Bible and remain constantly receptive to God's leading."

Adam hesitated before joining her on the verandah. "Your Miss Nightingale—she isn't married, is she?"

"No." Emma bristled. "And neither am I, in case you have forgotten our agreement. In singleness of purpose, Miss Nightingale and I are the same. She has no more need of a husband than I do. She is busy enough without a family to engage her time."

"Something wrong with children?"

"Miss Nightingale has other occupations that require her attention. She believes that the primary aim of life is to serve God. To that end, she reads prodigiously and puts her knowledge to use on behalf of those in her charge. She has written more than fifteen books on topics pertaining to medicine and nursing. But I assure you, Miss Nightingale draws no attention to her own achievements. Christ, she told me at tea, is the author of our profession. He is the Great Physician, and prayer provides the means by which we know His will."

Emma could just make out the glimmer of blue in Adam's eyes, but his face—as usual—was a mask. He hid his emotions so very well.

"What would your Miss Nightingale do about a missing sister, a deceased father, a big inheritance and a man who has his sights set on making her his own?"

"You refer to Mr. Bond, and I can tell you that I have no intention whatever of allowing him to own me. I came to Africa to find a mission hospital—"

"I was talking about me," he cut in. "Emma, I'm that man. What are you going to do about me?"

She held her breath, almost afraid to exhale. And then without thinking, she took a step toward Adam, wrapped her hands behind his neck and pulled him near. His lips were warm and he hesitated only a moment before drawing her against him.

"Emma," he groaned her name. "What are you doing to me, girl?"

"I'm kissing you," she whispered, feathering her fingers through his hair. "At the moment, it's what I want to do. And it's all I can do."

He wrapped his arms around her and crushed the air from her lungs. "Emma, where did you come from? How did you find your way into my heart?"

He punctuated his words with kisses, grazing his lips across her cheek and nuzzling her ear. She shivered, powerless in his embrace.

"Adam, please tell me to go away," she pleaded. "Send me to my room. I'm too tired to think clearly."

As she spoke, she felt something press against her shoulder. A small round object. But he was speaking against her ear.

"I'm not letting you go again," he murmured. "Emma, I will never send you away."

"But don't you see?" She set her hand over the object in the pocket of his shirt. "You must help me, too. I can't be strong for both of us, Adam. I need—"

Her entreaty broke off as she lifted the small golden disk she had discovered. The fading light gave it a hazy glow, and she knew at once what she held. A woman's locket.

Chapter Eleven

Emma dangled the necklace from her fingers.

Adam stiffened. "Let me have that," he said, reaching for it.

Tightening her hold, she pried open the locket. The face of a beautiful woman filled the small oval frame. She had deep-set eyes, curls that hung in ringlets to her shoulders, a full and pouting mouth. She was not smiling.

Emma snapped the locket shut. Chilled, she pressed the memento into Adam's hand.

"Clarissa." He said the word softly, never taking his eyes from Emma's. "A woman I knew in America."

Emma could only stare at him. Then, very deliberately, she stepped away. Adam had told her he was not married, but Clarissa's name marked the letter he had torn in Mombasa. She had signed it as his wife.

Ashamed, Emma had no choice but to admit the truth. She had kissed another woman's husband. She could blame no one but herself for the pain and humiliation she now felt. Adam belonged to Clarissa and he lacked the strength of character to tell Emma. She had played the fool. Now she must pay the price.

Adam felt nothing for her but physical attraction.

In the presence of that knowledge—in the despair it gave her—Emma knew suddenly, overwhelmingly, that she loved Adam King. She loved him not just a little, but with her whole heart. She loved his smile, his voice, his gentle ways, his intelligent mind, his ambition, even his stubbornness. She loved him and she must never let him know.

Without looking back, she walked across the verandah toward the door that led into the house.

"Emma." Adam's whispered voice was urgent. "Emma, listen to me."

Too late to listen now. She had done too much damage, she admitted as she drifted down the hall and into her room. Numb, she poured water into the basin. The night was hot despite her chilled skin, and she blotted a cool, damp towel over her face.

Tears of repentance welled in her eyes as she wandered to the window. Why had God allowed Adam into her life? The man had complicated and blurred the certainty of her call. She could only believe that God had put a test before her in order to determine her faithfulness to Him. A test she had failed completely.

Beyond the verandah, the sea surged and crashed across the shore. Emma closed her eyes, finding peace in the sound of the waves as she confessed her transgressions. She had known about Clarissa from the start. Even so, she allowed Adam to fill her thoughts and take possession of her heart. He had never once said he loved Emma. He never gave anything of himself but his kiss.

A traitor's kiss.

She brushed a tear from her cheek as she recalled Nicholas Bond's warnings, and she berated herself for failing to heed him.

The moon had risen fully now, casting a curling ribbon of white over the indigo ocean. On an impulse, Emma raised the window. The sea breeze blew her hair out around her shoulders. Sighing, she rested her head against the cool pane.

"You all right?" The voice came from the shadows.

Adam leaned against a verandah post a few paces from Emma's window. He had waited there, hoping she would emerge. He knew he couldn't tell Emma about Clarissa, about how he had tried in vain to get her to come to this land. Clarissa was afraid, uncertain. She thought it would be dirty and dangerous. And the people . . . "Are they all really so very black?" she had asked. No, she didn't understand at all. She didn't know Endebelai, Sendeyo and Kiriswa. She probably never would. Maybe he was a fool to think any woman could.

Then Emma had opened her window. The moon silvered her skin and lit her long hair with a glow that burned in his chest. But seeing the anguish in her eyes, he regretted lingering.

"I suppose one is allowed errors in judgment now

and then." She spoke in a low voice. "I intended to take the high road. I failed."

"I've made my fair share of mistakes." He shifted from one foot to the other. "But you didn't make a mistake with me tonight."

"You love another woman."

"There have been women I cared about."

He didn't like to talk about feelings. He had never been able to put his finger on them the way women could. Women were complicated and difficult. He was a simple man.

Except when he looked at Emma. Then he didn't feel simple at all. A strangling fear had gripped him when he saw her sprawled on the sand that night. He had begged God to spare her life, and when she had opened her eyes, he had never felt such gratitude.

Even now, the wave of her hair down her shoulders, the curve of her cheek, made him feel things he couldn't even name.

"I do believe," she said, "that I have behaved quite foolishly with you."

"No, Emma." Adam started toward her. He needed to say something. "You haven't been foolish with me, Emma. You're a woman and I'm a man. What we feel for each other is natural and right."

"Natural?" She shook her head. "It might be natural but . . ."

"But what?" he asked.

Without answering she withdrew and shuttered the window. His mind finished the sentence for her . . . but it is not right . . . but I don't need you . . . but this won't last forever . . . but don't fall in love with me.

"Roll out there, honey-bunch!" Soapy's voice reverberated through Emma's sleep-fogged brain. "Wake up and bite a biscuit!"

She struggled to her elbows within the cocoon of white bedspread in which she had fallen asleep the night before. Carrying a breakfast tray loaded with food, Miriam entered the room—followed at her heels by Soapy. In silence the woman set the tray beside Emma on the bed and gave a quick little nod, then hurried away.

"The boss wants you to shake a leg so we can get going," Soapy told her. "He said to tell you to put on somethin' simple without all them doodads and fancy fluff, but honest to Pete, I think he—"

Soapy stopped and scratched his head. "Well, it don't matter what I think. The boss wants to get to town and fetch your supplies, so's when the money comes in at the bank we can head out. See, he got a message this mornin' from the ranch that Tolito—"

He caught himself again and shook his head. "I ain't supposed to say nothin' to you about that."

"About Tolito?" Emma sat up fully, her eyes wide.

"Aw, shucks, ma'am. They ought to hire me to keep the windmills goin'. I can talk the hide off a cow." His gray eyes clouded and he hung his head for a moment. "The boss said nobody's supposed to give you no trouble from here on. You're in charge of the outfit, not him. He told me just to come in here and get you up and goin' and then back out. And don't say nothin' else. 'Specially 'bout Tolito."

Emma had to smile. "Don't worry, Soapy. I shall not let Mr. King know you did anything but wake me up. But I should like to know more about Tolito. Is this the ill person I'm to attend?"

"Yep, but I can't say nothin' else. If you knew what happened and how things come to be the way they is, you might not want to help Tolito." Soapy began backing toward the door. "And you just got to help Tolito."

Emma rose to her knees. "I have never refused to assist anyone for any reason. And I never shall."

"That's what I done told the boss. I said I thought you was a real good woman and real kind, too." Soapy grabbed the door handle. "But he said you was as hard to pin down as smoke in a bottle."

Soapy stepped into the hall and shut the door behind him. Emma stared at the blue-painted wood for a moment. So Adam thought her hard to pin down? Good. Very good. God must have forgiven her missteps and clouded Adam's memory of her reckless kiss. Best of all, Adam had told Soapy she was in charge. And with God's help, she would be.

She had confessed her failings. Forgiven and filled with a newfound peace, she felt a surge of assurance. She had made a mistake in letting Adam into her heart, but God was permitting her to rise above error and misjudgment. His plans for her were far more important and would cause far less pain than any beguiling emotional entanglement.

Therefore she would simply label Adam King as the man he was—her employee. She would speak to him as such and treat him as such.

Without pondering further, she devoured the breakfast Miriam had brought and set about to dress herself. Adam did not want her to wear *fancy fluff?* From her trunk, Emma pulled a brilliant turquoise gown with black-and-silver bows at the shoulders, intricate whorls of black velvet across the skirt and an artfully curved neckline. After dressing, she stepped into a pair of matching high-heeled shoes.

A visit to the mirror over the washbasin saw her hair swiftly pinned and a sweeping, wide-brimmed hat with three blue ostrich feathers fastened atop the curls. She pinched her cheeks, pulled on turquoise kidskin gloves and stepped out of the room.

"Good morning!" she sang out the words as she paraded into the parlor. "I do hope the carriage is waiting."

Adam turned from his position by the door where

he had been engaged in conversation with Soapy. His eyes widened, taking in the tossing feathers and swishing skirt as Emma strode across the room. Both men stepped aside to let her walk between them onto the front verandah.

"Do come along, gentlemen." Emma lifted her skirts and glided down the steps. "We don't have all day."

Determined never to need a man's help again, she climbed into the carriage by herself. It was the Stanhope, its axle replaced and its seat newly polished.

"Are you driving this morning?" he asked, breaking into her thoughts.

The man's disarming grin put her on the defensive. "Of course I'm not driving. I have a letter to write."

Adam climbed up beside her. "You'll have a rough time of letter writing on this road."

"I mean to compose my message to my aunt and then pen the letter as soon as may be. It must go out on the next ship." She ventured a glance at Adam's blue eyes. "Start the carriage, sir. We have a full day of work ahead."

"So tell me about this aunt of yours," Adam said as he released the brake.

"Prudence Pickering is married to my father's brother."

"You have other relatives in England?" He pushed his hat back on his head. "Do you have somebody to live with? Is there a house waiting for you?"

The morning humidity had begun to intensify, and Emma regretted her long gloves. It was hard enough to be sitting this close to Adam without the very air heating up around her.

"My father owned two homes," she told him. "One house is in London and the other is in the country. We lived in town after my mother died. I requested the country home as part of my inheritance. It's beautiful—near Wales and the sea, but I knew I would never have it because of my father's stipulation."

"That you get married before you could inherit."

Emma nodded. She didn't know if this arrangement with Adam would hold up in England. So quickly begun . . . so quickly over. Probably not.

"How did your mother die, Emma?"

"Aunt Prue said it was a broken heart. She had suffered a great loss."

Adam stopped the carriage on a street lined with buildings. "I'm sorry, Emma," he said. "Sorry for your loss."

She clutched her bag and sat forward, fighting the tenderness for Adam that was creeping into her heart again.

"Is the bank nearby?" she asked.

"It's just down that street."

"Very well." She drank down a deep breath. "I'll accompany you in purchasing the best equipment we can find. We shall not stop until I know who is holding Cissy."

"Holding her?" A note of skepticism crept into his voice.

"You said if she's still alive, then she's with someone." Emma heard herself reaching out to him for reassurance. "You said she would be in someone's care."

"That's my guess. But, Emma—"

"I know what you think. I know what you and Nicholas and everyone thinks." Her voice quavered and she fought to control it. "But I shall not rest until I know what has become of Cissy."

"Okay, okay." Adam stretched out his hand and almost took hers. Catching himself in time, he took the reins. "I think your sister is alive, too. I do. We'll find her."

"Yes, we shall. I hope it won't take long to outfit us for the journey. I feel as if we've been at it for days."

"We have been." Adam jumped down from the carriage and hurried around to help Emma down.

She was pleased, indeed, that when he got to her side, she had already stepped to the ground and was beckoning him from the nearest merchant.

"I feel like a child in the sweetshop," Emma said in a hushed voice. They had just stepped from the large whitewashed labor office after hiring six African porters to accompany them on their trek.

That morning they had traveled from one shop to another. Adam spoke fluent and rapid Swahili to the local shopkeepers, some of whom were African and some Arab. Emma provided the stamp of authenticity, wealth and immediacy as she stood beside him in all her finery. Not a soul refused to deliver the enormous number of goods they ordered—solely on credit. Adam rattled off items while Emma nodded, looked imperious and wealthy, and it was done.

In the process, Emma saw that Adam could have managed very well without her. In his years in the protectorate, Adam had established quite a reputation for himself, and everyone was eager to do business with him. If she hadn't thought the cordial treatment might stem from his involvement in illegal activities, she would have had to admire his acumen.

Despite her concerns, their teamwork lifted her spirits. She laughed along with him and joked at their small victories as they walked the narrow streets between rows of shops with craftsmen calling to them.

A heady aroma of spices—cinnamon, cloves, sandalwood incense, curry powder, red chilies—wafted around them along one street. As they turned a corner, the smell of drying fish, roasting maize and boiling Arab coffee rose up. This olfactory feast, mingled with the scent of seaweed, sand and salt, was served on the sea air.

"It's so different here," Emma remarked. "I am utterly astonished."

"I could say the same myself." One dark eyebrow lifted as he gave her an appreciative glance. "You amaze me, Emma."

"I do?"

"You were smart to dress in all that finery. It got us the attention and respect we needed. You have a good head for business, too."

"But I was speaking about Mombasa. Africa astounds me."

"It's a strong land. The smells are strong, the people are strong, the animals are strong, the earth is strong. A man can do things here."

Emma glanced at him. She had seen that look of vision in Adam's eyes before. It drew her. "A woman can do things here, too," she said. "I intend to make my mark."

He nodded. "A woman could do a lot here . . . if she—"

"Oh, my goodness!" Emma's exclamation cut off his words. She knelt in the street. "Look at this poor child."

The boy's leg was wrapped in dirty rags that failed to hide a festering sore. Emma peeled off her turquoise gloves, tossed them to the dusty street and gently examined the wound with her fingers.

Adam crouched at her side and spoke to the boy, who answered haltingly. "He says he burned his leg on his father's coffeepot fire. His father sells coffee from one of those big brass urns we've seen on the street corners."

"It's a serious burn. He's in pain." Emma looked into the deep black eyes of the frightened child. He had edged back against the wall as far as he could go. "The injury occurred some time ago, I think. Perhaps a week?"

Adam spoke to the boy again. "He can't remember when it happened. He wants us to go away."

"Please tell him to have no fear. I want to help him."

Adam relayed the message as Emma began to remove layers of bandage. She had no qualms about her action. Miss Nightingale taught that true nursing ignores infection—except to prevent it. Indeed, the evils of filth and poor ventilation were proved anew as Emma saw that the burn was crusted with dried pus and fiery red around the edges.

"Poor dear," she murmured. "Does it hurt dreadfully? I'm sure it must."

Emma talked quietly while she worked, and Adam translated her words into the soothing rhythm of Swahili. Unaware of the growing crowd of curious onlookers, she could see only the boy, his large, tear-filled eyes gazing into hers. She could hear only the words of Miss Nightingale and the instructors at St. Thomas's school of nursing.

"One of the commonest observations made at a sick bed," she recited, "is the relief and comfort experienced by the sick after the skin has been carefully washed and dried. Adam, I must have water. And I need clean cloths and soap, if you can find them. Please see to it."

He laid a hand on her arm. "Emma, I don't want to leave you here. These people aren't sure about what you're doing. The boy's father is right behind you."

Emma looked up in surprise at the crowd about her. For an instant her determination wavered. But it was obvious the boy was in pain and needed care.

She gave an impatient sigh. "If you cannot go, please send someone to fetch the water and cloths. Surely they see his suffering."

Adam touched the leather pouch that hung from the child's neck. "This is his medicine. It's an amulet, Emma. Inside are herbs, powders, maybe some hair and grass. The parents believe this will heal their child. Even if you clean him up and send him to a doctor, his family won't do what they're told."

"But why not?"

"The people don't understand. They haven't learned about diseases. Nobody has taught them."

"Then they must start to learn now."

He shook his head. "They believe evil spirits cause illness. This amulet is supposed to fight the spirit that's making him sick."

"Are you telling me to leave him here? Am I simply to walk away and let this wound fester?"

She looked away, fighting emotion born of frustration. "This child is just like the one in the village, isn't he? He's just like all the other ill children in this land. No one is doing anything for them."

"You." Adam caught her hand, forcing her to meet his eyes. "You, Emma. You can do something for the sick children here. You can teach the families about dirt and infection and all the things your Miss Nightingale taught you. You can help change this country, but it's going to be slow. You need to find your sister first."

Dear God, Emma prayed. *How am I to make any difference? I'm torn into pieces. What can I do?* As she begged God's assistance, Adam spoke to the boy's father, who nodded and loped away.

"He's going to get cloth and water," Adam explained. "I told him you bring healing powers from England that will drive his son's evil spirits away."

"Healing powers? But I can't promise anything."

"I expected to find you in the midst of trouble, Mr. King." Nicholas Bond's voice cut through the babble around them. Adam and Emma broke off their conversation as the Englishman descended from a trolley. "I've been out to your house this morning. Potts told me you'd taken Miss Pickering into town to spend her money."

Emma's spine prickled. "Good afternoon, Mr. Bond."

The crowd parted for Nicholas, who removed his

top hat and made a smart bow. "Emmaline, what are you doing here?"

"This child is badly burned, as you see. I am tending him." Emma instinctively addressed him just as she had her father. Her heart beat with a familiar irregular rhythm as she braced her shoulders.

"My dear, you are too refined and mannered a woman for this sort of nonsense." Nicholas took her hand to help her rise. "Kneeling in the dust is no place for a lady."

"But it is *my* place." Emma withdrew her hand. "Nursing is my passion and profession. Do not presume to dismiss my calling, Mr. Bond. I shall never be denied."

"King, I have no doubt you're behind this." Nicholas's eyes narrowed at the man beside Emma. "You're up to no good, and I warn you to watch your step in my country."

"*Your* country? Funny you should warn me about anything, buckaroo. I've got enough dirt on you to—"

As Adam bit off his sentence, Emma saw the Englishman's face drain of color.

"Just back off," Adam continued. "This woman and I have been taking care of business. Her business."

"Emmaline, may I speak with you please?" Nicholas's face suffused with red as he took her hand. "Come with me."

Before she could object, he pulled her through the crowd to the other side of the street. "Release me at once!" she cried, struggling to free herself from his grip. "I shall not be treated in this manner."

Nicholas halted and swung around, his brown eyes blazing. "You've allowed Adam King to control you and you're making mistakes. Start to think for yourself, I beg you. Listen to me if you wish to find your sister."

"I'm listening," Emma said. "What have you learned?"

"No more than you. But I am far more likely to find her than that American. My men are combing the bush even now, yet you place your life in a renegade's hands."

Emma glanced across the street to see Adam kneeling beside the boy. His father had returned with a bowl of water and a white cloth. "I have listened to you," she told Nicholas. "But to this point, I am unable to verify a single accusation against Adam King."

"No? We've had word that your friend has received another shipment."

Emma caught her breath.

"A shipment of guns," Nicholas went on. "Ammunition. Supplies for the native rebellion he's helping to foster. Five crates arrived yesterday morning. Through bribery or stealth, he managed to get them past the customs officials unopened— as usual. We know he has a warehouse, a headquarters, if you will, where he stores the crates until they can be transported for distribution."

Five crates . . . yesterday. Emma tried to recall what Soapy had told Adam. *Everything made it safely past customs . . . nothing opened. They're all sealed up tight and stored at the warehouse.*

She could see Adam leaning over the child. He had soaked the cloth and was dabbing the wound. With eyes full of trust, the boy regarded the tall man in his big black hat. Emma turned away, uncertainty tearing at her heart.

"You are right about the crates, Nicholas," she whispered. "Mr. King received five crates yesterday morning. He told me they contained farm tools."

"Tools?" Nicholas gave a dry laugh. "If you can call rifles and bullets tools, then I suppose he's telling the truth. Dearest Emmaline, you don't believe him, do you?"

"I shall not believe anything until I've seen for myself. I hired Mr. King to find my sister. That has nothing to do with other occupations in which he may—or may not—be engaged. I need his assistance."

"You need *my* assistance. Allow me to take you to the border of the protectorate, Emmaline." His brown eyes deepened with warmth. "The Germans who guard the boundary line will not divulge information to the daughter of Godfrey Pickering. Your late father's role in the construction of the railway made him the kaiser's enemy."

"But Mr. King is a neutral party."

"Hardly. Adam King is in the Germans' employ. His loyalties lie with them."

"I cannot believe him capable of such duplicity. Surely you're mistaken."

"I tell you, the man is deluding you, Emmaline." He touched her cheek. "Listen to reason. As representative of British interests in the region, I can ask to speak to the German soldier who courted your sister. A refusal would mean he is missing and likely to be in her company. Either way, I am far more likely to find the girl than an American with dubious motives and connections. Once the truth is out, you and I may announce our attachment and prepare a happy future together."

"Stop. Stop speaking, Nicholas." Emma stepped away from him, rubbing her temples to ease her sudden headache.

All her life she had been ordered to obey her father and ignore the voice of God in her heart. But she had listened anyway. Her faith had given her hope to go on living after her mother's death. Her faith had led her to become a nurse. Her faith had told her to come to Africa and make a life here. Even though she had suffered for heeding God's call, He had never led her astray.

"Emma?" Adam's deep voice echoed into her troubled thoughts. "I've cleaned up the boy. Come take a look."

Emma turned to the Englishman. "Thank you for

your concern, Mr. Bond. I shall inform you if I learn any pertinent information. Good day, sir."

"Emmaline?" Nicholas tried to catch Emma's wrist as she pushed past him, but she edged away in time. "Emmaline, listen to reason. Where do you go now?"

Electing to ignore him, Emma started across the street.

But Adam called out. "We're going to the bank to get her money." With a broad wink, he tipped his hat to Nicholas.

Chapter Twelve

"Approval to disburse your funds has arrived from the Bank of England in London, madam." Mr. Richards looked up from the telegram he held. "Of course we cannot make the entire amount you requested . . . er, five thousand pounds . . . available to you at this time. It would deplete the bank's resources. I'm certain you understand."

"I require only one thing from you now, sir. Your bank must cover my accounts immediately." She took a list of that morning's expenditures from her chatelaine bag. "Here is the record of my purchases."

He read the catalog of supplies. "The local merchants will not expect you to pay them today, madam. You could wait until the balance of your funds arrives from England."

"I prefer to establish myself as a reputable businesswoman in the protectorate. When my funds do arrive, you are to release them to no one but me. At the moment, however, I wish for you to draft a check for one thousand pounds, payable to Adam King."

"Of course, madam." The banker pursed his lips, wrote out the check and handed it to Emma. "And if you should need other funds?"

"I shall be traveling in search of my sister, but I'll send . . ." Emma glanced down at her bare hands. She had left her turquoise gloves in the street. She slipped the brass ring from her finger. "I shall send this token as proof the request is mine. Do not entrust the money to anyone—not even my husband—unless that person has this ring in his possession."

"Of course, Mrs. King." Mr. Richards took the ring in his round fingertips and held it to the light. "But this is not gold. It's brass."

"As you see."

"Very well, I shall look for a brass ring, slightly bent. I'll release nothing without it."

Emma returned the ring to her finger. "I intend to depart Mombasa at dawn and I shall not return until I have found my sister."

With a polite farewell to Mr. Richards, she stepped out of the bank to find Adam slouching on the carriage seat, his black hat tipped low on his forehead so that she could barely see his eyes.

"Did you get your business worked out, Mrs. King?" he asked.

"Nicely, thank you, Mr. King." She handed him the check.

He didn't bother to read the slip of paper, but folded it loosely and stuffed it into his shirt pocket. Emma waited a moment, wondering if he would assist her into the carriage. He made no move, so she gripped the sides of the Stanhope and climbed up beside him.

"You needn't be miffed that I conduct my financial affairs in private," she told him. "Secrecy is the hallmark of good business."

Adam straightened and took the reins. "Who taught you that one—your father?"

"You taught me that one, dear husband."

With that, she leaned back and closed her eyes. They rode in silence. The sun was setting, and she felt so grateful for a reprieve from the heat.

"Emma?" The deep voice dragged her from the depths. "Emma, we're almost home."

She opened her eyes but saw only darkness. "Where am I? What time is it?"

"You're here, with me." Adam brushed a strand of hair from her cheek. Then he bent and kissed the spot where it had been. "You fell asleep in the buggy."

At his touch, she sat up straight, her heart beating wildly. "You must not kiss me, Adam. It's improper. We established the terms of our agreement."

"We established a marriage." He guided the horse toward the house. "We did do that, didn't we?"

"It was a business contract, nothing more. I should think we've been over that enough times."

"And I should think we've been over this enough times." He kissed her lips. The blue in his eyes mixed with the golden light of the lamps along his verandah, and they shone a catlike glow. "Emma, we've been dancing around each other for days now. All I can think about is you."

He dropped the reins and let the horse amble where it pleased as he took her in his arms. Dismayed, she stiffened. But only for a moment. Then melting against him, she nuzzled her lips against his neck. His kiss found her ear, his warm breath sending shivers through her . . . and she drew up sharply again.

"Oh, Adam," she exclaimed in a breathless whisper. "You must stop at once."

Instead, he took her trembling hand and covered it with kisses.

Every shred of righteous indignation evaporating, Emma wrapped her arms around his broad shoulders. "I want you. I want you so desperately . . . but I can't bear this fear, this confusion, this storm of remorse you stir up inside me." She gasped out the words. "You're going to destroy me."

"Destroy you?" He drew back. "Is that what you think?"

"You'll try."

He was a man, wasn't he? And hadn't she learned by now the true nature of men?

She covered her face with her hands. All she could see before her was the woman in the locket. The curls, the unsmiling mouth, the staring eyes. Clarissa.

The horse had come to a stop near the verandah. Emma grabbed her chatelaine bag and stepped down from the carriage. Unwilling to speak even a word of farewell to the man who had turned her life topsy-turvy, she threw open the door and hurried to her room.

"Howdy, howdy!" Carrying a lantern in one hand and a steaming platter in the other, Soapy barged into the dining room Emma had just entered. "I've got your eggs just how you like 'em!"

Miriam followed him like a wispy black ghost in the dim light of early morning. Emma watched them scurry around lighting lamps, setting plates and silver on the long table, filling glasses with fresh milk.

"The fellers you hired for the trek are here, ma'am," Soapy was saying. "They're out by the stables puttin' everything in order. Looks like a good crew."

Soapy was even livelier than usual. "This is the first wagon train I been on since seventy-eight, when my pa took us young 'uns out west to new territory. Ma had died of the fever right after I was borned. Then Pa up and died right after we had barely got settled. If the King family hadn't took us in, I don't know what would've happened."

Emma raised her eyebrows. Soapy was a wealth of information about Adam. "You lived with the King family?" she asked.

"With their ranch hands. All nine of us kids." Soapy looked out the window with a faraway expression. "Adam was like a second father to me. He ain't that much older, but he acted kinda fatherly in his way of takin' care of me. 'Course he always kept himself apart. Never lets nobody know what he's really thinking, Adam don't. He's a loner. He won't let on that he cares, but he does. That I know."

She wondered at this. His intentions toward her had seemed clear the night before. Adam was loyal to his friend and drawn to Emma. But what of Clarissa?

Emma crossed to the window. The sun was rising out of the sea, a great ball of flame dripping with golds, oranges and pinks that spread out across the sky and onto the water. Soapy had gone back out with Miriam, and Emma closed her eyes in the silence of the room. There was only the smell of eggs and bacon and hot coffee, only the sound of the waves lapping on the beach.

"Emma . . ."

She turned to see Adam walking toward her, his

hat in his hands. "Emma, there's something I need to tell you," he said. "I'm sorry about last night. You made it clear how you felt, and then I just did what I wanted to anyway. I'm sorry."

Emma held her breath as she gazed into the deep blue eyes. She shook her head and sighed. "Oh, Adam. I don't know what to do about you any more than you know what to do about me."

"Hot sausage! Fresh mango juice! Whoa, there. Excuse me, folks." Soapy stopped in his tracks, his eyes darting between Adam and Emma.

"Looks like a great breakfast, Soapy." Adam broke from his stance and walked across the room. He pulled out a chair for Emma, then took his own place at the table.

"This is our last decent meal till we find that sister of yours," he told Emma. "Miriam's had a hand in this breakfast. You ought to taste what our camp cook thinks are eggs."

Soapy gave a snort and hitched up his pants. "Now just a minute there, boss. Them's fightin' words!"

The wagon train set off down the road between the rows of palm trees just as the sun climbed into the pale blue sky. Adam had greeted the six Africans Emma had hired. He helped them hitch the teams of oxen that pulled the wagons laden with supplies. A string of horses followed.

One wagon held the shipment Adam had

received in Mombasa. The five crates were strapped with steel bands and padlocked. Red dust rose as the caravan made its way onto the open plains. Before long they had left the sea behind to follow a narrow, rutted trail leading toward the German-British territorial border.

As days of travel stretched to a week, Emma rode Soapy's horse. She became skillful at guiding the surefooted filly around antbear holes, beneath thorn trees, over narrow gullies, up and down steep ravines.

They slept under the starlight, each rolled in thick blankets to ward off the night chill. Emma slept between Adam and Soapy, with her head toward the fire. Adam kept a rifle beside him.

They ate Soapy's cooking, which was better than advertised. Usually he created a stew from the gazelles or impalas Adam shot each day to feed the men. They drank water from canteens.

Emma marveled at the vast stretches of open land as they traveled toward the towering purple Kilimanjaro with its snow-capped peak. Herds of giraffes, gazelles, elephants and Cape buffaloes observed the caravan. A pride of lions sprawled in the shade of acacia trees. There were soaring vultures and marabou storks. But Adam knew the land was void of humans save the occasional wandering Maasai warrior or the rare village the wagon train happened to pass.

They asked the few people they met about Cissy,

but no one had seen her. With each disappointment Emma grew more despondent over the fate of her sister. If they didn't hear even a rumor of the young woman, Adam knew prospects of finding her were dim.

Adam spent the days riding at Emma's side. He took it upon himself to educate her about the habits of each animal species they encountered. Then he taught her about the different tribes living in the protectorate—the Maasai, the Samburu, the Kikuyu, the Luo, the Wakamba—each with its own unique customs and language. She drank in the information and begged him to teach her Swahili, the tongue understood by nearly every group. As they rode, he pointed out objects and told her their names. Hour after hour, day after day, they conversed. Emma's skin was burnished by the sun, even though she never took Adam's hat from her head. She left her long hair hanging down her back, where it bleached a light silver gold.

"We've been riding forever, it seems," Emma said one afternoon. "By this map, the border station should be a short distance to the west."

Adam studied the peaks of Kilimanjaro—one smaller and jagged, the other rounded and snow-capped. "Just ahead," he told her. "In those foothills."

Emma slipped her compass into the saddlebag. "I wonder if they will have a bathtub. I long for clean water and soap. I'm sure I've never been in such disarray. My hair is a tangle and my skirt is six inches deep in dust."

Adam knew she was speaking meaningless words to keep her thoughts from the reality facing them. She had to make decisions now, real decisions. "Emma, how are you going to feel if the soldier boy is still in the ranks? If he hasn't deserted?"

"I never know how I shall feel about anything until it happens. I only pray they will tell me the truth." She pushed her hat back on her head. "Adam, do you know any of these Germans?"

"Not many," he said. "As a rule, they don't come through Mombasa or travel the interior. Relations between the kaiser and your queen are unfriendly."

"Look, there it is!" Emma's excited voice ended the discussion.

Adam focused on a compound of whitewashed buildings at the foot of Kilimanjaro. The structures were bordered by a fence. Guard dogs set up a raucous barking at the approach of the wagon train.

"Time to find out what they know about a missing English girl," Adam said. But Emma had already spurred her horse toward the gate.

As she neared the compound, Emma's heart sped up to a frantic pace. Could Cissy be here, hidden away until the English government protested and turned the incident into a political scandal? Did Adam know where she was, as Nicholas had intimated?

She looked at the man beside her. His narrowed eyes were focused on a group of approaching guards. Nicholas's warnings rose to the forefront of her mind, and all she could think of was his condemnation of Adam. Her fears contradicted the man who had sung ballads by the campfire, the man who had taught her so much of what he had learned in his years in this land, the man who had protected her on the long trek. Was he instead the rogue Nicholas had painted—a slave trader who supplied ammunition and guns to native rebels, a traitor who worked with enemy Germans while living in English territory?

"Good afternoon," Adam said as four mounted men reined their horses before the wagon train.

"Good afternoon to you, Herr Koenig." The blond German in the foreground greeted him with a smile. "You are far from your home."

At the surname he used for the American, Emma's doubts surged higher. "We wish to speak to your commander, sir," she told the German.

"Commandant Doersch is occupied today, madam. We are training a new battalion."

A bilious panic rose in her throat. "But I've come from Mombasa to speak to the commandant."

"Have you authorization papers? Documents?"

Adam leaned forward. "Now let's be reasonable, Lieutenant Burkstaller." With that, he launched into a string of German words, of which Emma—who had studied French and Latin—could make very little. The blond German nodded twice, then looked back at his companions.

"Ja, ja," he said at last. "Very well, you come inside. I shall speak to the commandant on your behalf."

As Adam moved his horse in line behind the Germans, Emma turned to Soapy. The cook grinned and shook his head.

"I ain't never seen the end of what the boss can pull out of his bag of tricks," he told her. "Next thing you know, he'll be talkin' Chinese. I'll get the wagons rounded up for the night. We can camp under them trees yonder."

Emma agreed to Soapy's plan and followed the other men through the gates into the compound. As they dismounted, Burkstaller stepped into the main office building. Beyond it, a training ground displayed soldiers marching in formation. All wore the same uniform Dirk had worn on the ship, and Emma scanned their faces.

"Commandant Doersch, I present Herr Koenig and his wife." The lieutenant accompanied a slender man with graying temples. They halted a few paces from the visitors. "Frau Koenig brings a request from British authorities."

Panic fluttered in Emma's breast as she dipped a curtsy. "Commandant Doersch, how good of you to see us."

"What is your request, Frau Koenig?" The man's steel-gray eyes allowed no room for wavering.

"May I speak with you in private, sir?"

"Come with me." He turned toward the office building. Adam started to follow, but Emma gestured for him to remain behind. No secret messages this time, she thought. Nothing spoken in languages she could not understand.

"Commandant Doersch," she addressed him when they stood in the shade of a verandah. "I must know if you have here a recent arrival by the name of Dirk Bauer?"

A flicker of recognition sparked in the gray eyes. "What information do you have for me about this man?"

"First I must know if he is here."

"Why is Bauer of interest to you?"

"Is he here or has he gone? Sir, you must tell me. Lives depend upon your answer."

Emma noticed that Adam was deep in conversation with Burkstaller. How had he known the man's name? And why had she been so foolish as to leave Adam's side?

"Frau Koenig, what do you know about Bauer?" Doersch asked. When she said nothing, he continued. "You expect a German commandant to give you—an Englishwoman with no diplomatic standing—information about my battalion? You waste my time. Return to your husband. I am busy."

He gave her a curt nod of dismissal, then stepped into the building and shut the door behind him. Emma stared after him in dismay. All this way to learn nothing? No! She pounded on the door. "Commandant? My sister is missing. You must tell me what you know."

"Emma." Adam's hand covered hers. "We've worn out our welcome. Come on."

"Let me go," Emma exclaimed as Adam steered her off the verandah. "I can't leave now."

"We have no choice. And there's no time to lose."

He hurried her out the gates and across the open ground toward their companions. Tears of disappointment and frustration spilled down Emma's cheeks as they entered the circle of wagons.

Soapy straightened from the fire he had built. "Good news, boss?" He saw Emma's face. "Uh-oh. What happened?"

"A little run-in with the commandant."

"Maybe this'll help." Soapy lifted a kettle from the fire, poured a cup of tea and handed it to Emma. "I made it just how you taught me."

She took the cup and mumbled a word of thanks. Through tear-blurred eyes, she gazed across the empty plains. The late afternoon sunlight threw long shadows over the grass as the sky deepened toward darkness, shrouding the looming mountain in deep purple. What difference did anything make now? The meeting was over, and she had failed.

"Emma?" Adam took a step toward her, his voice full of concern. "Drink your tea. You'll feel better."

She could see the eyes of her hired men as they observed her from a distance. But she didn't care what they thought of her tears. Cissy was dead. Suddenly she was certain of it. She had failed to protect her sister, failed to find her, and now she would never see her again. Never even know what had happened to her.

"Emma, come here." Adam patted a blanket he had spread near the fire. Too numb to resist, Emma collapsed into the cradle of his arms. He tilted her head and wiped her cheeks with a soft handkerchief . . . and suddenly it was as though she were a little girl again—a child cradled in a different man's arms while he dried her tears with his big white hankie.

"My . . . my father used to—" Emma bit off the sentence and convulsed into sobs.

"Tell me about your father." Adam's voice was low but firm.

"It was different before." Hoping to calm herself, Emma put the mug to her lips and sipped the hot tea. "We were a family once . . . before my mother died. Before the duke. My mother met him on holiday on the Continent. They were staying at a spa in Bavaria, and . . ."

Adam dabbed the handkerchief across Emma's cheeks again. "And your mother fell in love with the duke."

"She swore she never meant to care for him. She begged my father to release her, but he refused. So she ran away."

"Where were you and Cissy?"

"With Aunt Prue during the worst of it. My father went to find my mother, and he . . . he shot the duke in a duel and brought my mother home."

The words poured out, their release easing her pent-up emotion. The pain over her mother's subsequent death had tormented Emma, yet she had never told anyone the whole story. "After that my mother grew ill, very ill. She lay in her bed at our country home—saying nothing, eating and drinking nothing—until she died."

"And from then on, your father was—"

"Angry." Emma took another sip of tea. "He feared that Cissy and I would do what our mother had done. There was justification in his worry. Men adore Cissy. She's forever threatening to run off with one or another of them. Father was irate all the time, and she longed to escape. I was to keep watch over Cissy, but I never did it well. Now look."

Emma's tears welled again. Adam took the mug from her hand and set it on the ground. He wrapped his arms around her and kissed her cheek. "Your father was angry at himself for not treating your mother right. Maybe he didn't treasure her love for him the way a man should."

Adam's voice lulled her as he went on. "He wanted you to protect Cissy—and yourself—and when you failed, he saw himself failing all over again. That's why he hurt you, Emma. He was angry with himself, more than with you. And still hurting over your mother."

Emma swallowed. She had never looked at it that way before. All she had known was the brunt of her father's fury and she couldn't see beyond it. Even now her mind felt fogged and befuddled. Cissy's face kept emerging in the flickering flames of the campfire.

"I've lost my sister forever," she whispered. "This country is too big and I have no way to find her."

"I talked to Burkstaller," Adam said quietly, his breath warming the hair around Emma's ear. "Bauer deserted his battalion the night they left Mombasa. He was unhappy, got into a brawl with his commanding officer. No one saw him go, but Burkstaller told me everyone thinks he left to find the woman he had been seen with on the ship . . . the Englishwoman."

Emma went rigid in Adam's arms. "How did you find out?"

"I paid Burkstaller to tell me," he answered. "With your money."

Chapter Thirteen

———❖———

"You paid Burkstaller?" Emma was incredulous. "But I gave you a check."

"There was money in your little bag."

"That's my property. You stole my money." She pushed her way out of Adam's arms. "You robbed me. Nicholas said you would. I didn't believe him, but now I see it must be true."

"Emma, did you hear what I just said?" Adam stood beside her. "Dirk Bauer never made it to the border. The battalion was marching down the coast, and he slipped away the night before Cissy thought she heard him calling."

"Could he have made it to Tsavo station by the following night?" Emma's heart beat louder, throbbing in her ears.

"If he were on horseback, he might have done it. There are a lot of villages along the coast. He could have found a horse."

Emma held her breath and closed her eyes. Dirk could have found a horse. He could have ridden to Tsavo by the next night. He could have been calling Cissy's name outside the railcar.

"Then she must be alive!" Emma exclaimed. "She's with Dirk. I knew it!"

"Now, Emma, don't be too hasty."

"Cissy!" Emma hugged herself.

Spotting Soapy near the fire, she danced over and gave him a warm hug. "My sister!" she cried. "Cissy is alive!"

"Ma'am, we ain't found her yet." Soapy reached for his hat as it began to slip from his head. "We still got all of Africa to look for her in, remember."

The words penetrated Emma's joy. She sobered as she realized they hadn't found Cissy and they had no idea where to look.

Nicholas's caution echoed again. *Believe me, if your sister was abducted by Germans, you can be certain your so-called protector knows about it.* She could almost hear him add, "King will say the German army told him Dirk Bauer deserted. It's a ruse."

She stared across the plain toward the military compound. Was Dirk there after all? Was Cissy there, too, or being hidden somewhere else? Did Adam know where she was even now? He had taken her money and given it to his German friend. What else might he do?

"Adam?" Her voice tinkled like a thin, broken bell.

He touched her elbow. "You'll do better with a meal and a good night's sleep."

As he spoke, the men were gathering around the fire. Soapy dished out bowls of stew and everyone ate. Before long, Emma lay in her customary place between Adam and Soapy. She had no opportunity to question Adam again, but her thoughts whirled. Although she did not expect to sleep at all, sometime in the night she stirred a little and realized she was curled in Adam's arms.

The sun's rays had just slipped over the horizon to cast a pink tinge on the snow of Kilimanjaro when Emma woke to the sound of low voices. She raised on one elbow and studied two figures standing behind a wagon. She recognized the deep timbre of Adam's voice. The other man was Burkstaller.

A shiver raced through Emma as she got to her knees, gathered her skirts and ran in a crouch across the dewy grass. When she reached the side of the wagon, she dropped to the ground and gripped the wooden wheel.

"And what did they say?" Adam asked.

"Nothing," Burkstaller answered in English. He was smoking a small cigar that smelled dreadful. "They said they had found no sign of the woman."

"And the soldier—Bauer?"

"The same. They know nothing of his whereabouts."

Emma swallowed. Who was the German talking about?

"Anything else?" Adam asked.

"You are followed."

"Bond?"

The German nodded. "He left Mombasa two days ago."

Adam muttered something under his breath, then reached into his back pocket. "Here's the rest of the money. Keep the information quiet for a while, will you?"

"Of course, my friend." The German dropped his cigar onto the ground. "Good luck with your search."

"Ma'am?" The word was spoken loudly behind Emma. Gasping, she turned to find Soapy standing with a lantern. In a moment, Adam was beside him and the German had vanished.

"Emma?" Adam's voice was harsh. "What are you doing out here?"

"What are you doing?" she snapped back. "I heard every word you said to that German, Adam King. I know it all."

"Good. Then I don't have to tell you anything."

He started to walk away, but she caught his arm. "Stop right there and tell me what you were talking about."

"I thought you heard it all." He shrugged. "I had Burkstaller telegraph Delamere in Mombasa—a message to keep an eye on the search for your sister."

"You're trying to get the Crown involved, aren't you? You mean to incite trouble in the protectorate."

"What are you talking about?" Adam crossed his arms over his chest. "Burkstaller came this morning to tell me about the telegraphed answer from Delamere. He said the British haven't found any sign of Cissy. Nothing. I took that as good news. She might still be alive. Delamere said no one has seen anything of Dirk Bauer, either. That means we have two missing people who just might be together."

"And you paid him for this news?" Emma asked. "You paid Burkstaller?"

He clamped a hand on her shoulder and dropped his voice. "You don't get a German officer to give you information about his battalion and telegraph the British government in the middle of the night for free."

Adam glared at her until Emma looked away. "What about Nicholas?"

"You heard what Burkstaller told me. Bond is following us."

"Why would he do that?"

"Because he wants you. Hasn't he told you that enough times himself? He thinks I'm a no-good skunk out to steal you blind and he wants to save your poor helpless little—"

"Boss." Soapy stepped forward and laid a hand on Adam's arm. He gave him a cup of steaming coffee. "We ain't gonna profit none by stirrin' things up with Nick Bond. You told me that yourself."

Adam snorted in disgust. "What else, Emma? Can we get on with this day now?"

She stared at him in silence. The rising sun had lit his blue eyes with a fiery glow that seemed to mirror the anger in his heart. What had passed between him and Nicholas? she wondered for the hundredth time. Who was the man to trust, if either?

"Burkstaller," she said at last. "How do you know him?"

"I met him in Mombasa five years ago." Adam took a sip of coffee. "He had just arrived from Germany. He left a woman behind—his wife, I think. He was drunk and rowdy."

"The boss took him back to Seastar and—"

"That's enough, Soapy. Burkstaller and I got to know each other."

"I see." Emma longed to ask him all the questions in her heart. Had she misread the conversation as badly as Adam would have her think?

Never mind, she thought. The truth would come out with time. Either they would find Cissy and Dirk, or they would not. The British government might step forward and accuse the Germans of duplicity, or it might not. Nothing could be certain until it happened.

The camp had begun to rouse, and Emma could see men loading the wagons. Soapy wandered over to the fire, stirred it and started pulling out pots and pans. She knelt and began rolling up her blankets.

"I thought we would head for my ranch."

Emma squinted into the sun to find Adam standing behind her. "What about my sister?"

"We'll look along the way. Stopping in villages, talking to people."

She nodded. What else could they do? If Adam was telling her the truth, there was little point in returning to Tsavo or to Mombasa. Delamere had reported no news of Cissy or Dirk. They would learn nothing else from the Germans. Continuing searching the trackless plains was the only option. At least Adam's ranch gave them a destination.

The days and nights blurred into one another as the wagon train rolled away from Kilimanjaro across the burning plains of the protectorate. Adam spoke with the people of every scattered village they passed. No one had seen or heard of a white woman in the area.

For Emma's benefit, Soapy told the story of his arrival in Africa. He related how happy he had felt to get the letter asking him to come, how seasick he had been on the ship, how good it was to sit by the campfire with his friend. The little cook talked about the King family in Texas, and he repeated the story of how the Kings took in all the brothers and sisters when their father died.

Soapy didn't mention the painful moment when Adam had left his parents' home in Texas. Adam's father had always said that a man needed to be free. But when he chose not to take over the family ranch but to make his own way in life, his father had been disappointed.

"Let him go, Ma," Adam heard him say. "Just let the good-for-nothing go. Don't ever let anybody get ahold of your heart. They're sure to fail you— even your own son."

The words had hurt, and they were seared on Adam's mind like a brand on a calf. Long ago, he had let Clarissa into his heart, but his father's warning had proven true. So he had stifled the feeling that anyone could matter to him. Until Emma.

From the moment Adam met her on the wharf in Mombasa, Emma Pickering had beguiled and fascinated him. The day the carriage axle broke and she tumbled onto the sand, he understood how much she meant to him. The thought of losing Emma was a torment that led him to accept her belief that God loved and cared for His creation. Now Adam prayed daily, hourly for her protection.

And his own release. He begged God to excise the woman from the place she had taken in his heart. His inability to detach from Emma—his certainty he could never do so—caused a palpable ache he could not dispel.

Every evening Soapy would stretch out by the fire, shake his head and groan, "I'm afraid we're almost back to civilization." Adam would nod and answer, "Nearly."

Finally one morning he looked at his compass and pointed toward a small knobbed hill in the distance. A familiar grove of acacias grew beyond it at the base of another low rise. In the shimmering sunlight he made out a faint area of glistening white.

"King Farm," he told Emma. "My place."

At mid-afternoon they rode up to the fence enclosing the cluster of whitewashed buildings. Soapy swung down from his horse and lifted the wire that secured the gate. One by one the wagons rolled into the farm.

"She stretches north and south," Adam explained, his eye on the rambling white cottage atop the rise. "Twenty thousand acres of prime grassland. Water's scarce here, but I've brought two pumps and I'm collecting rainwater in my tanks. I plan to build a dairy when the railway comes through here on its way to Nairobi station."

He studied the fine lines of Emma's profile as he spoke. Her eyes were trancelike, as if she were seeing things he couldn't.

"I drive my cattle to the coast now," he told her. "But one day I'll have a station right down there." He pointed to a level spot in the distance. "The cattle will go by train. I'm counting on that railway."

Adam looked at Emma and wondered if she knew what he was really saying. Why would he stir up trouble for the protectorate when his very existence depended on the British railway? Why would he work with Germans against the English?

"This is my home," he declared. "I will defend her with my life."

Like other homes in this equatorial land, Adam's had a shiny tin roof, whitewashed walls and a wide verandah. But he had built his house of stone—to last forever.

He dismounted and lifted his hands to Emma. She slid into his arms. For one moment they stood together, their eyes taking in the lines of the home, their arms entwined. Then around the corner of the verandah bounded two huge Irish wolfhounds, their feet sliding out from under them as they raced toward their master. Barking in excitement, they barreled down the steps and leaped on Adam.

"Hey! Whoa, there, Theseus!" He stumbled backward, laughing. The larger of the dogs jumped up to lick his cheek, and his hat tumbled onto the ground. "Emma, meet Theseus. And this one's Hercules."

"We just call 'em Seus and Herc, ma'am," Soapy confided. "Another one of them foreign languages the boss picked up somewheres. Named his dogs some heathen tongue."

The little cowboy ambled off, leading the horses toward the stables behind the house.

Adam spotted two Africans waiting for him on the verandah. One wore a floor-length white cotton caftan and a red fez. The other was dressed in skins. His hair was plaited and ochered and he carried a long, leaf-bladed spear in his right hand.

Taking Emma's elbow, Adam escorted her up the path. She bent and petted the fawning wolfhounds before ascending to the verandah.

"Emma, I want you to meet my top men." He gestured toward the skin-clad warrior. "This is Lenana, the ranch foreman. He's a Samburu, a close relative of the Maasai tribe. They live to the west. Most of the villagers to the east are Wakamba, like Jackson here."

"Jackson?" She sounded surprised.

"He worked for missionaries in the interior for a couple of years. He took that name when he was baptized. Jackson runs the house, takes care of the cooking and cleaning and all that."

"*Jambo,*" Emma said, using the Swahili greeting.

"*Jambo, memsahib,*" Jackson replied. "Welcome."

"He learned English from the missionaries," Adam explained. "Jackson will show you your room. When you're ready, there's someone I want you to take a look at."

"Tolito?"

Adam nodded, wondering how she learned the name. But Jackson was already leading her into the house. So he signaled to Lenana, and the two men strode down the verandah steps toward the wagons at the base of the hill.

"This way, please," Jackson said. Emma followed the sweeping white caftan through the house. The design of the home was spectacular—a flagstone entryway, smooth wooden floors, white walls, fire-places in every room. Most rooms opened onto a verandah, and each verandah framed a magnificent view of Africa. Every detail of the dwelling had been thought out and executed to perfection . . . yet, unlike Adam's house at Seastar, this one had almost no furnishings.

The rooms were bare save a few wooden chairs, a table, a straw mat and an old lamp. The bedrooms Emma passed as she accompanied Jackson down the long hallway stood empty. But when they came to a large room near the back of the house, Jackson pushed open the door as if showing Emma an inner temple.

"The room of *Bwana* King," he said in a hushed voice.

Emma peered around the door at the enormous bed stationed against one wall. A writing desk stood beside the door. Boxes of books lay scattered about on the floor. Several volumes were stacked on the desk beside sheets of writing paper.

"Why has Mr. King not furnished this house?" she asked Jackson.

"He is waiting, *memsahib.*"

"Waiting for what?"

"He is waiting for *Memsahib* Clarissa to arrive. She brings the chairs and tables."

Emma lowered her eyes for a moment. Of course, Clarissa would bring her own things. "Has she not come to this house before?"

"No, *memsahib.*" Jackson shook his head as he spoke. "*Bwana* King says she will come soon. But he has waited many years. We think she will not come. Not ever."

Emma frowned. So the woman had never seen this wonderful land? Never seen the home Adam had built for her? Never known his world, his life? How could that be?

"You will sleep in this room, *memsahib.*" Jackson led her to a door down the hall. "It is for guests."

"And who are Mr. King's guests?" Emma asked, stepping into the shadowed chamber.

"We do not have many guests. *Bwana* and *Bibi* Delamere visit. Others of the English government also. Sometimes *Bwana* Burkstaller comes."

"Burkstaller?"

"Yes, *memsahib*." Jackson drew aside the thin cotton curtains to let in the sunlight. Before Emma could ask anything else, the African men who had traveled so many miles across the plains from Mombasa came into the room with her baggage. In hesitant Swahili, she asked them to place the trunks and hatboxes along one wall. Then she dismissed Jackson and the others and stood alone at last.

She wandered across the room, took off her dusty black hat and set it on the windowsill as she gazed out across the darkening plains. Thorn trees dotting the grasslands cast long purple shadows. A pair of giraffes wandered up to a fence and bent their graceful necks to examine the foreign obstacle. Undeterred, they lifted their long legs, stepped over the fence and sauntered across the grass toward a leafy acacia.

Emma sighed. Even though Adam had said he was not married, he could never deny Clarissa's importance. It didn't matter that she was far away in America and that she had never bothered to join him in Africa. What did matter was that Adam had built this house for her and left it unfurnished for her things. He carried her portrait and surely he dreamed of her at night.

Emma reflected on the laughter she and Adam had shared as they rode side-by-side across the plains. She must forget his touch, his smile, the jangle of his spurs when he walked. She would have to let him go in order to get on with her own life. Not only was Clarissa alive in Adam's heart, but God had commissioned Emma to serve as a nurse. Although the Lord had allowed Adam into her life, He had never changed her calling.

Shaking off sadness, she lifted her chin. A pitcher beside her bed held fresh water, and she splashed her face and hands in the basin, arranged her hair into some semblance of order and set off down the hall.

Entering the bare sitting room, she found Adam leaning into an open leather-bound trunk. Bottles clinked, and he gave an occasional mutter of disgust.

"Adam?" Emma asked.

"There you are." He lifted his head. "This is all I've got. Dug it out from the stables. I haven't had much use for it. Not sure it's worth anything."

The serious tone of his voice concerned her, and she knelt on the floor beside him. Dark brown bottles lay scattered among rolls of dusty bandages, paper-covered boxes and foul-smelling jars.

"Dr. John's Asthma Cure," she read, studying a particularly odorous bottle. "Guaranteed permanent cure. Asthma, hay fever, influenza, catarrh, cramps. Ordinary colds in the head."

"You won't need that." Adam took the bottle and replaced it with another. "How's this? Dr. Baker's Blood Builder."

"Adam, take me to Tolito."

He gestured at the chest. "Do you want any of these bottles?"

"What's wrong with your friend? What are the symptoms?"

"You'll have to see him for yourself."

Him? With Soapy's innuendos and Adam's strange behavior, she had almost decided Tolito was a woman.

"This way." Adam took Emma's elbow and led her out of the room down the verandah steps. They crossed the darkening road toward a small stone house with thatched roof. Red curtains hung in the windows. Adam swung open the green door.

Emma went before him into the lamplit room. The house contained a small sitting room and two back bedrooms. At the sound of their entrance, Soapy stepped out of one of the bedrooms, hat in hand.

"It's bad." He sighed and shook his head. "He's sufferin', boss. I think it's gone putrid."

Adam halted, his jaw tight. Without a word, he turned and strode out of the house.

Soapy shrugged. "Adam and Tolito is like brothers." He motioned for Emma to follow. They entered a room lit by three lamps. An African man lay on a wood framed bed, his face a stoic mask.

"Can you speak to him, Soapy?" she asked in the crisp tone she had adopted at St. Thomas's Hospital.

"He can talk English, ma'am." The cowboy addressed the man in the bed. "This here's Miss Emma. She's gonna help you get better."

"My name is Tolito." Each word was an obvious effort.

"Think I'll check on the boss," Soapy said.

Hardly hearing him, Emma sat on a three-legged stool near the bed. "Now, Tolito," she said softly, "tell me what happened to you."

"Lion," he answered through trembling lips.

Emma swallowed. "A lion attacked you?"

Tolito grimaced. "I was foreman of the farm . . . now Lenana's job. One night lions attack cattle by the pump house. They take two calves. I cannot lift my shield and—" He stopped and closed his eyes.

Emma laid her hand on the man's furrowed brow. He stiffened momentarily at her touch, then relaxed. As she ran her fingers across his skin she saw scars from old wounds. Perhaps a knife, she thought.

"Why could you not lift your shield?" she asked him.

The brown eyelids slid back. "*Bwana* King say I cannot tell you about old trouble. Just lion."

Emma frowned. Adam King certainly had many secrets to keep. She returned to her patient.

"You must let me see the lion wounds, Tolito." She began to pull back the blanket, uncertain how this warrior would feel about a woman seeing his body. "I am a nurse . . . a healer of sorts. I shall take a look at what the lion has done to see if I can ease your pain."

She continued to speak in a low voice as she examined Tolito's limbs. Trying to keep her expression neutral, she assessed the lion's ravages. It was clear at once that the beast had come down on Tolito's shoulder, raking its claws down the man's body. At least one rib was broken. Again, she was surprised to see the markings of old wounds—raised and puckered scars tracing their way across his dark skin. Had he been attacked by some other creature as a child?

Emma touched the raw gashes that ran down his left leg. They were healing, and he might eventually regain use of the limb. However, it would bear the lion's marks for the rest of Tolito's life.

"We must bathe your wounds," she explained. "Each day, they should be cleaned well. I shall bind you tightly to set the rib. Now let me see your back."

Tolito rolled to his side. Here the lion had done great damage. She pulled aside the layers of crude bandages and gazed at the still-raw wound where the claws had torn into muscle.

"And now your shoulder." Emma peeled away the blood-soaked dressings and drew back in disbelief. The wounds lay open and raw, the joint dislocated. Even though someone had been tending the shoulder, Tolito must see a doctor. If not, he would die.

"Why has Adam not taken you to the railway doctors? Dr. McCulloch is a good man."

"No!" Tolito half rose from the bed, then fell back in agony. "No! Not the railway doctor . . . no, no."

Emma sat silent. Why would he refuse to be treated by Dr. McCulloch or Dr. Brock?

"Then you must go to Mombasa," she told him. "I will care for your other wounds, but I cannot put your arm right. You must see a doctor."

"I die." The words escaped the man's lips as if with his last breath. "Evil spirits curse me."

"You shall not die," Emma's retorted. "And you most certainly do not have evil spirits. We must get you to a doctor. I shall speak to *Bwana* King. First, I shall bathe these wounds."

"No!" Tolito's half-shouted word fell on deaf ears as Emma pushed through the door into the adjoining bedroom. It was shrouded in semidarkness, but a figure sat up from the bed when Emma entered. Both gasped.

"Who are you?" Emma peered through the gloom at the approaching silhouette. The veiled figure stopped before her and lowered the concealing folds of fabric.

Emma's mouth fell open in astonishment. She was staring at the most beautiful woman she had ever seen.

Chapter Fourteen

"Who are you?" Emma asked again in a low whisper.

The woman removed the red-patterned cloth from her head. Her skin was dark, yet it glowed with a golden sheen, heightened in the dim lamplight. Her deep brown almond-shaped eyes were heavily rimmed in kohl. Her nose was thin, her lips full, her cheekbones high, her neck long and slender. Her hair, as black and shiny as onyx, fell to her waist in tight, rippling waves.

"Linde?" Tolito called from the other room. The almond eyes turned their mesmerizing gaze from Emma's face.

The woman slipped around Emma into Tolito's room. For a moment Emma stood unmoving. She had never been face-to-face with such exotic and mysterious beauty. She had always considered the height of female attractiveness to be someone like Cissy with long golden hair, fair skin, blue eyes, an hourglass figure. Yet this woman was fully robed and as dark as King Solomon's beloved queen.

More intriguing, Tolito had not wanted Emma to see her. Why?

Emma stepped back into Tolito's bedroom. The woman, now crouching on the low stool, had rewrapped her face in the red cloth.

"Who is your caretaker, Tolito?" Emma asked.

Two pairs of dark eyes turned on her. Tolito ran his tongue over dry lips.

"She's his half sister." Adam's voice came from the doorway behind Emma, and she turned in surprise. "Her name is Linde."

"Half sister?"

"Tolito is a Maasai." Adam entered the room, his hat in his hand. "He's from the clan we stayed with out on the plain. Remember Endebelai? She's their mother. But Linde is half Somali."

Emma recalled the old blind woman who had served her breakfast in the Maasai village. So these two were her children.

"Tolito's clan roamed north several years ago looking for grass," Adam continued. "Their cattle were raided by a band of Somali warriors, and some of the women were taken."

Emma studied Adam's expression as he spoke. His friend was suffering and he was in pain because of it.

"Tolito can recover from his wounds," she told Adam. "I'll make a tincture to bathe them. But he must see a doctor about his shoulder."

"No," Adam said. "No doctors."

"He needs a surgeon if he's to have use of his arm again."

"He didn't have use of it before."

"Why not?"

"Old wounds. He's a warrior, Emma." Adam

reached down and straightened the edge of Tolito's blanket. "Anyway, he won't see a doctor."

"He told me that, but I don't understand. Surely Dr. McCulloch would tend him."

"No, he wouldn't. I talked to McCulloch. He said Tolito doesn't work for the railway, so he's not entitled to care."

"That's preposterous. This man needs immediate medical attention, and Dr. McCulloch has no ethical right to refuse him. I shall speak to that man. My father—"

"Your father is dead, Emma," Adam cut in. "You'll have to stop relying on his name. Take my word for it. They won't treat him."

Emma shook her head in exasperation. "This is ridiculous," she muttered, striving to keep the tremor from her voice. "I shall speak to Lord Delamere as soon as I return to Mombasa."

"The doctors in Mombasa are attached to the government."

"Have you some sort of trouble with the government as well as with the railway?" When Adam didn't answer, Emma set her hands on her hips. "When did this happen?"

"Just before I left for Mombasa. I was going to try to get a doctor to come back here with me, but then . . ."

"You found me."

"We made a deal, and this is your part. Can you work on him tonight?"

"Now, without delay." Emma unbuttoned her sleeves and began rolling them up. "I shall need assistance."

"I'll help you," Adam said.

"What about Linde?" Emma lifted her eyebrows at the woman waiting in the shadows. Her long, thin fingers reminded Emma of Miss Nightingale.

"She can't speak much English."

"We'll get by."

Emma knew this silent woman had played an important role in Adam's life. He had wanted her hidden, kept apart. Why? Could she be his lover? An arrow of panic shot through Emma's heart, and she glanced up at the woman again. The mysterious almond eyes gazed back.

"Do you need anything from the main house?" Adam turned up the lamps as he spoke. "This is Soapy's house and he doesn't keep much here."

"Soapy's? But where do they live?"

"Tolito lives down in the village. He has a wife and three children."

"I see."

Adam had not said Linde lived in the village. Was she Soapy's mistress? Or perhaps a slave?

"I shall need that chest of medicines and some clean water," Emma told him. "Bring me a bedsheet, too. Linde can make bandages."

Adam started for the door.

"And a needle," Emma called after him. "Find me a needle and some thread."

Adam looked back, his brow furrowed. "A needle? I don't think I have a needle."

"I have." Linde rose from the shadows. Her voice was low and husky. "I have needle."

Emma looked from one to the other, hoping for a clue to the past between them. Then Adam was gone, shutting the door behind him.

For the remainder of the evening, Emma concentrated on Tolito. Adam and Soapy carried down the chest. Emma created a tincture of various medicines in an effort to create a healing, numbing wash for Tolito's wounds. She set Linde to work tearing the sheet into strips for bandages. Soapy elected to spend his time in the stables.

"I reckon I'm 'bout as helpless as a froze bull snake 'round here," he told Emma. "Hope you don't mind if I make myself scarce."

Emma was relieved to see him go. She feared there would be too many people in the room with both Adam and Linde at hand. Yet she wanted to watch them interact.

As Emma began to work, Adam sat beside Tolito and held his hand, gripping tightly as the pain increased, stroking his forehead when it subsided. He bent over and murmured words in Tolito's language, words to which the African nodded and sometimes even smiled. And finally Adam began to sing.

Emma had heard his voice occasionally crooning a cowboy tune as they rode across the plains, but he had kept the words mostly to himself. Now, in the lamplight, his voice echoed soft and melodic.

Linde hummed along, tearing the sheet methodically. When Emma began cleansing Tolito's leg, the dark woman glided to her side. Adam joined Linde in helping to calm Tolito's torn, writhing body. Emma was surprised at the way the young woman worked beside her, never flinching at the gory task. Instead, she seemed to anticipate Emma's needs with a clean cloth or a fresh bandage.

"This, you see, has started to heal," Emma explained as if Linde were her student. "It will make a scar, but your brother will not have pain here after a few weeks. You can see he already has many scars."

Linde nodded, her eyes intent on Emma's face. "Arm?"

"We shall clean it, but we can do nothing more tonight. The flesh is badly torn." She eyed Adam, hoping he would see that guarding his secrets could cost this man's life. "Tolito must go to a doctor in Mombasa."

Adam gave a tense nod. "I'll get him there."

Satisfied, Emma bent again to her work. She lost track of time as she wrapped bandages around Tolito's ribs and cleansed the wound in his shoulder.

"There," she announced at last, trying to straighten her back. Adam stopped singing and looked up from his trancelike fixation on the wall. Tolito had drifted to an uneasy slumber in his arms.

Linde rose from a crouch. *"There,"* she echoed.

Emma smiled at her eager pupil. "You have done well, Linde. Now Tolito can begin to heal. Do you understand?"

The woman inclined her dusky head. "I like."

Emma was puzzled. "What do you like?"

"I like *you*." She took Emma's hand and kissed it. "Thank you. Thank you."

"She's been worried," Adam explained. "She hasn't left his side for a minute. Not even when his wife comes."

"But when I came, you made her go to the next room." Emma couldn't hide her annoyance. She was weary . . . and tired of the mystery. Why did Adam have secrets? Why must he build walls around himself?

"Let's go up to the house." He took her arm. "Thank you, Linde. Send for me if he needs anything."

Adam escorted Emma through the chilly night air. "Why did you hide Linde from me?" she asked as they reached the main house.

"I didn't hide her." He opened the dining room door to a table spread with cold meats, crackers, fresh sliced bread, fruits and hot tea. "She was in the next room, wasn't she? If I'd wanted to hide her, I could have done a better job than that."

"But you didn't want me to see her."

"Let's eat." He pulled out a chair for her and began piling a plate with food.

She wanted to be angry with Adam, to insist that he explain himself. But she felt drained, too spent to rail at him. As she ate, her empty, knotted stomach relaxed and she began to feel stronger. She had no idea what time it was, but the moon shone bright through the open windows. Adam slouched in the chair across from her, his own plate empty. He was staring at the table, his face unreadable and his blue eyes deeply shadowed.

"I'm going to my room." She stood. "Good night."

Adam looked at her. "Thank you, Emma . . . for Tolito. You were good with him."

Forcing away the urge to soften, she made her way down the hall. Stepping into the bedroom, she shut the door and leaned against it, breathless. Tears welled, and she crumpled in exhaustion to the floor.

She loved him. She knew too well it was forbidden, hopeless and utterly impossible, but she could not suppress it. Even though she might find Cissy, might even start her nursing work, her life would seem meaningless without that love. Without Adam.

Her own willfulness, she saw, had led to this agony. Since setting foot in Africa, she had hardly taken time to pray or seek God's leading. Instead, she had forged ahead on her own. Now she was caught in a snare—trapped body, heart and soul. How, in the darkness of the African night, could she ever see her way into the sunshine again?

Adam stood in his favorite place on the verandah. By the light of the moon, he could see the landscape he loved bathed in silver. He would not trade this vista for a chest full of gold. On this land, he had planted his dreams and would reap his future.

He leaned one shoulder against a rough-hewn post. After dinner, he had gone to his room, bathed and made an attempt to sleep. Too restless to lie still, he rose and stepped outside. An hour of pacing and pondering had left him no closer to peace.

"Adam King."

He turned to find Emma standing in the shadows just outside her bedroom door. She wore a white robe embroidered in white roses that caught the moonlight as she stepped closer.

"May I speak to you?" she asked. An edge of flint in her tone belied the softness of her hair and gown.

"Sure," he replied.

"I want the truth from you. I want it now. No more lies."

He scrutinized the woman as he moved toward her. She held her shoulders high. Her stubborn little chin jutted forward. But as her eyes followed him, he saw her tremble ever so slightly.

"The truth, Emma?" he said, lightly taking her

shoulders. He pivoted her toward the trees in the distance. "Look out there. That's the only truth I know."

He pointed to a baobab. Two large spotted cats crept along the limb, their thick tails twitching gracefully from side to side. They moved toward something else . . . the shape of an animal hanging in the forked branch. The leopards pawed at the dead antelope, its horns hanging askew toward the ground. Then they tore into their catch, grunting with pleasure as they feasted.

At the sound, Emma gasped. She stepped backward into him, her breath shallow. "Adam, let me go. I'm frightened."

"You wanted the truth, Emma. There it is. The truth is that we're no different from those leopards. They schemed to catch that gazelle and they caught her. Then they dragged her up into the tree where no other animal could have her. They left for the day, and tonight they came back."

"I see them." She hugged herself. "What are you trying to tell me?"

He turned her to face him. "Every man is out to get the most he can for himself, Emma. He'll plot and scheme and stake out his claim. Then he'll move in for the kill. Once he's got what he was after, he'll hide it away where no one else can have it, so that he can enjoy it for himself."

As he spoke, he searched her eyes. Tormented to a mossy green, they darted across his face.

"And that's what you're like?" she whispered.

"That's what everyone's like," he told her. "That's what you're like, Emma."

"No, you're wrong. Look, I came here to help you, Adam. By helping Tolito."

"I forced your hand. You didn't want to come. You have your own plans. You want to be a nurse, right? Never mind that someone might want you to—"

He bit off the words and looked away. His pulse roared and he clenched his jaw against the throbbing in his temples. Why was he hurting her like this? What had she done to deserve his cruelty? It wasn't Emma he was angry with . . . it was himself.

"You've done everything possible to make your dream come true." Emma's voice wavered. "Haven't you?"

"Not everything." Again he stopped himself. No, he couldn't tell her. He couldn't bring it out again. He had hidden it so well. But she had forced him to look at it again—that old longing, that hunger to share his life with someone.

"What is it, Adam? Is there more to your dream?"

He let out a breath and walked away. No, he wouldn't tell her. He didn't need to add another heartache to his life. He had angered his parents, turned them against him. And Clarissa—look what he'd done to her. He had allowed Tolito's life to be ruined. So many mistakes.

"Adam, tell me." Emma came after him and

caught his hand. "I want what's best for you. Don't be mistaken about me. I love you—" She stopped, her eyes wide with dismay. "I shouldn't have said that."

"No, you were right to say it." He looked away, anxious as a big caged cat. "I've gone wrong so many times, Emma. So many lives. But not this time. Not with you. I love you, Emma."

His eyes met hers, the knowledge between them almost too stunning to bear. And then the desire they had tried to deny drew them together with unimaginable power. He embraced her on the moonlit verandah, and she met his kiss.

"Adam, I've been so tormented," she whispered.

"I'm yours, Emma. Every day, every hour." He wanted her to know it all. He wanted to hold nothing back now, nothing. "I love you, Emma. I've never known anything like this feeling I have with you. It's so right, so good."

She nestled her head on his chest and spoke against his shirt. "Just hold me, Adam."

He tried to focus his thoughts. "Emma, I want you to stay."

She looked up. "Stay? But I must find—"

"Cissy, I know. I'm going to help you find her. But after that—" She covered his mouth with her fingertips.

"After that," she said gently. "After that, I have my mission to fulfill. Working as a nurse in Africa is . . ."

She stopped speaking, and he felt sure he knew why. "I don't want you to turn from your calling, Emma. Every dream I've had, I've made it come true. I've forced it to come true, even when the odds were against me."

"This is different." Emma drew back from him. "You cannot force this. You cannot force God."

"Emma, please." He reached for her.

"I should go back to my room now. We must forget what was confessed here tonight."

Adam watched her walk away. For the first time in his life, he had found what he had been seeking, and she would not come to him. She refused to be his even though he had vowed to be hers.

He knew what he must do—go to Emma and tell her everything. That was what held her back—the secrets he'd kept. He would tell her the whole story. But there was more to it. Something else was keeping her from him even more powerfully. Clarissa? Cissy? The determination never to belong to any man? Her dead mother's past? What was it?

God, he realized, was at the heart of it all. Emma was called by God, and no man could ever truly have her.

He leaned against the post again, his gaze fixed on the moon. Never mind that life promised only emptiness without her. For now, for this moment, he knew that Emma loved him. That was enough.

Chapter Fifteen

"Lions. We have a lot of trouble with lions." Adam buttered a thick slice of bread as he spoke. Emma observed him across the table, her eyes following his every movement. Framed in the light of dawn, he seemed almost to glow. His dark hair, blue shirt and deeply tanned skin set up a vibrant contrast with the emerald and pink of the landscape behind him. He was onyx on a field of rubies and sapphires, more brilliant because of his darkness.

"They get old, you see, and their teeth and claws start to fall out. Then they can't hunt as well and they start to search for easy prey. That's when they go after my cattle."

"They could decimate your profits, I imagine." Emma lifted her teacup to her lips.

"Exactly. I supply a lot of beef to Mombasa. And when the rail line comes through my land, I'll be able to build up my herds because the transportation will be so much simpler."

Emma nodded. The dreamer was speaking, and she warmed to this part of Adam that merged with the dreamer in her. It was good to be here breakfasting with him. She had slept well, relieved to have confessed her true feelings. They had an understanding now. They cared deeply for each other but would never let their attraction take control.

As Adam talked, she scanned the landscape beyond the large windowpane. The sun had just risen over the acacia trees behind the house. A warm pink glow colored the white tablecloth and lit up a pitcher of water.

"We talked before about the town to be built inland," Adam was saying.

"Nairobi?"

He smiled. "That's right. Nairobi will be built in the highlands, where the best farmland is. That will create more demand for my beef."

"If you can keep the lions away."

"There is that," he acknowledged.

Emma reflected on Nicholas's excited panoply of schemes. Somehow his plans sounded different from Adam's. Nicholas's words had conveyed greed, gain for gain's sake. Adam spoke as though striving for his dreams was more important than achieving them.

"Everyone's talking about Nairobi." Adam downed the last of his coffee. "Frankly, I've got some reservations about it. Civilization ruined the American West and it'll destroy this land, too, if someone doesn't commit to take care of it, starting right now."

"But there's so much empty land. So many animals."

"Huge herds of bison used to range across the West. Now you'd have trouble finding a single animal. It could happen here, too. Sometimes I see

264

a family of elephants wandering toward a water-hole, and the line stretches farther than I can see. But at the harbor I've seen rows of tusks piled up by the hundreds. For a few dainty earrings, an elephant dies. For a dagger hilt, a rhino is slaughtered."

"You'll put a stop to it," Emma murmured.

A question mark furrowed his brow. She laid her hand on his. "You won't let them destroy the land and the animals. I'm sure you can work with the government. You'll be named to some post, some ministry, perhaps. Minister of wildlife—that sounds appropriate."

"I'm an American, Emma. The British have their grip on this country so tight it'll be years before the Africans get it back."

"Get it back?"

"Do you think the people are going to sit around and let you tell them what to do forever?" He glowered out the window at the wakening farm. "Africans have their own government, their own way of managing. They have a civilization, no matter how savage your government thinks they are."

Emma listened, wary. Was Adam speaking treason? Would his outrage lead him to try to sabotage England's rule of a promising new colony? Did he imagine the Germans to be good for Africa?

"If you plan to stay in the protectorate, Emma, you'd better know what's going on." He broke into her thoughts before she could sort them out. "One of these days, things are going to get troublesome. A smart woman will know where she stands."

He didn't give her time to answer before changing the topic. "So, how about a ride? I'll show you my land."

"Ride? On a horse?"

Adam gave a low laugh. "I don't have a Stanhope out here. Not enough roads. If you're not up to it, you can stay here and rest."

"I'm certainly up to riding a horse. I'm quite a good rider now, if I do say so myself."

"Indeed, you are."

"But what about Tolito?"

"He's comfortable. I checked on him this morning. We can drop by on our way to the stables. Linde is there and she takes good care of him. I'd like for you to see my ranch."

Emma nodded. She wanted to share it with him, more than almost anything.

"We'll visit the villages," he said. "I can ask if anyone has news of your sister. We'll be back here by noon. And I have an English saddle at the stable. You won't even need to change clothes."

The brass ring on her finger caught the sunlight as Emma absorbed his words. It would be Clarissa's saddle, of course. This was her house, too. And the man she loved. Emma was ready to refuse Adam's invitation when she looked into his blue eyes.

"A ride would be lovely," she murmured. "I should very much like to see your land."

"Wait here in the barn. You'll be warmer there. I'll bring the horses in to saddle them."

Adam studied Emma as he spoke. She watched bemused as he reached out and fastened the top button of her wool jacket. "Go on inside before you freeze. Soapy's probably still asleep in the loft."

Thrusting her hands into her pockets, Emma hurried into the barn adjoining the stables. Like the barns she had meandered through as a child on the family's country estate in England, Adam's smelled of sweet hay and well-used leather. Saddles rested on a long beam supported by sawhorses. Bridles and other tack hung from bent nails on the wall. Bales of hay stood stacked in one corner, and a pile of loose straw covered part of the floor.

While Adam worked with the horses, Emma ran her fingers along brightly colored wool saddle blankets as she strolled toward the dim recesses at the back beneath the loft.

During breakfast, she had managed to sort the confusion in her mind into manageable boxes tied with pretty bows. Cissy was with Dirk, and soon Emma would find her. Tolito would get well after a trip to Mombasa to see a doctor. But Emma knew she had made a difference, and before long she would find a hospital where she could work.

Perhaps she would start a clinic here, on Adam's ranch. She could live in a little house like Soapy's and sew curtains and learn to speak the native tongues as well as Adam did. Sometimes she and Adam would ride out together, as good friends often do.

Emma bumped her knee on something hard and unmoving, and her thoughts vanished. In the faint light, she felt a rough wooden edge and realized with a start that it was one of the crates Adam had brought from Mombasa. He had them hidden here. She touched the padlocks and cool metal straps.

Farm tools? Nicholas's laughter echoed as she traced her fingers over stamped black letters: King Farms Ltd., Mombasa, British Protectorate of East Africa.

"Who's there?" The click of a gun being cocked followed the words. "I said who's there?"

"I . . . I'm Emmaline Pickering."

"Well, glory be." Soapy's voice registered relief. "What're you doing pokin' around back here, ma'am? You coulda got killed."

Emma tried to smile. "Forgive me, Mr. Potts. I didn't mean to frighten you. I was waiting for Adam."

"Mornin', cowpoke!" Adam's hearty voice boomed through the barn. "You're up just in time. Come help me saddle this worthless old mare of yours."

"Anything you say, boss." Soapy shuffled toward

the light, muttering as he went. "Ol' Red can't rightly be called mine no more. Your little woman's pretty much took her over."

Before joining Adam, Emma took a quick look at the crates. She had ridden with them all the way to the border and on to the ranch, and here they sat. So intent had she been on finding Cissy that she had hardly given them a thought. But now she understood this might be her last chance to learn the truth about Adam. Inside these crates were either guns and ammunition or farm tools—proof of his guilt or innocence.

The chests were locked, but tools hung on the nearby wall. Closing her eyes for a moment, she lifted up a prayer and made her decision. She must open a crate.

"Emma?" Adam called out. She could hear the horses stamping impatiently.

"Coming!" With a deep breath for fortification, she hurried out to him. She would be calm and sensible now. And when the opportunity arose, she would seize it.

"I used to sit in our barn in England," she told Adam as she approached. "I would read for hours, and no one knew where I was. Father called it a waste of time, but Mama defended my dreaming. She believed that without dreams, life was worth nothing."

Emma slid her boot into the stirrup and started to pull herself up when she felt Adam's hands at her waist. He helped her onto the saddle and then adjusted the reins.

"One time I run off, too." Soapy was settling his hat on his head. "Took a apple pie off the kitchen winder and stayed gone three days. Slept in a ol' ditch and got rained on. When I decided to go home, Pa took one look at me and tol' me to go milk the cows. He never even knowed I'd been gone."

"We would miss you around here, Soap," Adam told him. "Stick around, old partner."

"I ain't goin' nowheres 'cep' down to the house for some grub. That trail cook you got is plain terrible."

Tolito was sleeping when they looked in, and Adam was glad Emma chose not to wake him. Linde had bathed her brother's wounds in the night. Even though she had hardly slept, her dark eyes sparkled with life. Emma gave several instructions before she and Adam left the little house.

The morning ride could not have been better. The horses pranced through the dewy grass, shaking their heads and snorting in the crisp air. Thomson's gazelles, their black-and-white tails flicking briskly, glanced up at the riders, then took flight with springing bounds. Hartebeests, with their ears and horns in perfect parallels, observed the pair on horseback. A mother rhino lifted her two curved gray horns into the air as a warning to the passers-by before returning to grazing beside her baby.

Adam took Emma to his pump house and showed her the inner workings of the valuable machine he had imported. Drawing water from a borehole dug deeply into the ground, the pump supplied a lifeline for the cattle. Next they rode along his fences to check for breaks in the wire. Adam stretched his arm across the land to show Emma the boundaries of his ranch. As far as the eye could see, endless acres stretched unfenced and unmarked.

He showed her his three large ponds and pointed out lion pugmarks sunk into the muddy shoreline. When Emma told him they looked like her Aunt Prue's kitten's paw prints—only bigger—he had to laugh. Emma seemed delighted when he introduced the hippo he had named Jojo. The creature had wandered away from its family during an exceptionally rainy year and had found his ponds. The two riders dismounted and sat on a warm rock to watch Jojo blow streams of mist into the blue sky.

Later, they stopped at two villages, one of the Wakamba tribe and the other Samburu. Neither group had seen nor heard of a white woman or a white man wandering across the plains. In fact, they had never seen a white woman at all—as evidenced by the African children's curious, half-frightened inspection of Emma.

On returning to the farm complex, they went

271

straight to Tolito. He was awake, staring listlessly at the ceiling. Adam hunkered down on the stool and took his friend's hand. Leaning over, he spoke quiet words of encouragement.

Emma hung back for once. Adam could see that she was transfixed by Linde, now dressed in a brilliant green gown and peacock-blue head wrap.

"Linde," she spoke up. "Where are the bandages you stitched together? We must rebind Tolito's ribs."

The young woman glided into the adjoining room and returned with a basket filled with fabric. Linde had poured the tincture Emma mixed the day before into bottles, and they, too, lay in the basket.

"She has an instinct for nursing," Emma remarked to Adam. "Observe her sense of order and cleanliness."

"You should rest, Linde," Adam suggested. "I'll sit with Tolito."

She shook her head. "I do not rest."

"But you've been awake most of the night," Emma reminded her. "You must be tired."

"No, *memsahib*." Linde looked away as her lower lip started to tremble. "I will not leave Tolito. My brother saved me. I will not—"

"Linde," Adam cut in. He stood abruptly, knocking over the stool. "We'll be back this afternoon. Send word to the main house if you need help."

The young woman nodded. Adam took Emma's arm and started to lead her out of the room.

"I beg your pardon, sir." Emma tugged free of his grip. "You interrupted Linde as she was speaking to me. That was rude. And I have more to do here. I must change my patient's bandages."

Adam looked from one woman to the other. It would be unwise to leave Emma alone with Linde, but he didn't seem to have much choice.

"I'll be at the house," he said abruptly, before walking out of the room and shutting the door behind him.

Emma sat near the bed and observed Linde and Tolito speaking in earnest tones. The woman's voice wavered to the point of breaking until Tolito reached out and touched her arm.

"*Memsahib,* Linde wish to help you." Tolito's English was halting but clear. "She say you powerful woman from far land and she wish to be your servant."

"Oh, dear Linde, I am hardly powerful," Emma replied. "I'm a nurse, that's all. I am trained to care for sick people. I do not have need for a servant."

Linde lowered her eyes. "I am not anybody."

"But of course you're somebody. You are Linde. You are Tolito's sister."

"No, *memsahib,*" Tolito told her. "Linde not anybody. She mixed blood. Not Maasai. Not Somali. Not marry. Not wife. Not children. Not home."

To her chagrin, Emma understood all too well what Tolito was saying. She knew what it was to

273

feel as if one didn't belong. Linde had begun removing Tolito's dressing. She spoke words of comfort while her careful fingers eased away the bandages. And then Emma saw it all.

"You shall work with me, Linde," she announced. The young woman's dark eyes widened. "After I've found my sister, I shall start a clinic. My own clinic for the Maasai and the others. You must be my assistant, my helper. I'll train you—although anyone can see you have more natural skill than most of the women at St. Thomas's. Perhaps one day we shall bring a doctor from England and build a small hospital."

To Emma's surprise, Linde was weeping. Tears rolled down the woman's cheeks into the folds of her peacock blue scarf.

"Come, Linde," she said. "We shall begin even now. I can see you're as eager as I was the day I first heard Miss Nightingale speak."

For the remainder of the day, Linde worked alongside Emma. Teaching the essentials of nursing lifted Emma's spirits. After the early morning ride, she struggled to turn her thoughts away from Adam. The warmth in her heart toward him now blazed even brighter, but she knew she could never be his. She must look in the crates to prove him innocent and clear his name with Nicholas Bond and the British government. And she must prepare her own future in this land.

This was where it would unfold. Here in Africa

among the ill and needy. Here with the woman she would train to be a nurse. Her future did not lie with Adam in the big house at the top of the hill. That would never be her destiny.

Looking for Emma, Adam pushed open the front door of Soapy's house and stopped in amazement. The living room had been transformed. The curtains had been pulled back and the windows stood wide open. His rough wood table was spread with neat rolls of clean white bandages. The bottles from the medicine chest had been removed and most of them emptied. He could hear them rattling in a vat of boiling water on Soapy's little cookstove. Two chairs and an old board had been fashioned into another table and covered with a white cloth.

"Oh, Adam, there you are!" Emma's smile brightened as she bustled out of Tolito's room. She had rolled her sleeves to the elbow and tied a white apron over her blue dress. Her hair was up in a knot and her cheeks were a pretty pink that set off the sparkle in her green eyes. Adam had never seen the woman so radiant.

"Emma, what are you doing here?" He stepped onto scrubbed floorboards that squeaked beneath his boots. The setting sun gave the windowpanes a golden rose shine, and newly washed walls reflected the light.

"Adam, you should just see this." Emma caught

his hand and tugged him across the room. "We've actually begun. Linde and I have started to prepare the clinic. I am training her, you see, and she is my assistant. I'm teaching her everything I know. She is perfect. Brilliant, in fact, and so clever."

As the stream of excited words poured forth, she pulled Adam into Tolito's room.

"Emma." Adam stopped the rush of words by kissing her cheek.

She caught her breath and took a step backward. "Don't be silly now," she whispered. "You mustn't confuse me, because I'm content at the moment."

His eyes lingered on hers, then traveled down to caress the line of her nose and lips. He had wanted Emma to see his land. He had brought her here. And if God permitted, he would find a way to keep her.

"I've had a message from the crew on my western boundary," he told her. "They've got lion trouble. I'm riding over there and I won't be back until late. Soapy's going with me, but you'll be safe here. Take a lantern when you walk up to the house. I've arranged for your supper."

"Thank you." She took his big hand in hers and pressed it to her cheek. "You've made me so happy today."

He felt a surge of elation at her words. How it had happened, he couldn't say, but Emma's happiness had become more important than his own.

"I've arranged to put Tolito on the train to

Mombasa," he told her. "When you think he's feeling well enough, we'll send him. I've got men asking at all the villages on my ranch for any sign of your sister."

"You are too good to me," she responded.

Even though he knew Tolito and Linde were watching, Adam couldn't resist another peck. "I'll be back tonight."

"I'll be here." Emma touched his sleeve. "Be careful, Adam."

Before he lost what little control he had in her presence, Adam bolted out the door and ran down the steps to his horse.

The moon hung high in the sky when Emma finally left the little house and strolled toward the stables. She had eaten with Linde, and her heart warmed to the joy of a new friend. They spoke a disjointed mixture of English and Swahili, clear enough to get across their meaning.

Emma carried a lantern as she went into the barn. The soft call of night birds and the chirp of crickets were becoming as familiar to her as the squeak of her brass bed in London.

She walked across the barn floor and scanned the rows of pitchforks, rakes, branding irons and other implements hanging on the wall.

Spying an iron crowbar, she carried it to the crates stacked beneath the loft. After hanging the lantern on a nail, she inserted the tool between the hasp and the padlock of the largest crate. Leaning her body into the task, she pried with all her strength. Nothing budged.

Annoyed, she found a pair of wire cutters. Climbing onto the crate, she hoisted her skirts around her knees and began to snip at the iron bands encircling it. She quickly realized that method was hopeless as well.

Emma heaved a disgusted sigh. Adam was innocent, after all. She reflected on the ridiculous accusations Nicholas had made. Adam was no slave trader. Miriam, Tolito, Linde—such loyal workers could not be slaves. Nicholas had insisted that Adam sided with the Germans and knew what had become of Cissy. True, she had seen Burkstaller and Adam together, but treason was out of the question. That Adam might be inciting Africans to rise up against the British was ludicrous. He knew the native languages and employed members of at least three different tribes, but this hardly pointed to subversion.

Tossing the cutters onto the crate, Emma glared at it. Adam was just the sort of man she had always believed him to be, a man whose gentle nature she had witnessed again and again.

But was she naive? People could play roles, especially if they had a great deal to gain by doing so. Money. Power. Land. These were the stakes for which men played.

Her determination weakening, Emma searched

for another tool. As she looked up, she spotted a moonlit shape above her in the loft. Its dark rectangular sides glinted with soft silver light. Curious and a little afraid now, she raised her skirts and crossed to the ladder. Lifting the lamp from its nail, she began to climb.

Instead of hay and pitchforks, Emma discovered a tidy room with a wooden desk, chair and bookshelf. An iron bed with a patterned yellow-and-blue quilt stood against one wall. Soapy's sleeping quarters while Tolito was in his house, no doubt. But the desk? Surely Soapy did not keep Adam's books.

Emma sat in the chair and studied the array of pens, inkwells and paper. Then she opened a drawer to documents of various kinds—records of cattle transportation, sales, credits, charges and invoices.

She paused at an envelope labeled *Guns*. Did she want to see? Did she really want to know?

With trepidation, she looked over shipping orders, with delivery taken in Mombasa. She scanned them, praying she would find only things a rancher might have ordered. When she came to a registry of African names, she saw that a weapon was listed beside each man—shotguns, revolvers, rifles.

Emma blinked back sudden tears. Pushing the envelope to one side, she continued her search. *Warehouse,* another envelope read. She took out the documents and spread them on the desk—the deed for a building in Mombasa and a blueprint showing rooms labeled for office and storage.

Her stomach rolling in pain, she discovered documents with the name *Burkstaller* on them. Through blurred eyes she read: *Payment for Services Rendered* and *Transportation of Arms.*

Feeling faint, she scooped up the papers and tried to stuff them back into their envelopes. Unable to make her fingers cooperate, she stood, shaking. All her dreams had risen to a peak this day during her time with Linde. However, they came crashing around her ears when she opened Adam's records.

He would deny everything, she knew. Trusting him would be easy. Emma was too willing a victim, caught in his snare. She must escape this place at once. Find Cissy and leave. Nothing was as it seemed. What a fool she'd been.

Grabbing the lantern, she took a last look at the condemning desk. As she started for the ladder, light fell on a familiar shape in the corner beside the bed. She took up the rifle, determined to blast open the crate.

"Emma? Is that you up there?"

At the sound of Adam's deep voice, her heart stumbled. His tall form loomed in the moonlit doorway of the barn. With great care, she cocked the rifle.

"Stay away from me, Adam King," she warned. "If you come one step closer, I shall shoot you."

Chapter Sixteen

"**P**ut down that gun, woman!" He stepped into the moonlit barn. "It's me, Adam."

"You're not who I thought you were." Emma began to descend the ladder. "Move out of the way and let me pass. I'm releasing you from your contract, but I shall take a horse. Send my clothing to Delamere at Mombasa."

"Emma, what are you talking about?" Adam started toward her, but he stopped when she dropped down from the ladder, lifted the rifle to her shoulder and aimed it at his heart.

He wasn't afraid of the gun. She didn't have a clue how to aim the thing, and he had left it unloaded. But what had happened to send the woman off half-loco like this? He had seen Emma unhappy before. He'd seen her angry, too. But never this.

She moved toward him, and he could tell her arms were trembling as she struggled to maintain the heavy weapon at shoulder level. Headed for the door, she edged past him—making a valiant effort to keep one eye on him and see her way at the same time. If she hadn't been so upset, he would have laughed out loud and swept her up in his arms.

"I've seen your files," she told him. "I know everything. The guns. Burkstaller. Your warehouse in Mombasa."

"Really?" In a cobra-quick move Adam reached out and snatched the rifle from her hands.

"Oh!" She stiffened in horror. But her fear turned to rage as she squared her shoulders. "Shoot me, then, Adam King! Shoot me right now, because I am going to tell Nicholas Bond the truth about you. I am a Christian and committed to honor and justice. I am English, too, and I shall never betray my country. If you don't kill me at once, I'll reveal your treachery to the Crown."

"Treachery?"

"Don't pretend at innocence. I mean to inform the authorities that you have imported weapons."

"And assigned a rifle to each of my herdsmen," he added, still unsure what she was implying. "Their names are listed beside the make and numbers of their weapons. Is that what's got you riled up?"

He flicked open the Winchester's chamber and nodded in satisfaction. Empty.

"Emma, I arm my foremen and guards. Delamere and every other landowner in the protectorate does the same. Bond knows that as well as he knows anything."

"You're lying." She stood rigid, her cheeks flushed. "You always have a logical answer. But Nicholas told me about the secret warehouse where you carry out illicit operations."

"My warehouse at the edge of Mombasa is no secret. The building sits right beside the railway station. Bond walks past it every day. I tip my hat to him when I'm in town."

"Stop it. Just stop it, Adam." Emma buried her face in her hands. "Dear God, help me!"

"Emma, honey, don't fret about this." He could endure almost anything but a woman's tears. Wanting to hold her close, he settled for offering his handkerchief. She looked so forlorn standing alone in his barn, crying into her bare hands. "What made you go looking through my desk? What did you want to know about me?"

"I read your documents, Adam." She brushed away a tear. "I know Burkstaller brings you weapons."

"Of course he does. So does Delamere and anyone else coming upland from the coast. It's a tradition among the settlers to help each other deliver goods from Mombasa. In fact, one of the crates back there is for Delamere. I'll take it to him next time I visit Njoro. As for Burkstaller, he likes to spend his leaves on my ranch. The Germans wouldn't take kindly to the association between us, so we keep it quiet."

He paused as the situation came clearer. "Emma, who do you think I am, anyway? What kind of dirt has Bond put in your pretty head?"

She looked up at him. Her green eyes shone in the silver light. She was sad, but even the downturn of her mouth allured Adam. The soft blue muslin dress rippled in the night breeze, and all he wanted was to hold her.

"Look at my actions, Emma," he said. "If you want to know what kind of man I am, don't poke around in my desk or talk to some rattlesnake who'd just as soon put a bullet through my head."

He leaned the rifle against a bale of hay and took her hand, drawing her close. "I am what you see, Emma. Plain and clear. Haven't you figured me out yet?"

"What I hear and what I see are two different men. I can't trust you."

He chuckled. "Me? What about you, honey? One minute you're sweet as molasses, and the next you're pulling a gun on me."

"I rely on God. He is my strength and my shield. I shall not allow your words to trap me. I'll not be another of your victims."

"So you'd rather shoot me than believe what I say. Just what do you want me to be, Emma?"

"I don't know. I'm so confused."

"Come here, then." He pulled her into his arms.

"Oh, Adam. Why does this happen to me every time? Truly you must stop."

"Stop what, Emma?" He stepped back from her. "Do you want me to stop loving you?"

She looked away, her eyes luminous with unshed tears. "I think you must. And I am sure I cannot go on like this."

At that, he left her and crossed to the barn door. "Do what you think best, Emma. If you want to leave, take old Red. She's yours. But if you want to come back down to the house, you're welcome. I'll light a fire for you."

He left the barn. Soapy was coming up the path, and the two talked for a minute or two. A sick cow, a jackal in the henhouse, the usual things. Adam lingered, hoping, but Emma did not join them. After a moment, they ambled down the hill together.

Emma awoke and blinked in a beam of sunlight slanting across the bare wood floor. Adam. The first image in her mind.

She closed her eyes, recalling their conflict the night before. Her discoveries, the confrontation, the tears. What a mess she had made of everything.

The crates were sealed as tightly as ever. The proof of Adam's innocence—if it existed—was locked inside the crates. Even then, how could she be sure of him? Worst of all, she had lost her heart to a man who gave her no hope of a future. And she could think of no way to retrieve her heart before it was irreparably broken.

She tilted her face into the sunbeam, praying for an answer. But the storm inside her drowned out the voice of God. Sighing, she swung her legs from the bed.

The day was passing, and she needed to look in on Tolito. Afterward, she would speak to the men she had hired in Mombasa. They must prepare the wagons to depart at dawn the following morning.

By the time Emma dressed and ate, Adam had gone. Jackson told her the *bwana* was on rounds and would not return until lunchtime. She hurried down the path toward the little house and Tolito. Adam had promised to send his friend to Mombasa, and she hoped to make him comfortable for the journey.

As Emma entered the house, Linde rushed out of Tolito's bedroom. She wore a thin white gown and her hair tumbled about her shoulders as she grabbed Emma's hands and pressed them to her lips.

"What's wrong, Linde?" Emma asked. "Has something happened?"

"Tolito has pain!" The woman's brown eyes were wide with fear.

"Why did you not come for me?" Emma pulled away and ran into the room. She could see at once that Tolito's condition had worsened. Groaning in agony, he was curled into a trembling ball.

"Tolito, I am *Memsahib* Emma and I'm here to help you." She touched his shoulder. "Where is your pain?"

At that, the man burst into a loud, half-weeping explanation in a language Emma did not know. She gripped his hand and turned to Linde.

"His shoulder," Linde mumbled, gesturing. "The evil spirit of *Bwana* Bond was in lion. Now my brother die."

"*Bwana* Bond? Nicholas Bond?" Emma shook

286

her head in confusion. Whatever could they be talking about?

"Tolito, you are not going to die. Linde, give me the brown bottle. The laudanum."

The young woman handed her the drug. "I gave to him last night," she confessed. "Big pain. Bad spirit of *Bwana* Bond."

Emma poured a spoonful of the opiate. "Linde, if you want to be a nurse, you must stop this nonsense about spirits. Your brother was wounded by a lion. Mr. Bond and Mr. King dislike each other, but that's no reason to blame anyone but a wild beast for these wounds. When you saw Tolito suffering, why didn't you send for me at once?"

"*Bwana* Soapy say you angry with *Bwana* King and not come."

"Oh, for goodness' sake." Emma sighed in exasperation. "Just hold your brother's hand while I tend his shoulder. How I wish for a doctor."

Frustrated at her lack of knowledge and the ridiculous notion about spirits, she studied the collection of medicines and instruments. What could she really do for Tolito? She had watched surgeons at work, but to try a procedure herself was out of the question. Yet something must be done or the man might not survive the trip to the coast.

She breathed up a prayer as she turned to Linde. "You must assist me. Miss Nightingale would disapprove, but we shall do what we can."

"Yes, *Memsahib* Emma." Linde gave a hint of a smile. "You make Tolito well."

What seemed like hours later, Emma's stiff muscles protested as she stood to look out the window. A wild commotion of barking dogs and shouting children had erupted near the houses just below the office buildings. She could discern nothing amiss, so she returned to her patient.

Tolito lay on his back, looking up at her. His dark face was drawn, but he was alive. With Linde at her side, Emma had managed to move Tolito's shoulder back into place. Then she had cleaned his wound again, noting with relief that the infection seemed to be dissipating with frequent cleansing.

"You'll feel better soon, Tolito, but you will not be able to use this arm as you could before." Despite Miss Nightingale's admonitions to the contrary, Emma believed it was better for the patient to know the truth at once. "You will go to Mombasa as soon as you feel well enough to travel."

"Tolito's arm bad before, *Memsahib* Emma. Before lion." Linde gazed down at her brother as she spoke. "Tolito almost die. His arm die then."

Wondering at this news, Emma laid a damp cloth on her patient's forehead. "You must see that he takes the laudanum, Linde. Otherwise the pain will be too great."

"Thank you, *memsahib*." The women gazed at each other in silent understanding.

"You are my friend, Linde," Emma told her.

"My sister." Linde touched her bloodstained hands to Emma's.

"Yes, indeed," she agreed, thinking of Cissy. "Linde, you are my friend and my sister."

The dazzling sunshine blinded her as Emma stepped onto the small verandah. She groped for the post and leaned against it, breathing deeply the fresh air and letting her eyes focus on the red dirt road and the whitewashed buildings. Battling the truth that this farm was a place she loved, a place she could easily call home, she walked down the steps.

At the sound of hooves she turned to see a tall gray horse round the corner of the little house.

"Emmaline?" Nicholas Bond's voice rang out. "Thank God, I've found you at last!"

Shading her eyes with her hand, Emma took in the handsome figure on the prancing horse. Nicholas looked fine, indeed. Clad in proper English riding clothes—a white shirt, khaki trousers, knee-high brown leather boots, brown riding jacket—he swept his hat from his head.

"Good afternoon, Nicholas." Emma dipped a curtsy, aware too late of the blood splatters on her dress. "You've been riding all day?"

"And half the night." Dismounting, he strode toward her. "I have good news."

"Cissy!" She ran toward him. "You've found her! Where is she?"

"Not so hasty, dearest." Laughing, he caught her hands before she could touch him. "What on earth have you been doing? Slaughtering game?"

"Nicholas, where is my sister?"

"Calm yourself." He led his horse to the porch rail. "We've had a message."

"From Cissy? You must tell me everything at once."

He took a sealed envelope from his jacket. "The letter is addressed to you. I merely serve as the messenger."

Emma snatched the envelope and ripped it open with trembling fingers. *"To Emmaline Pickering,"* she read aloud. *"Your sister is alive.* Alive! There, that is wonderful news."

"Indeed, it is. Where is she?"

"We are holding her prisoner." The words took the breath from Emma's lungs.

She continued reading. *"She is well hidden. You will never find her. To secure her release, deliver a chest containing two thousand English pounds in gold coin to the waterfall in the Aberdare mountain range one week from the date of this letter. Place the chest in the cave beside the falls. Your sister will come out of the forest near the pool. Do not involve the government in any way. If you do not follow these instructions, your sister will die."*

Emma leaned against Nicholas to read the date. "But this was written two days ago. How shall we ever get there in time with the gold?"

"The Aberdares are not far. We can reach the place in a week."

"Adam will send his men to fetch the gold. I shall start for the waterfall immediately." She clenched the letter. "Who would dare to kidnap the daughter of Godfrey Pickering?"

"Germans, no doubt. Look at this warning. *Do not involve the government in any way.* But that is just what they want you to do."

"Create an international incident?"

"Yes. They want to provoke the English into commencing hostilities."

"I shall not tell anyone, and you must promise as well. I shall follow these instructions to the smallest detail."

Nicholas's smile was tender. "Dearest Emmaline, I had no doubt you would do everything in your power to save your sister. I'll assist you in every way."

"You are too good."

"But I must beg you not to give over the ransom."

"Not ransom my sister? How can you ask that?"

"I believe Adam King and his German conspirators are behind this. They will use the gold against the British government. Come away with me, Emmaline. Allow me to find your sister for you and spare you the cost."

He took her hands. "I love you, Emmaline. Surely you can see that. Leave Adam King—break your pact with him—and become my wife. I am asking you now to marry me. Will you make me the happiest man in the world?"

"Nicholas, I am . . . I'm touched by your endearment." She managed to fumble out the words. "But I shall never disregard the instructions in this letter. And I certainly cannot think beyond it to any future, with you or anyone. I must find my sister."

He nodded. "I expected such a response and I accept it. Of course I shall take you to the Aberdares. I've brought my most trusted men. They will return to Tsavo and telegraph the bank. But it is a great sum, Emmaline."

"I have it. There's nothing I shan't do to rescue Cissy. Oh, I do hope she has been treated kindly. If they have hurt her . . . or abused her . . ."

Emma covered her mouth with her hand. At once, Nicholas took her in his arms.

"Emmaline, my love, do not make yourself ill. The Germans want the gold. They want an incident. Harming your sister would serve no purpose. You must believe she is all right."

"What's going on here?"

Surprised, Emma looked up to find Adam glaring at Nicholas from his horse. In an instant he had dismounted and was striding toward them.

"What are you doing on my land, Bond?" He took Emma by the arm, turning her to expose the bloodstained clothing.

"Oh, no, Adam, it's not what you think. I've been

working." She gestured at the little house, then waved it off. "But look at this. I've had a message from Cissy's kidnappers."

"Kidnappers? Give me that." Adam scanned the letter. "You believe this, Emma?"

"Of course I do. Who would invent such a lie? And to what purpose?"

"Reads like something out of a mystery novel. The protectorate is filled with hardworking men, not criminals. No one's ever been kidnapped. And who even knew your sister would be here? This thing took some scheming."

Emma stared at Adam in disbelief. How could he expect her to do anything but obey the letter—even if it were a hoax, even if he himself were behind it?

"I don't care what you think," she told him. "I will get the gold and wait for my sister to come out of the forest."

"And if she doesn't?"

"Then I shall lose the money. It's a chance I must take."

Adam stared at the ground for a moment. Then he turned on Nicholas. "Where did you get this letter, Bond?"

"An African brought it to the station at Tsavo yesterday evening. I came at once."

"I'm sure you did. What kind of an African was he?"

Nicholas scowled. "What do you mean?"

"What tribe?" Adam barked.

"How should I know? They're all the same to me."

"What difference can it make?" Emma took the letter from Adam and slipped it into her pocket.

"The tribe would give us a clue where Cissy might be." He took off his hat and wiped his forehead. "Emma, I don't believe anyone's holding your sister. But I'll send Soapy after the gold, and we'll head for the Aberdares. When these kidnappers—if there are any—come out to get the gold, we'll surround them."

"No, Adam!" Emma caught his arm. "I must do as they say or they might kill Cissy."

"She's right, King." Nicholas bristled. "Don't try to use your cowboy heroics. You'll only get people killed. I shall escort Emmaline to the Aberdares. You're not needed, so just stay here with your cows."

"Get off my property, Bond." Adam reached for the rifle on his saddle, but before Emma could stop him she saw Nicholas suddenly go completely white. The blood rushed from his face, and his eyelids flew open as if he were seeing a ghost.

"Nicholas?" Emma started toward him, afraid that he was having an attack much like her father's. But Adam caught her arm. She followed the direction of Nicholas's shocked stare.

Silhouetted in the sunlit doorway of the little house stood what might easily have been a ghost. Tolito leaned against the frame, his clothing spattered with blood, his face thin and wasted with pain. But most astonishing was the glare of hatred in his eyes.

"Go," Tolito commanded.

Nicholas took a step backward. "That's . . . that's not . . ."

"You know me." The man in the doorway straightened. "I am Tolito."

"It can't be," Nicholas whispered.

"You know each other?" Emma asked.

"They've met." Adam untied Nicholas's horse.

His face wan, Nicholas gestured to Emma. "Come with me. I'll take you to find your sister."

She hesitated only a moment, listening to the whispered voice of her heart. "I shall go to the Aberdares with Adam. But when I have found Cissy, I'll return to Mombasa and discuss your proposal."

"No, Emmaline, don't make the wrong choice." His words were calm enough, but then he made a choking sound.

Now Linde stood in the doorway beside Tolito. She had changed into a vibrant purple dress with a flaming-red shawl. Her hair draped around her shoulders like a thick cape of lustrous silk. Her dark eyes sparked as she stepped out onto the verandah and raised a bronzed arm.

"Go, evil spirit," she commanded. "Leave us or be cursed forever."

Nicholas turned to Adam. "I shall do everything

in my power to bring about your downfall. Everything."

"And if I see you on my land again, you're dead."

Escaping the charged atmosphere, Emma started up the hill toward the big house. But with each step she took, she realized she had chosen to follow her heart. And her heart was held captive in the strong hands of a man with eyes the color of the African sky. A man she still wasn't sure she could trust.

Chapter Seventeen

Adam stopped at the doorway to Emma's room. She was packing a trunk and she looked up when he called her name.

"Soapy's at the stables," he said, noting how weary she looked. "I'm sending him to Tsavo alone. He'll ride faster that way. He's a crack shot and he'll guard your gold with his life."

"But I must catch him before he goes!" She brushed past Adam, gathered her skirts and started up the hill.

He followed, overtaking her halfway there. Soapy had just ridden out of the barn, an extra horse tethered to his roan. Emma signaled with a wave.

"Mr. Richards won't give you the gold unless you have a sign from me," she told him. Adam watched as she worked the brass ring free from her finger.

Breathless, she handed it to Soapy. "Telegraph the bank in Mombasa my orders to send two thousand pounds in gold immediately to Tsavo station. Tell Mr. Richards the brass ring will arrive on the next train. You must tell him it's urgent. He mustn't wait for the ring."

"There's only one train, ma'am. It'll be in Mombasa by the time I ride into Tsavo. I'll make sure the bank loads your gold before the train heads back up country. But if I don't get to Tsavo before the train leaves the coast, you ain't gonna get your gold in time to save your sister."

"Ride like lightning, Soapy," Adam ordered.

"Yes, sir." He held up the ring. "But what about this? Should I wait to put it on the train myself?"

"Give it to someone else," Adam growled. It was clear how much the ring—and their words of love—meant to Emma. "That thing isn't worth a pile of corn shucks anyhow."

"Whatever you say, boss." Soapy tucked the ring into the breast pocket of his shirt and smiled at Emma. "Don't worry your purty head, ma'am. I'll get that gold to you if it near kills me. My word is as good as a hangman's knot."

With that, Soapy spurred his horse down the hill toward the plains. Adam watched until his friend was no more than a speck moving across a sea of golden grass.

"You ready to go?" Unable to prevent the brusque tone of his voice, Adam started toward the house.

Emma hurried after him. "What about Tolito?"

"I ordered my foreman to take him to Tsavo when he's fit enough. Linde will ride the train with him to Mombasa."

"Thank you, Adam." She tried to slip past him as he held open the door to the house, but he caught her wrist.

"Why didn't you go with Bond?"

Her green eyes were depthless as they met his. "More important, how does Mr. Bond know Tolito?"

"You don't need to know that, Emma. It's history."

She freed her hand from his grip. "And you don't need to know my motivations. We each have our secrets, haven't we, Adam? That's what keeps us safely apart."

"Your inability to trust me keeps us apart."

"Should I trust you?"

"You should trust what I told you the other night," he answered. "You should trust that I love you."

"If you love me," she said quietly, "help me find my sister."

They rode alone. No wagon train would slow them this time, no heavy supplies, no plodding oxen.

Adam rode his black stallion, Emma the red mare. They took only what they could carry in saddle-bags.

For three days they journeyed toward the fertile highlands. The land changed from dry, shimmering grasslands teeming with wildlife to green hills dotted with trees.

"Coffee and tea country," Adam remarked. "Colonists are crowding these hills, running off animals and pushing Africans into tribal reserves. The English will profit no matter the cost."

"Will Nairobi be built nearby?" They had stopped to drink at a cold stream. Emma dipped her hands into the bracing water and took a sip.

"Right about here, I'd imagine." Adam studied Emma on the mossy stream bank. Wild passion fruit vines tumbled over the ground, and bird of paradise flowers bloomed in profusion. He could almost see the lush foliage give way to a bustling city with gray stone buildings, paved streets, courts of law, restaurants, rows of houses. And bursting onto the scene, the hissing steam locomotive of the British East African Railway.

"It would be a lovely place for a home," Emma said, rising to brush moss from her skirt.

She was buoyant now, anticipating her sister. It was all she wanted. But he was not so easily satis-fied. Emma had brought a sort of magic to his life. The future presented itself not just in terms of cattle, fences and coconut palms. With her talk of following God, her sweet innocence, her tender care for the hurting, Adam felt a new warmth, a hope for companionship and love.

But Emma didn't trust him. She had never admitted any desire to be with him after she found her sister. Instead, she planned to be a nurse at an outpost mission hospital, her world filled with patients and medicines instead of a home and family.

Adam took off his hat and studied the leather band around the crown as he lifted up a prayer. God was listening, he trusted that now. He had found a Bible while rooting in the old medicine trunk. As he thumbed through it, he understood what Emma had told him. The Creator of the universe took note of everything—even a simple cowboy with a hurting heart. But did God want Adam to let Emma go, this woman who had been sent to Africa to fulfill a mission? He waited for an answer but heard nothing except the gurgling stream.

"Adam, what is this flower?" She drifted toward him, a pink blossom cupped in her palms. "Such a rich perfume."

"It's a frangipani."

They had shared a kiss, tender words of love. Did that mean nothing? Did God expect Adam to walk away—when even now he struggled to keep from taking her in his arms? But Emma's holy calling superseded common human passion. Adam knew he must accept that and back away.

"Before we go, Adam," she said, "I want to thank you for helping me. I didn't know how much I was asking."

"I was glad to do it." He turned to his horse, but she caught his arm.

"And thank you for teaching me about this country. The language and the animals and people. I shall never forget what you did."

"No trouble. I'd have done it for anyone."

"Yes. Of course."

"You'll always be welcome at my ranch or at the beach house." He stroked away a strand of hair that had blown across her cheek. "You know that."

"I should like to visit. Your life will be back to normal soon. You can wear your gun again without me protesting. And it won't be long before Clarissa—"

He cut short her words with a kiss. His hands found her arms and drew her close. She leaned into him, her arms twining around his neck, her fingers weaving through his hair.

"Oh, Adam, I can't think of anything but you," she whispered. "Even poor Cissy is—"

"Wait." He drew back, listening for the tinkling sound he had heard a moment earlier. It came again—a giggle, and then another.

"Karibu." He spoke the word of welcome.

Like shy kittens, three African girls emerged from a thicket. Each carried a bundle of sticks on her back.

"They're from the Kikuyu tribe," he said, stepping away from Emma. "Maybe they can tell us how to find the waterfall with the cave."

He spoke some of the Kikuyu words he knew, using his hands to signal his meaning. One of the girls responded by pointing toward two jagged peaks that jutted into the sky.

"Batian and Nelian. The twin peaks of Kenya Mountain." He fixed his attention on the shimmering vision.

"Is the waterfall near?" she asked as the girls slipped away.

"If we travel toward the mountain, we'll come to the Aberdares and the falls. A fig tree stands at the base of a hidden gorge where a stream flows into a pool of water. The waterfall and the cave are above it."

"If the moon isn't shadowed by clouds," Emma said, "we can ride most of the night."

"We ought to be there by morning." He stepped toward his horse. "The girl warned that evil spirits live in the cave. Said we shouldn't go near the gorge."

"How odd. Tolito insisted that Nicholas Bond had cursed him with an evil spirit. Such a ridiculous notion."

"Maybe."

"You don't believe in evil spirits, do you?"

"I took you for a Bible reader, Emma." He stepped into the stirrup and mounted his stallion.

"Jesus cast out evil spirits everywhere He went. I seem to recall one time He sent a whole gang of them into a herd of pigs."

"Oh," she said, going pale. "You're quite right, of course."

"Time to move out," he announced, turning his horse. "Let's go find your sister."

After hours of trekking through thick bush, Adam and Emma finally had to dismount and lead their horses. They slogged through ankle-deep mud down steep gullies and into icy streams. Emma began to believe the whole land was cursed by an evil spirit.

The rainforest was mostly quiet through the day, but as evening lowered its dusky head, it came to life. Bush babies gaped with huge glowing brown eyes. Birds shrieked and bats fluttered by. A shy dik-dik—the tiniest of antelopes—peered at them with a minuscule face and horns smaller than a pen. Most startling to Emma was the small furry hyrax, whose shrill cry mimicked the wail of an abandoned child.

At midnight Adam insisted they stop. They huddled into the curved roots of a huge tree. They spoke little, too tired for the effort. Emma slept on Adam's shoulder, but he kept watch until dawn.

In the early morning when tendrils of mist curled over rocks and between fern fronds, they began the last leg of their trek. The horses struggled for footing in the mud, and Emma could not imagine how Soapy would ever arrive with a chest of heavy gold.

The sun had burned away the mist when Adam halted beside a stream. Emma looked up at a towering fig tree. In the distance a waterfall gurgled.

"I believe we're here," he said. "We'll camp near the falls."

"Today is a week from the date on the message. They will expect us to make the trade for Cissy."

"There's nothing we can do until Soapy gets here. If anyone is around, they've already seen us."

"Do you still doubt the letter Nicholas brought?"

"Do you still doubt me?"

She had to look away. "I don't know what to believe."

If Adam had plotted with the German forces, might Dirk Bauer be part of the scheme? Had Cissy been with him all these days, shivering in the cold forest and heartbroken by his treachery?

As she slogged through the mud, Emma wondered if the dense green foliage hid her sister. Could Cissy be watching her right now? Battling the urge to call out, Emma waded across the chilly stream and up the bank on the other side.

Deep in the heart of the gorge, vine-covered tree limbs arched overhead like Aunt Prue's lace-gloved fingers. The sky was a ragged ribbon of deep blue that clouded to gray as it began to rain.

Adam led Emma around a bend in the ravine.

Emerging into a clearing, both stopped and looked up at a torrent rushing over a lip of rock. The plummeting water scoured a face of smooth black stone until it calmed at last in a bubbling pool. From there it slipped into the narrow stream they had followed up from the fig tree.

"Do you see a cave?" Emma asked. Even though the crashing water blocked every other noise, her words seemed loud.

Adam pointed toward the cascade, and she followed the line of his finger until she spotted a deep black maw halfway up the side of the ravine. It would not be an easy climb.

"The wood's probably damp," he said, "but I'll see if I can start a fire."

"I hope Soapy arrives before dark. I don't like the thought of staying here tonight."

While Adam searched for dry wood and started a small fire, Emma sank into the long grass with relief. Her riding skirt was splattered with mud and her boots were caked. She wondered whether Cissy had lived in this damp jungle for many days. What would she have eaten? Who had protected her and kept her warm?

"Emma?" Adam touched her arm. "You all right?"

She nodded as he knelt beside her and held his hands before the flickering fire. They ate a little of the bread and cheese stored in their saddlebags. Curled beside him, Emma watched as the clearing deepened to emerald and the sky turned a dark rose. She drifted toward sleep, but a sudden sound jerked her awake.

Adam leaped to his feet and reached for the rifle hanging on his saddle. Then he stopped and began to grin. Emma struggled to stand on half-frozen legs. Below them in the gorge, a man with bright yellow hair guided two stumbling horses that pulled a small cart.

"Soapy!" Adam strode toward his friend. "You're a sight for sore eyes, partner."

"Just 'bout didn't think I could do it, boss." Soapy emerged into the clearing. "Them poor horses is nearly tuckered out. We had a time trekkin' up these mountains. If you two hadn't trampled down the bushes in this gorge, we never would've made it. Anyway, here she be."

Emma touched the chest. Her father's gold—her gold now. She would gladly give it all away to have Cissy safe and well.

"We must take this to the cave at once." She looked into Adam's blue eyes. "It's almost dark, and I must keep Cissy from another night of misery."

He studied the steep incline leading up from the pool. "Soapy, we have our work cut out for us. Emma, you stay here. If this kidnapping is for real, they might let your sister go while we're in the cave. Just lie low with her until we get down. Here's the rifle if you need it."

Emma took the weapon, her heart hammering as she watched the two men wind their way past the pool and start up the ravine. She searched the forest for any sign of life but saw nothing. She set the rifle next to the fire and tried to calm herself.

Adam was high above her now, almost concealed by ferns and vines as he guided the horses along the cliff face. His hat lay on a mound of moss near the base of the falls, and he had rolled up the sleeves of his white shirt.

Emma thought back to the first time she had seen him. Adam had scooped the small boy from the path of a tumbling wooden box and saved his life. She recalled how he had cradled the child in his arms. How strange and wonderful he had seemed with his soft shirt and denim trousers and his boots with their silver spurs glinting.

But she must not walk in her mother's footsteps. In marrying Godfrey Pickering, her mother had chosen the safe course. Following her heart so many years later had caused her family great suffering and led her to an early grave. Emma would be foolish to plunge heedlessly after a man like Adam King who could never commit himself.

Nicholas Bond had declared his love for her, proposed marriage, avowed his undying devotion to England and all that was honorable. He was upright and steadfast, just as her father had been. Once Cissy was safe, Emma could marry

Nicholas if she chose. Her money would provide a comfortable life for their children. And it would help fulfill his dreams of rising in authority with the railway and helping build the new city of Nairobi.

Nicholas did not love her. Emma knew that. She would never experience the kind of love that had sparked to life in Adam's arms. In the end, what did passion matter? Following God was the only path to true happiness.

Resolved, Emma watched the men climb toward the cave. But a movement in the forest caught her eye. The bushes parted and a familiar face emerged.

"Good evening, Fraulein Pickering." Dirk Bauer stepped into view, a broad grin across his face. And behind him came a disheveled, determined-looking woman.

"Cissy!" Emma's voice rang out as she threw her arms around her sister.

"Emma, oh, Emma, how I've missed you!" Cissy kissed her cheek again and again as the two clung to one another, shivering with happiness.

"You were with Dirk all along," Emma cried, tears spilling down her cheeks. "Oh, Cissy, you can't imagine how worried I've been."

"Save your happy tidings, ladies." The harsh voice startled Emma, and she saw Dirk's eyes widen as he reached for a pistol. Before he could draw it, a figure brushed past the women and slammed a rifle butt into the German's abdomen, doubling him over.

"Nicholas?" Emma stared in astonishment. "But what are you doing here?"

"Business, Miss Pickering," he spat. "Throw it down, Kaiser."

Dirk dropped his gun to the ground and Bond snatched it up. He grabbed Emma and pulled her close, keeping the rifle trained on Dirk. "I want the gold," he told her. "Tell your American friend to bring it down. Now."

Emma looked up to see Adam and Soapy scrambling down from the waterfall.

"Help!" Cissy yelled. "He's going to kill us!"

"Emma!" Adam's voice thundered through the clearing. He dashed ahead of Soapy, but stopped short when Nicholas turned the rifle on him.

"The gold is up by the cave," Adam shouted. "Let the women go."

"What's goin' on, boss?" Soapy darted past Adam, his pistol drawn.

A deafening blast exploded next to Emma's ear, and she saw Soapy clutch one thigh and fall to his knees. Before she could react, Nicholas threw her to the ground. He stepped forward, working the bolt action on the rifle.

"You told her," he barked at Adam. "You've ruined me."

Emma could see Soapy writhing in pain. Unarmed, Adam crouched beside his friend.

"Nicholas," she called out, fighting with her tangled skirts to rise from the mud. "Nicholas, listen to me."

"No." He stepped toward her, trapping her dress beneath his muddy heel.

Rage flooded through Emma. She had been pinned before, held back, held down, cowering beneath a man's wrath. But no longer.

"Stop, Nicholas!" She jerked her skirt free. But as she stood, he took aim at Adam's heart. Without thinking, she lunged between the two men.

"Don't shoot him!" she screamed. "I love him, Nicholas. I won't let you do this."

His face blanching, Nicholas started toward Emma, the rifle barrel now pointed at her. "Get out of the way, Emmaline."

"Emma!" Adam leapt forward, caught her around the waist and swept her behind him. "Soapy, Bauer—get her out of here."

Emma shrieked as Nicholas took aim a second time, but somehow Soapy and Dirk were grabbing her arms and dragging her away.

"Adam!" she cried as the men pulled her across mossy rock toward the thick brush where Cissy had taken cover. In the tangle of undergrowth she lost sight of Adam. Soapy scurried down the ravine, and Emma felt hands grasping her.

Cissy's voice called out, but Emma could only continue to fight against Soapy's grip. She must help Adam. Otherwise Nicholas would kill him.

She glanced up into the jade canopy of leaves and saw a dark shape descending toward her head. Through the flash of pain that preceded unconsciousness, she heard from the clearing the thunder of a gunshot.

Chapter Eighteen

Emma shut her eyes against the invading light. No, she did not want to see. She did not want to feel. All she could hear was the echo of a rifle firing again and again. A cool hand stroked her forehead and she wondered if she were dreaming. Everything was confused and jumbled.

"We're at Tsavo station." Cissy's voice. "Try to wake up, dearest."

With effort, Emma opened her eyes and gazed into her sister's face. Cissy looked pale but she was smiling.

"Where is Adam?" Emma asked.

"Lord Delamere sent a contingent to the Aberdares. They left a few hours ago."

Emma struggled to sit up. The room tilted, and her head felt as if it held nothing but clouds. "Tsavo station?"

"Yes, and you've been given laudanum. Quite a lot, actually. Emma, darling, you've had a nasty bump."

"You stumbled in the forest." Dirk Bauer moved

into view. His blond hair gleamed in the sunlight, but his handsome face was somber. "You fell and your head struck a stone."

Emma frowned, unable to recall the moment clearly. She took Cissy's hand. "What happened at the waterfall? Where is Adam?"

"Oh, Emma," Cissy murmured. "We don't know. We had no choice but to flee. You and Soapy were both injured. Gravely so. Please don't think about this now. You must rest."

"Did you bring me here?"

"Yes." Cissy hesitated. "I was told about Father, Emma. His grave is nearby. I waited until we could go together."

Through the small window above the settee on which she lay, Emma saw an azure sky and dazzling sunshine. This was the office where once she had talked to Nicholas. She had seen Adam walking just outside . . . near the track. The train was in the station and workers bustled about. But Adam was not here.

"Let us visit the grave, then," Emma proposed. "I'm well enough now."

Cissy and Dirk helped her stand and supported her across the room. They stepped out onto the verandah and walked around to a small plot of ground enclosed with an iron fence. Several markers had been erected, but Emma saw only a small cross where their father had been laid to rest.

"I ordered a large headstone of Italian marble,"

Cissy said. "His name and the dates will be engraved on it. You are free now, Emma. Free of our father's domination."

"And free to love him again as I once did."

"As we both did when Mama was still with us."

Dirk cleared his throat. "Excuse me, ladies, but the train is leaving for Mombasa."

"And Mr. Potts is on it," Cissy added. "He needs you, Emma."

"Herr Potts refuses to allow anyone but you to treat his leg wound," Dirk concurred. "He says the railway doctors worked for his enemy, Herr Bond. May I escort you?"

Emma accepted Dirk's arm and he led both women to the train. Her head throbbing, she climbed aboard and moved unsteadily down the aisle. A seat had been made up into a bed, and Soapy lay still and pale upon it.

"Afternoon, ma'am," the cowboy greeted Emma. "Think you could patch me up? The bullet went clean through and near took all my blood with it."

She knelt beside him. "Oh, Soapy, I'm so glad you're alive! But why did you force me away? I needed to go to Adam."

"The boss told me to get you out of there. I figured I'd better do what he said, shot or not. Me and Dirk there had to get you two ladies off that mountain and away from that loco and his rifle. He woulda shot all of us dead."

"Nicholas Bond."

313

"Yeah, that's the one. And all because he thought Adam told you about him."

"Told me what, Soapy? I don't know anything."

He grimaced as the train jerked to life, its whistle sending a mournful cry into the afternoon air. "I'm jiggered if I can pull it all together myself, ma'am. Ya know I ain't got nothin' under my hat but hair."

Cissy looked at Emma, her blue eyes questioning. "Can you understand what he's saying?"

Emma gave her a wan smile. "I'm learning to. All right, then, Mr. Potts. Let's have a look at your leg."

Soapy took off his hat and put it over his face as Emma peeled back the sheet and began to examine the injury. "I apologize, ma'am," he muttered, "but I'm as yeller as mustard without the bite."

"If that means you're a coward, I shall have to disagree. You were very brave."

"It's the pain," Soapy groaned. "Oh, the pain."

Emma frowned. "Cissy, I need water."

"Will this help, madam?" Dirk was striding down the swaying aisle, his fingers wrapped around the handle of a steaming kettle. "I got it from the kitchen car."

Emma nodded in surprise. "Yes, thank you."

"Dirk is always so helpful," Cissy said. "We went everywhere looking for you, Emma, and we could hardly believe it when we saw you climbing into those mountains. Whatever were you doing there?"

"You were following *me?*"

"Of course. Dirk called to me that night when we were in the railcar. He left his battalion and came to find me. I had no idea he was going to do it, but once we were together . . ." She looked at the man beside her, and he drew her into his arms. "Dirk is in a great deal of trouble, Emma. The German army is looking for him. We're in a rush to get to Mombasa to plead for the British government to grant him asylum. We intend to marry."

"Are you certain, Cissy?" Emma searched her sister's blue eyes for assurance. "Perhaps you should rest before you agree to such an attachment."

"Emma, this man is to be my husband. I have no doubt."

"I have some savings," the soldier added. "Enough to buy a small farm here."

"Here?" Emma glanced at Cissy. "In the British Protectorate?"

"I love this country, Emma. Oh, I know it's hard to believe I could give up my parties. Truly I cannot explain the change in me. In Africa, I've found what I've been looking for all my life."

"I see a peace in your eyes, Cissy."

"While tracking you into the mountains, we found a lovely place for our home. Dirk wants to plant beans and corn and have a farm of his own."

Emma dabbed at Soapy's wound. Adam had foreseen the future of the protectorate. It would be a busy place, a fertile land where a man and his wife could carve out a good life for themselves and their children.

"I'm happy for you both," she whispered, leaning over to give her sister a kiss. "I'm certain your farm will be a great success."

Cissy beamed. "That night when I ran away, Dirk wanted us to go straight to Mombasa. But I knew you would be worried and I insisted we go back. We've been trying to catch up to you ever since. In fact, we arrived at Mr. King's ranch only hours after you had gone. His man Jackson sent us in the right direction. You can imagine our surprise when we found ourselves under the barrel of Mr. Bond's rifle only moments after we'd found you."

Emma sighed. She hardly knew what to make of all this information. Blotting away the last of the wash water, she leaned toward her patient. "Mr. Potts, are you still under that hat?"

The buckskin cowboy hat slowly slipped from in front of Soapy's eyes. "Am I gonna live to see tomorrow?"

"Your wound is clean and it should heal well. A doctor in Mombasa will treat it." She turned to Cissy. "If you'll excuse me, I shall look for some bandage material."

Dirk leaped to his feet. "I shall go for you, madam."

"No, no. Please sit down." The pain in Emma's head increased as she started toward the door of the car. "I need to be alone."

She gripped the backs of the leather seats to

316

make her way down the aisle. It was growing dark, and she could see the conductor lighting lamps. Nearly paralyzed by her sense of loss, Emma had all she could do to keep from crying. Where was Adam? Had Nicholas killed him?

Dear God, why did this happen? And how am I to go on?

From the things Cissy had said, Emma realized Nicholas must have written the ransom note and planned to take the gold for himself. He had been more surprised than Emma to see Cissy and Dirk emerge into the clearing.

But what had made him behave in such a villainous manner? What had driven him to such a rage that he would shoot Soapy and kill Adam?

Her vision blurred by tears, Emma was startled when she laid her hand on a seat back and felt warm fingers close over it.

"Memsahib?" Linde floated up from the seat and pressed her forehead to Emma's palms.

"Linde, what are you doing here?" As Emma stepped closer, she saw Tolito smiling at her.

"My arm good, *memsahib*." The African's eyes were warm. "You drive evil spirit away. Now we go to Mombasa, as you wish."

Emma sat beside him. "Tolito, has anyone told you about *Bwana* King?"

"No, *memsahib*. He is here with you?"

She shook her head. "We had trouble in the Aberdares. Mr. Bond came after us."

"That man?" Tolito's face contorted in anger.

"What happened, *Memsahib* Emma?" Linde asked.

Emma gave a brief recounting of the story. "Mr. Potts was wounded by Mr. Bond," she concluded. "The last I knew was the sound of gunfire. I was unconscious when the party brought us to Tsavo."

"*Bwana* King die?" Tolito asked.

"I don't know. I pray he is still alive." Emma fell silent for a moment. "Tolito, how did you come to know *Bwana* King? And what caused the trouble between him and *Bwana* Bond?"

Tolito closed his eyes and began to speak. "*Bwana* King come to my country many years ago. He is not of the British. He buy land from the land office, but the British send him from Mombasa with a bad map. He get lost. In those days, I am the *olaigwenani*—the spokesman—of my clan's age set. The men of my age set go to hunt a lioness, but we see she hunts something to eat. It is *Bwana* King. He near to death. Vultures sit in trees to wait."

Emma gazed out the window as the sun slipped below the horizon. Black skeletons of thorn trees stood against an orange sky.

"We take *Bwana* King to our *manyatta,* where we live," Tolito continued. "He get strong again. Then I go with him to his land. I become head man. We work hard, and two years pass. *Bwana* Potts come from America. He work also."

318

"I stay with my brother and his wife," Linde spoke up, her voice a murmur. "I am happy there."

"One day *Bwana* King tell Linde and me to go to Mombasa." Tolito paused, his brow furrowed as if he could not bear to summon the memory. "*Bwana* King say we get crates and woman."

"Clarissa," Linde put in. "That is why I should go also. But woman not come."

"No." Tolito shook his head. "We put crates on train. We ride train and see *Bwana* Bond also going. That day, he sees my sister."

"*Bwana* Bond want me." Linde's words came with difficulty. "I not want this thing to happen with *Bwana* Bond. I tell him no, no. But he tries to . . . force."

"Oh, no." Emma touched the young woman. "I am so sorry."

"We come to station," she continued. "It is night. *Bwana* Bond chase me, and I run and shout. Tolito fight him. *Bwana* Bond has knife and cuts Tolito. Try to kill him. Every part of Tolito is blood."

"My arm very bad," Tolito added.

"Then comes *Bwana* King to meet us at station. I cry to him what happened, that *Bwana* Bond want me and that Tolito dying. *Bwana* King fight with *Bwana* Bond. Then *Bwana* Bond run away."

As Linde's words faded, so did the last of the light. Emma sat beneath the lamp and stared out at the darkness. So Adam knew everything. Nicholas must have lived in dread that he would one day make public what had happened. Such a story, related to Godfrey Pickering or another railway director, could destroy his ambitions and career.

When Emma had come to the protectorate—an heiress and, upon her father's death, a wealthy woman in her own right—Nicholas had seen the chance to make his dreams come true. But he knew Adam might tell Emma the story and ruin his chance. No wonder he hated Adam.

"Emma?" Cissy appeared at her side. "What are you doing?"

"This is Adam's brother Tolito," Emma replied, touching the African's arm. "And this is Linde. She's going to assist me in my clinic . . . if I have a clinic."

To Emma's surprise, Cissy gave them a curtsy before taking her sister's hand. "Perhaps Miss Linde would be willing to look after Mr. Potts. I've never heard such groaning in my life. He does believe he's going to pass on."

Linde rose at once, and the three women made their way down the aisle. Emma settled into a sleeping berth, and Cissy drew a shade over the window.

"Sleep, my poor love," she whispered as Emma closed her eyes. "You shall have a hot bath at Government House and you'll feel much better. We shall find your Adam and bring him to you. I promise."

Chapter Nineteen

The heat and humidity of the ancient port bore down on her, and Emma still felt dazed as the trolley rolled toward Government House. Lord and Lady Delamere hurried down the steps to meet their guests. The couple were eager to hear the news and more than eager to ensure that Godfrey Pickering's heirs left the protectorate with much goodwill to take back to England and her prospective colonists.

Lord Delamere exclaimed in dismay over the tragedy in the Aberdares. He vowed to find Nicholas Bond. Justice would be served. Adam King would be given a gentleman's burial. The entire protectorate would mourn.

Lady Delamere's sadness was overtaken by the joy of Cissy's engagement and plans to settle in the highlands. There must be a reception this very night, she insisted. The wedding would take place on the Delamere farm at Njoro. Her husband declared Dirk's desire for sanctuary a "bit of a sticky wicket," but he assured the couple that all would fall into place.

Amid the excitement, Emma started toward the house. She was crossing the lawn when she heard Lord Delamere addressing Soapy.

"I'm told Adam had one of my crates," the

Englishman said. "Do you know if he took it to Njoro?"

"Sorry to say it's still in the barn on King Farm," the cowboy told him.

"Well, we'll just pop 'round for it. I shall need that plow on my return to the farm."

A plow. Emma reflected on the crate and all its mystery as she stepped inside the house. How could she have doubted Adam? But she had. Nicholas Bond had been the serpent in the Garden of Eden, whispering poison into her ear. All along, he had been the evil one.

In the room where she and Cissy had stayed before, Emma bathed and dressed in a soft gown. Then she took a chair near the balcony door Adam had once entered. He had wanted to take her away then, but she would not go. And now he was gone.

It seemed she was always losing those she loved most. The terrible truth of her losses was more than Emma felt she could bear. As she thought of Adam, his body lying in that cold damp gorge, tears streamed down her cheeks.

Where was God in such a time as this? She had heard Him so clearly as she listened to Miss Nightingale. His call on Emma's heart could not be mistaken. Her path to Africa had been made straight, and her future unfurled before her like a soft carpet.

Until she met Adam King. Confused, tempted

and deeply in love, she had struggled to pray. God's voice became so hard to hear. What was He telling her? What was she to do? She had tried to listen. She had done her best to obey.

But now she had lost the love she had never wanted. She had been torn from a man she could never have. A future she suddenly desired more than anything else was ripped away by a single bullet.

She watched as the sun sank. The stars were just coming out when the door burst open. Breathless, Cissy flew into the room, begged Emma not to cry and announced happy plans for an impromptu reception that night in honor of her engagement. Lady Delamere had offered to lend her a gown! Slippers must be found, to say nothing of a hat! Blue eyes sparkling, Cissy whirled away in a flutter of excitement.

Under a moonlit sky, trolleys and carriages began to arrive. Emma observed elegant men and women promenading into the hall below. Laughter, music and the tinkle of crystal floated up to her in the darkened room.

Emma knew she had no choice but to carry on without Adam. Her heart would hold him always, but she must move forward with her plans. A hospital would be found where she could serve. Linde would be at her side. Cissy and Dirk would marry and have children. Emma would visit often. She would go to England and tell Miss Nightingale about her work. Perhaps they would drink tea together.

"Emma, where have you got to?" Cissy rushed into the room again. At the sight of her sister still seated beside the window, she exclaimed in exasperation. "Oh, Emma, you're here all alone. I've been cruel to stay away. How heartless of me."

Cissy turned up the flame in a lamp on the table. Emma watched her butterfly sister for a moment. The joy of seeing such a loved one alive was enough to warm a shattered heart.

"I've needed to be alone, Cissy." Emma turned from the light to gaze out the window. "I loved him, you know. It was very wrong, but I couldn't help it."

Cissy wrapped an arm around her sister's shoulders. "I know you loved him . . . and he loved you, Emma. I knew it the moment I saw you together. He was wonderful, wasn't he?"

"Yes, but I shall go on. I had made up my mind not to be like Mama, not to follow my heart. But I found out that's quite impossible for me. I believe I shall always go where my passions lead me. But I won't be ruled by them. Unlike Mama, I shall not pine away from my loss. I shall not die of this."

"Of course not. You are far too strong." Cissy smiled. "We are women of fortitude, you and I. Lady Delamere is thrilled about the wedding, as you know. She wanted to host the event at their farm at Njoro, but instead we've set it right here tomorrow afternoon."

"So soon, Cissy?"

"Why wait? Everyone we know is in Mombasa already. Lord Delamere says that after Dirk and I are married, he'll have no trouble getting a residency permit from the British government. So it is good to be hasty in such a situation."

"I'm happy for you, then." Emma took her sister's hand. "Truly I am."

"Will you come down? It would mean so much to me. I won't make you dance."

"Certainly I shall. An occasion such as this is not to be missed."

Emma had to laugh as Cissy twirled about the bedroom in Lady Delamere's pink gown with long feathers sweeping from the velvet sash. A soft blue-green silk gown was chosen for Emma herself. She pinned her sun-streaked hair into coils atop her head and slipped on a pair of gloves.

The two young women swept down the stairs to a chorus of ahs and the gentle applause of the assembly. Emma learned she and Cissy were viewed as heroines of a sort, having endured hardships in the wild and come through impossible adventures unscathed.

Cissy vanished into the sea of celebrants. Emma greeted several guests before stepping into the ballroom. Leaning against the cool plaster of a back wall, she sipped at a glass of punch and watched the dancers whirl around the room to a lively waltz. Cissy and Dirk, enraptured in one another's arms, did not even see her as they swept past.

"Well, howdy, ma'am." Soapy's voice broke into Emma's reverie, and she turned in surprise to find the little cowboy standing close beside her. His yellow hair, parted in the middle, had been slicked back on either side. Even more astonishing, he had washed his face, and for the first time Emma realized that he had freckles. His broad grin belied the despondency Emma was sure he must be feeling.

"Mr. Potts, how lovely to see you," she said. "You're looking well."

"They got a purty good doc over at the government clinic. He says I'll be back in the saddle good as new afore long." Leaning on a cane, Soapy pulled at one of his black suspenders and snapped it against his chest. "You might like to hear I was right there when the doc took a look at yore handiwork on Tolito. I never heerd such fine talkin'. He said you done good . . . real good. He was purt' near happy as a flea in a doghouse. Says he wants to meet you—" Soapy stopped speaking and scratched his head. "What's goin' on over there?"

Emma looked up to find that the music had faltered and the instruments were falling silent. The dancers had stopped, every eye turned toward the door. Voices, arguing, growing louder, filled the ballroom. Three African doorkeepers surrounded a figure who rose head and shoulders above them.

Standing on tiptoe, Emma felt the blood rush from her head as Adam King took off his black cowboy hat and started across the room toward her. No. It was impossible.

She caught her breath at the man she hardly recognized in such a clean white shirt, black coat and gray trousers. His sun-bronzed face wore a smile and his eyes shone like blue diamonds. Even his hair, shiny black in the lamplight, bounced with life as he strode through the frozen dancers.

"My lord," one of the servants protested, "this man insists on entering the consulate without invitation."

"Mr. King!" Lord Delamere called out.

"Lord Delamere." Adam never took his eyes from Emma's. "Mind if I join you?"

"Not at all. Welcome!" Delamere turned to the military band. "Carry on, gentlemen."

As the music started again, the dancers swung back into the waltz. But no one could refrain from watching as Adam swept Emma up in his arms.

"You're alive!" She threw her arms around his neck, unable to believe that he was really here—holding her tight and spinning her around and around.

"You didn't really think Bond could get the best of me, did you?"

"That ol' tenderfoot weren't no match for a cowboy!" Soapy exclaimed. "Coulda told you that, ma'am."

Adam set Emma down and stepped back to look at her. "The dress makes your eyes look almost blue," he declared. "Or have you been crying?"

When she couldn't answer, he led her out onto the verandah where once they had strolled together.

"Bond is laid up at the ranch right now," he told her. "He's got a couple of slugs in him, if you'd like to practice on someone new."

"You shot him?"

"I couldn't help but wing him. He was pretty determined, if you'll recall. I returned your gold to the bank a little while ago. Richards was glad to see it."

Emma shook her head. She still couldn't believe he was here . . . and yet she could feel his arm around her shoulders, rest her head against his chest, hear his heart beating loud and strong.

"I wanted to bring you this." He stopped walking and turned Emma to face him. Reaching into his shirt pocket, he took out the brass ring. It rested on the tip of his right index finger, and he looked down at it as he spoke. "When I first met you, Emma, I knew right away there was something different . . . special . . . about you. You proposed that crazy business arrangement, and I went along with it because I needed a nurse for Tolito."

"And the money," she reminded him.

"I inherited a little shipping business when my pa died. I'll make things right with him when we meet up again. And now I know we will."

Emma smiled. "We can both look forward to reconciliation. God has given us that gift."

"Your father was wounded and in pain, but he loved you. And he was right when he recognized my name. Pa wouldn't leave me the ranch in Texas. I was too unreliable. But he gave the ships to his son who had wandered away and never come home."

"Ships," she repeated. "Then you didn't need my money at all."

"I thought the ranch and Seastar would fill up what I was missing in my life—that empty feeling I tried to ignore. But it didn't go away . . . until you came along. Then I had to face the truth, Emma. I don't want to live without you in my life. Will you come back to the ranch with me? Will you be my wife?"

Emma looked up into the clear blue eyes. "But what about Clarissa? Your heart belongs to her."

She stepped away from him before continuing. "The day we met on the pier, I saw you tear a letter. It blew across my path, part of it, anyway, and I could not resist reading it. She signed it, *your wife*."

Adam shook his head, a slow grin forming at the corners of his mouth. "You read half the letter, Emma. Half. The whole message read, *Your wife-to-be.* I was engaged to Clarissa for a long time. My parents thought it was a good match. But I've never been one to do the thing I was supposed to do. I tore up the letter, remember? And I wrote to her the day you found the locket. It's over, Emma. It had been for a long time."

"I've never done what I was supposed to do either," Emma whispered. "But I know one thing I must do—and that is to spend my life with you."

Adam took her into his arms and kissed her lips. It was a lingering kiss, one that erased the bewildered ache in her heart and sealed the vow in his. Then he took her left hand in his and slipped the brass ring onto her finger.

"Care to dance, Mrs. King?" he asked in a low voice. "I'm not much of a high-toned dancer, to tell you the truth—especially when the prettiest nurse in Africa has got me all knock-kneed."

She laughed. "You must pay a visit to my clinic on King Farm about those knees, sir. You'll find I have a wonderful cure for that sort of thing."

"I'll bet you do." With a smile, he drew her even closer. "It sounds like our song in there."

Emma barely heard the strains of the "Blue Danube Waltz" as Adam led her back into the ballroom and whirled her around the room. The other couples drifted into corners to watch. Emma threw back her head in joy as she swayed close against Adam. Her curls tumbled to her waist, and her skirts billowed around her ankles. But all she knew was Adam's shoulder against her cheek, his hand at her waist, and both of them moving as one.

Dear Reader,

Maybe you've never been a nurse in Africa, as Emma was, but all of us have experienced a strong desire to do something meaningful with our lives. Are you doing the important work God prepared just for you? Are you even sure you know what it is?

Emma felt God "calling" her to become a nurse in Africa. I used to wonder about that concept. As the daughter of missionaries, I'd heard it all my life. People reported that "God called me to do this." Or "I experienced God's calling on my life." Or "I'm definitely not called for that purpose."

What is a call from God? What does it look, feel or sound like?

I've been writing novels for twenty-three years, and I knew I was being obedient to the Holy Spirit's quiet guidance. God prepared me for this "call" in many ways. He gave me a love of reading, an unusual childhood in Africa and Bangladesh, an ear for language, a vivid awareness of sensory details and, of course, the ability to tell a story.

Two years ago, I experienced a "call" that wasn't quiet or even rational. While visiting a refugee resettlement area in Atlanta, I felt an overpowering certainty that I was supposed to move to Atlanta and minister to refugees. *What?* I was living in Missouri . . . in a house by a lake . . . in a cozy little town . . . with family and friends close by. My husband reminded me of all this when I told him about my new "call."

I could have chosen to put in spiritual earplugs and continue my former life. But God soon called my husband, too, and here we are in Atlanta! I'm happier than I've ever been. Each day is a joyful miracle.

God may not be calling you to move to Africa, or to help refugees in a city far from home, but He definitely is calling you to do something for Him. Are you listening? I hope so! If you hear His voice and obey, you'll be blessed a thousand times over. I sure am.

Love,

Catherine Palmer

QUESTIONS FOR DISCUSSION

1. Emma feels that God has called her to be a nurse in Africa—have you ever felt a similar call in your own life?

2. Do you think Cissy makes the right choice when she gives up everything to run away with Dirk Bauer?

3. Cissy has fallen in love many times—do you believe her love for Dirk is different? Why?

4. Emma and Adam both agree to a marriage of convenience to save people they care about. Do you think this was a wise choice on their part, or could their goals have been accomplished in another way?

5. Adam and Emma both follow their dreams to Africa, even though their families disapprove. How important do you think it is to follow your dreams?

6. How do Emma's dreams change over time?

7. Although Emma and Cissy had the same upbringing, they are very different. Why do you think they have such different personalities?

8. Everyone believes Cissy was killed by the lions, but Emma refuses to give up. Do you think Emma was right not to give up hope? What would you do in this situation?

9. Do you think Adam was right to keep secrets from Emma, or should he have told her everything from the start?

10. Even though Adam clearly hates Nicholas Bond for assaulting Tolito and Linde, he never tells anyone else what happened. Do you think this was the right decision? Why?

11. How well do you think you would adapt to living on a different continent?

CATHERINE PALMER

The bestselling author of more than fifty novels with over two million copies sold, Catherine Palmer is a Christy Award-winner for outstanding Christian romance fiction. Catherine's numerous awards include Best Historical Romance, Best Contemporary Romance, Best of Romance from Southwest Writers Workshop and Most Exotic Historical Romance Novel from *Romantic Times BOOKreviews*. She is also a *Romantic Times BOOKreviews* Career Achievement Award winner.

Catherine grew up in Bangladesh and Kenya, and she now makes her home in Georgia. She and her husband of thirty years have two sons. A graduate of Southwest Baptist University, she also holds a master's degree from Baylor University.

Center Point Publishing
600 Brooks Road ● PO Box 1
Thorndike ME 04986-0001 USA

(207) 568-3717

US & Canada:
1 800 929-9108
www.centerpointlargeprint.com